Love Like the Movies

Victoria Van Tiem, like her protagonist, is an artist,
a gallery owner and a former creative director, with a
background in marketing and brand development.
Love Like the Movies is her first novel.

VICTORIA VAN TIEM

Love like the Movies

PAN BOOKS

First published in 2014 by Pocket Star Books,
a division of Simon & Schuster, Inc.

This edition published 2014 by Pan Books
an imprint of Pan Macmillan, a division of Macmillan Publishers Limited
Pan Macmillan, 20 New Wharf Road, London N1 9RR
Basingstoke and Oxford
Associated companies throughout the world
www.panmacmillan.com

ISBN 978-1-4472-6973-1

1 3 5 7 9 8 6 4 2

A CIP catalogue record for this book is available from the British Library.

Printed and bound by CPI Group (UK) Ltd, Croydon, CR0 4YY

Visit **www.panmacmillan.com** to read more about all our books
and to buy them. You will also find features, author interviews and
news of any author events, and you can sign up for e-newsletters
so that you're always first to hear about our new releases.

For my husband, M, my forever leading man,
and our two wonderful boys, Kirklen and Garrett—
your unwavering encouragement and support
is nothing short of epic.

For AJ,
a woman who lives inspired, and by doing so,
inspires the best in everyone around her
You are Hollywood Glamour in the everyday,
and I will forever be in awe and just a little starstruck.

Now Showing

CHAPTER ONE

Almost Thirty, Flirty and Thriving

WHEN I WAS NINE, I fired my mom. I simply wrote in bright red marker "you are fired." I also drew a smiling daisy and a frog.

Okay, the flower was firing the frog and the words were in a cartoon speech bubble above its head. But if you looked really close you'd see Mom's favorite necklace around the frog's neck.

It was my satirical debut.

Sadly, that still didn't get her attention. It was tossed into the kitchen drawer with all the others; the penguin I sketched from a photo, the cat I spent days on to get just right, even the butterfly with my art teacher's handwritten note of "wonderful, such talent!"

Today, however, I don't have to worry about getting Mom to take notice. The sparkly diamond wrapped around my left ring finger all but guarantees it. Bradley's a complete catch. Blond, brawny, and refined, and he wants to marry me. I'm going to be Mrs. Kensington Connors. My insides flutter just thinking about it.

So why am I so nervous? Bradley catches me admiring my ring, flashes me a reassuring smile, and takes my hand as he opens the front door. He knows how anxious I get around my family and how excited I am to finally show them the ring and start planning the wedding.

We make our way into the kitchen, where Mom and Ren are cooking away. The aroma of sickly sweet pastries instantly fills my nose. I try to ignore the familiar pang in my gut. Instead of a confident twenty-nine-year-old, I'm thirteen again and desperate to win their approval.

"Hi," I say with a nervous smile. Bradley gives Mom a kiss on the cheek and waves hello to Ren. He gives a quick wink my way before heading toward the sitting room, where Dad and my brother, Grayson, are discussing health care loudly enough that I can hear pieces of the conversation.

Mom sets the batter bowl down and wipes her hands on her apron. "There she is! We never see her anymore, do we, Ren?" She says this like I'm the visitor instead of the one who grew up here. She reaches to me for a hug.

"Hi, Mom." It's a quick squeeze. I notice she's in one of her casual Jackie O sheath dresses with a shabby-chic apron tied around the front, and Ren is . . . *wow*, she's wearing about the same thing. They're like mother-daughter twins. I'm suddenly a tad envious. I want to yell, *Get your own mom!* But I know she lost hers when she was young, and I should understand.

"Hi, Kensington, you're looking well," says Ren with an abbreviated smile. No hug. She eyes my brand-new Coach bag. The one I saved up for. "I saw those were out. Everyone seems to have them already. I've got my eye on the new Burberry satchel."

I smile and nod my acknowledgment that yes, she still reigns supreme.

"So let's see. Give us a look," Mom says, waving to my hand.

I feel the swell of a victory in my chest; a small win on the horizon for Team Kenzi. Yes, sadly I keep track. To date, I've never come out ahead. The overall standing looks something like this:

Team Ren: Two hundred and seventy-five.

Team Mom and Dad: I've lost count.

Team Grayson: Forty-five exactly. Although, since I've been with Bradley, he's not as critical.

Team Kenzi: Four. And that's including today.

Four check marks for a lifetime of coming in second. I was on the homecoming court, but not the queen. I graduated in the top ten of my class, but I wasn't valedictorian like Grayson. I'm creative director at a prominent ad agency, but it's not a serious profession like medicine. My dad, Grayson, and Ren are all doctors.

My first real win was when I brought Bradley home to meet everyone. They worship him. In fact, he fits into my family of Kennedy wannabes better than I do. The second mark is from staying together past a year. The third, from when Bradley and I got engaged this past week. And now, this mega-ring is a surefire winner to rack in my number four.

I hold my hand out so the light from the kitchen window gleams off it, creating the most perfect sparkle.

Ren pulls my hand up to take a better look. "Oh! It's stellar, Kensington. Bradley is just too good to you."

What she really means is Bradley is too good *for* me. At this exact second I'm proud of Bradley for being able to afford such a quality piece and having such refined taste. It doesn't matter if it's not my personal taste. It's from Tiffany's, it's huge, and it hits all the marks.

Ren flinches. "Oh, you should really get those nails done, though. With so much attention on that hand, you don't want the presentation marred by unkempt cuticles. You owe that to Bradley."

Ding. Team Ren: Two hundred and seventy-six.

She digs in her bag, pulls out a business card, and hands it to me. "Here, call and ask for Cindy. She's fab."

"Yes, we just went for a girls' day, see?" Mom holds her pink polished nails out to me and wiggles them. I notice Ren's are the same shade of pale pink.

Girls' day. Without me.

I admire them and smile. "They look great. I'll be sure to call. So, what do you think, Mom? Bradley did good, right?" I ask, hopeful to lock in the check mark. I know it's pathetic.

"Oh, yes, dear. Bradley did wonderfully." Smiling, Mom directs Ren to grab some blueberries from the fridge and again busies herself with the batter.

"Do you need me to do something?" I ask, feeling a bit out of place. "I could set the table or start bringing dishes out?"

"No, we've got this down to a science, don't we, Mother Shaw?" Ren crinkles her nose at Mom.

For a moment, I just stand and nervously fiddle with my ring. I guess that's it. Round one of the Shaw Sunday brunch is officially complete. I'm sure we'll talk about wedding plans over lunch. Of course we will. No way will I let *this* be shoved in a drawer.

Why didn't I get my nails done?

I wander up the stairs and head for my old room, which was completely gutted and is now Mom's scrapbook studio. A huge square project table was constructed to look like the one from Pottery Barn, but this one is on steroids with a million drawers and cubbies, each filled with different sticky letters and embellishments. The only *me* left in the room now resides on the closet's top shelf in a fabric zip box marked *Kensington*.

With a sigh, I fish out my phone and click on the Facebook app. I'm always peeking at my phone to see what people are up to. Then I compare it to what I'm doing, or not doing, and it makes me think of what I should be doing. The thing is . . . I don't really end up doing anything different. I just lose hours of my life doing it.

Since we only told our families about the engagement over the phone, I've been waiting until after today to officially announce it. And it's killing me.

Two new friend requests. I click the icon and accept the first one, a girl I know from the gym. I freeze over the second. *No way.* I bring the phone closer, staring at the tiny photo icon. My chest constricts. It can't be. Oh my God. *It is.*

It's Shane.

Shane Bennett.

The same Shane Bennett who ripped my heart out after four years together. Now he wants to be friends?

Seriously?

A swell of emotion wells up inside. No tears, though. I've shed my tears for him, hundreds, maybe thousands of them. What I'm feeling now are only aftershocks of hurt that surface anytime I stumble upon a reminder of him. Little ripples of what once was.

He moved to the Midwest from England to live with his grandparents for high school and stayed on for college. That's where we met. I don't remember why, but we started talking and never stopped. We were always together. He was all attitude and messy hair. I loved his hair.

He was my first real love. My first real heartbreak. My first real *everything.*

I glance at my Kensington box in the closet. It should really be labeled *Kensington and Shane.* Every card that passed between us and all our little mementos are securely locked inside. I walk over and stand on my toes to jab at it until I have a good grip and pull it down. There's one photo I'm desperate to see. I used to have it in a frame next to my bed; it's how I remember him.

Placing the box on the project table, I unzip the top slowly, as if the memories I've trapped could somehow escape.

I push through the loose contents, searching. Cards are stacked and tied together with string. A terry wristband is lying loose. I lift it to my nose and inhale. The scent of him is long gone, but the memory of me wearing it while I slept isn't. I set it down and wade through the photos.

My mouth presses into a hard line when I spot it. Shane's leaning against the wall with his collar popped and his notebook hanging low in his hand. That's the face I said good night to, the one that greeted me in the morning, and the one I missed for so long.

Looking between the old photo and his Facebook profile picture, I compare them. Same wavy dark hair. Same honey-brown eyes. Same Shane.

He's older. But it's definitely him.

A heavy sigh blows out. Why didn't he tell me it was all a lie? I would've believed him. I wanted things to stay the same. I wanted him. But he didn't say anything, just that he was sorry. And that it wasn't something he could explain because—

"Kenzi?" It's my Aunt Greta.

"I'm in here," I say, throwing the photo inside the box and replacing the lid. Quickly, I zip it up and toss it back on the shelf.

"Thought I'd find you up here. They're ready to eat."

She has on dark jeans and a billowy white tunic. A turquoise necklace brings out the blue in her eyes and pops her newly red locks.

"Like the hair," I say and smile, quickly clicking my phone off.

Aunt Greta flips her shoulder-length curls. "Your mom hates it. Says it draws too much attention."

I raise an eyebrow. "Isn't that the point?"

She laughs a warm, deep laugh. "It's a bonus."

I'm not sure if she means that it's a bonus because it bothers my mom or that it gets attention. Most likely both. Aunt Greta is considered the black sheep, the unconventional one, because she doesn't care what anyone thinks. She's one notch below me, the never-get-it-right-but-at-least-she-tries hen in the Shaw family pecking order.

She pulls my hand out to admire the ring and whistles. "Wow. That had to cost a mint. What'd Renson say?"

Aunt Greta's the only one who knows my nickname for the Ren and Grayson super duo. I grin and stifle a laugh.

She smiles. "Trust me, she'll have additional stones fitted on her band next time you see her." Releasing my hand, she nods toward the door. "Come on, might as well get this shindig started."

Trailing behind, I fish out my phone again. I still don't know why Shane would contact me now, after all this time. *Wait.* The friend request is gone.

Where's the request?

A knot forms in my stomach. I tap on the app so my profile wall pops up. It reads, "Kenzi Shaw is now friends with Shane Bennett and one other person." *What?*

AUNT GRETA'S LATEST BOY TOY is called Finley. He seems nice enough, but I don't bother to get to know him, because he won't be here for the next brunch go-round. He shows far too much interest in Ren, who is politely ignoring his nonstop questions about her culture.

"Ren's from Chicago, Fin," Aunt Greta says with a stern, enough-already look.

"So how's the hospital been treating you, Grayson? Were you able to use the 3-D video to assist with the thorascopey?" Dad asks as he adds hot sauce to his eggs.

Grayson pauses with his empty glass in the air. "You know, I did get my hands on it last week. It's an effective tool. I'm suggesting to the board that we invest."

"Good, good," Dad says and passes some sausage-rolled pan-cake things to Ren.

"Anything exciting over in Pediatrics?" he asks her and takes back the serving plate.

"Oh, well, there's always something of interest when working with children," Ren says with a smile.

Dad nods his agreement, manages a few more bites, and turns to Finley. "So, Finley, what do you do?"

Bradley piles two more sausages on his plate and waves Mom away when she tries to add a few pancakes.

"Bradley doesn't eat carbs, Mom," I remind her.

Finley sits up and clears his throat. "Well, sales. Phones now. I've always worked in sales of some sort."

"Good, good," Dad says. "Bradley's the sales manager at Safia downtown, biggest ad agency in Indianapolis. Handles all my media buys." Dad owns a medical spa here in the Village, where you can have Botox, a lip plump, and a plastic surgeon consult-ation, all under one roof. It makes no sense to me that he and my mom are so proud of Bradley for his position, but mine as a creative director is considered frivolous. We're at the same agency and both hold titles.

Bradley nods and waves his fork to make a point. "That reminds me, I have some numbers crunched for the Channel Six afternoon blitz we talked about."

I wait for Bradley to finish talking about when housewives with 2.3 kids in private school and a disposable income over six figures watch television. I outwardly nod and smile, but inside I'm bubbling with excitement, impatient to discuss our wedding plans.

Aunt Greta winks at me and interrupts Bradley's long-winded ramble. "Kensington, have you two set a date yet?"

All eyes turn to me. I beam. I'm up. *This is it.* My stomach turns cartwheels.

Bradley grabs my hand and flashes a warm smile. "No firm plans as of yet, but maybe next spring? What do you think?"

"Maybe," I say brightly at the thought. "Spring could be really nice—"

"Oh! I can't stand it anymore. Guess what will be here next spring as well?" Ren blurts out the question with an unusual amount of bubble in her voice. "A baby! We're pregnant!"

"Oh! Oh my goodness!" Mom squeals and is up running around the table. Her arms wrap both Ren and Grayson in an awkward bear hug. "She's pregnant! I'm going to be Grandma Shaw!"

Everyone's yelling and clapping. It's like Vegas when the slot machine hits.

Ding. Ding. Ding. Ding. Team Ren: Two hundred and seventy-seven. No, three hundred! Five hundred! It's too many to count. She's hit the frickin' jackpot!

My dad's going on about being called Grandpa. Grayson explains they couldn't put off kids forever, what with Ren being twenty-nine and all. I mean, my God, she's *almost* thirty. Even

Finley is pumping my dad's hand in congratulations. Mom yells over to me that I have no time to waste, that Bradley and I had better have a quick wedding to get things moving.

Aunt Greta looks at me and gives me an "I know, honey" kind of look. I force a half-smile to show her it's nothing. I mean, of course I'm happy for them.

A baby.

It is the jackpot.

I'm not thirty yet, so there's still time.

Glancing at my engagement ring, I imagine a new *you're fired* sign in thick red marker. This time it's for my sister-in-law. No flowers or frogs for her.

She already has a baby.

WE DIDN'T EVEN TALK ABOUT the wedding.

I toss my bag on my kitchen counter, peel off my coat, and head to the fridge for wine. It's been a long day. Instead of feeling excited and happy, I'm drained. Thoughts of today's Shaw family brunch, Shane's sudden reappearance, and Ren's big announcement are swirling around in my head making me dizzy.

A bottle of white is opened and chilled, so I pour a glass. Bradley prefers the good stuff, but keeps my apartment well stocked with the less expensive sweet wine because he knows I like it. I take a sip and lean against the counter, letting the fruity blend push down the lump that's been stuck in my throat.

A baby *is* big news. It's the first grandchild. I'm sure after the shock wears off Mom will want to discuss the wedding and help me with all the details. Of course she will. I'm her only daughter and there's so much to do: find a dress, pick a venue—we don't even have a date yet.

She did like the ring.

I hold up my hand to admire it. What's not to like? It sparkles and radiates all the four Cs: clarity, cut, consistency, and carats. Maybe I should include one more. Crazy. Because *I* don't like it.

Well, I mean, I like it—it's just not the ring I would have chosen. It's traditional and really big. Maybe a little too big. My mouth lifts up in a smile because Bradley says I'm worth it.

The ring doesn't matter anyway, it's beautiful and I'm happy. I'm getting married and one step closer to starting a family. Bradley wants lots of kids, a whole football team. I'd be happy with one. Maybe two.

At least one girl.

Staring blankly, I imagine ballet classes and dance recitals. I could be a class mom and help with costumes. I once made my doll a tutu from the petticoat of one of my dresses. I remember Mom screaming because it was from some hoity-toity designer. I wonder if my daughter will be born with hair? Bradley was bald, and I barely had enough to clip a bow in. Mom had to tape it to my head.

Ren will probably have a girl.

It's fine. I'm next. There's time.

Finishing my wine, I promptly pour another glass. I do this after every Shaw family brunch, torturing myself with my tally of mental check marks to see how I've stacked up to my family's expectations. I never win. I'm not sure why I thought today would be any different.

One more long drink to fortify myself, and I walk over and sit at my desk, logging in to Facebook.

I held off for a whole fifteen minutes.

My heart beats a little faster as I type "Shane Bennett" in the search box. Small sparks of excitement flutter around inside as his face appears, listed as one of my friends. All grown up. *But did he really grow up?* Shane had big ideas, but lacked follow-through. He barely made it to class. In fact, I did a lot of his papers.

I take another drink and study his photo. His hair is still in loose, messy waves, although it's shorter. He has the beginning of scruff across his jaw. There's a hint of a smile.

God, he's still gorgeous. It's frickin' annoying.

The demon plan I've hatched includes posting several photos of my uber-ring, random posts about how wonderfully happy and successful I am, then after a few days—I need to make sure he's had time to see it all—I'll delete him.

Again.

Forever.

Goodbye.

I blow a wayward strand of hair from my face. Tonya, a girl we hung out with and I now work with, was the one who found out he'd cheated. I didn't want to believe her, but when I questioned him about it, his face did that thing where the expression doesn't quite match the words, and inside, I knew. I could feel it.

After that, when he tried to explain, I wouldn't listen. Then he left for the UK to work with his dad, and I was left here alone. It was done.

We were done.

I sigh. *I'm* done. I log off and change.

My mind's reeling with babies and Shane Bennett. I need to settle. We have a big presentation at work tomorrow. Bradley wants us well rested and ready. But I'm not resting, well or otherwise.

I burrow into my pillow and pull my covers up. If Bradley were here, I'd at least be warm. He's like my own personal furnace and my feet are cold. I should've let him stay over, but I told him I wasn't feeling well. I'm really not. My heart's sitting in my stomach.

In *13 Going on 30*, Jennifer Garner's character, Jenna, wishes to be thirty and with wishing dust she wakes to find she is, and her life is everything she'd hoped for. Until she digs in deeper and discovers it came with a price. But she gets a do-over.

Where's my do-over?

I'm almost thirty and my life is . . . *what?* Everything it's supposed to be, but still it's not good enough. *I'm* not good enough. Fighting back tears, I stare at the ceiling. Today was supposed to be one of those special moments you always remember. The big feel-good scenes like you see in the movies. Where the dad can't believe his little girl is really getting married and the mom sheds happy tears.

Instead, I'm the only one with tears, and my moment ended up on the cutting room floor.

CHAPTER TWO

Ten Minutes' Notice

$\mathcal{S}$ITTING IN THE AGENCY'S parking lot, I scan my Facebook feed. Shane hasn't updated anything. He friended me, so looking is allowed. My mom and Ren, however, both have a new status. Ren's reads, *Baby on board*, followed by a slew of congratulations and likes. Mom's says, *This is Patrice Shaw. I can't wait to be a grandma!*

There's no mention of my engagement. Not that I've announced it either, but still.

With a deep breath, I force back the emotion that's much too close to the surface and type, "Congratulations Ren and Grayson." It shows I'm happy and a part of things. Even if I'm really not a part of things . . . I *am* happy for them.

I click off the screen, throw my phone in my bag, and head inside to prepare for my pitch. The big meeting is for the Carriage House, a trendy restaurant trying to attract the date crowd on weekends. It's part of a larger company, and Clive, our general manager, wants the entire account.

If I lock this in, he's promised me a bonus. The extra money could be used for the wedding, since Bradley's bent on paying for most of it. Growing up without much, it's really important for him to stand on his own. He won't even consider letting my parents help like they did for Grayson and Ren. This is one of the things I love about him. Unfortunately, it also means a smaller wedding with even more scrutiny.

I *need* that bonus, so I need to embody a woman who's persuasive, someone like . . . Lucy Kelson, Sandra Bullock's character in *Two Weeks Notice*. She's smart, influential, and came up with the deciding factor between two seemingly like-styled envelopes by taste. Extremely clever girl. She'd get that bonus.

I run a mental check as I walk in. I look the part: smart pencil skirt, crisp white blouse, and frizz-free straightened hair. I know the part: present three visual variations for an effective brand launch. Now all I have to do is play the part to win them over. Think clever, smart, and confident.

When I enter the office, Clive's standing by my desk. I'm set up in a huge, open room with the other designers so I'm close to my team.

"Good morning," I say, sliding into my chair and waking up the computer.

Clive's eyeing the disarray of papers scattered about and his thick brows are creased in frustration. I have a process. It's messy. He needs to get over it.

"Morning. I was hoping to see today's conceptuals again." His hand taps excessively against his leg. "I want to make sure everything's in the pocket." He's dressed in his black power suit with white shirt and brick-red tie. It's the same thing he wears for every big meeting. He says it's lucky. Let's hope so. I want that bonus.

"I set them up last night," I say with bright enthusiasm. "They're all ready to go in the conference room." I hate his last minute look-sees. It's too late to change anything. Lucy Kelson's boss never questioned *her* choices. Of course, her boss was Hugh Grant. Clive's more like Howard, the brother character, but with hair.

"Thirty minutes," he says glancing at his watch, and heads off to inspect them. For whatever reason, Clive has been particularly anxious about this account.

He's making me nervous.

The moment I log in, I pop open Facebook, just to see if, oh I don't know, my engagement's been announced in the last five minutes. My chat window pops up with the familiar chime. Ellie must be in. My eyes swivel down.

My heart jumps. *Not Ellie.*

SHANE BENNETT: Hi, Kensington.

It was never Kenz or Kenzi. Always Kensington, and I loved how it sounded on his lips. I'm frozen, vacantly staring at his name and photo icon. It's been years and yet . . .

I can feel him through the computer.

Feel him.

Okay, breathe. *It's fine.* Just keep it short and say you've got to go. I sit up a little straighter, place both feet flat on the floor, determined to be poised and nonchalant. As if I'm composing some major literary masterpiece, I type two letters with an exaggerated exactness, then hit Enter.

KENZI SHAW: Hi.

SHANE BENNETT: You look great.

I look great? I don't respond. Instead, I stare inanely at the words, jaw clenched, eyes wide.

SHANE BENNETT: The business shot is nice, but the one with paint in your hair is my favorite.

He went through my albums?

I quickly scroll through my images and find my business shots, all professional and perfect. Bradley loves these, says I look like a million bucks. I search down and find the one Shane mentioned. I'm sitting in front of a canvas, a brush in my hand, paint on my face, and my knotted-up pigtails are covered in splashes of yellow and blue. I'm smiling and a mess.

I should change my profile picture to one of me and Bradley from this summer's pool party at my parents'. We're laughing and being silly. Plus, his shirt's off in most of them and he's seriously ripped.

SHANE BENNETT: Still there?
KENZI SHAW: Working. Getting ready for a big presentation.

I type this like we talk all the time and there was never anything between us. My emotions are bubbling around wildly, as if they're carbonated and someone shook the bottle. It was ages ago. *What is he doing? Why is he contacting me now?* I'm perched on the edge of my chair, gawking at the screen in disbelief. My heart resides in my throat. This is crazy.

SHANE BENNETT: I returned to the States about six months ago.

My hand covers my mouth. He's *here*? I don't respond. Instead, I blink hard and wait, breathing deeply through my nose.

SHANE BENNETT: Caught *Pretty Woman* on TV. Remember that one?

Only every line. I'm smiling in spite of myself. It's one of my favorites. Okay, they're all my favorites. There's something so innocent and sweet about romantic movies. The world doesn't always make sense, but in a good romantic comedy, I'm guaranteed a happily ever after. The girl always gets the right guy, the guy that really *gets* her at the most basic level.

In *Pretty Woman*, Edward sees Vivian as a bright, special woman. She wants desperately to believe that about herself.

A bubble of bliss swells in my chest. I bet Shane and I watched *Pretty Woman* at least fifty times. Late at night snuggled on the couch. Laughing, saying the lines. Kissing in between them.

There's a familiar tug on my heart followed by a twinge of guilt. My smile drops. I shouldn't be thinking about this.

I'm happily engaged.

I lean over and type with speed.

KENZI SHAW: Really need to work. Sorry.

Oh my God. Clicking off Facebook, I sit gaping at the screen. With a quick gasp of air to clear away the confusion, I lean back. What *was* that?

I need to get my focus back on track. I have a presentation. A *fiancé*.

I need to see Bradley.

Swiveling my chair, I jump up and head toward his office, peeking into Tonya's as I pass. She has a potential client with her and looks bored. I can always tell because her eyes glaze over and her smile's painted on. If she hasn't closed the deal in thirty minutes, she's ready to kick them out. "It's a numbers game, sweetie," she always says.

Tonya attended the same college as Shane and me. We used to be somewhat close. In fact, she was the one who told me the creative director position here had opened up, although I think it surprised her when I got it. *Does Tonya know Shane's back?*

"Hi." I smile at Bradley and settle into one of the club chairs across from him. I catch the scent of his aftershave. It smells like the forest, all woodsy and fresh.

Looking up, he flashes a smile but then his expression drops. "You okay?"

My head kicks back. "What do you mean? Yeah, I'm great." I'm not. I'm a cocktail of confusion. *Is it that obvious?*

Bradley's big shoulders fall. "You're still upset about yesterday, aren't you?"

I shrug, dismissively. "Yeah, of course." Actually, I hadn't thought about it for at least fifteen minutes. But before that, yes, definitely still upset. "It's just . . . well, the timing of Ren's announcement." He hates the whole Ren, Mom, and me thing. I'm not sure he really understands it.

"Kenz, everyone's just excited. It's the first grandchild."

I cross my arms defensively and furrow my brows. "I get that, trust me, I do. A baby's exciting. But so is a wedding. *Our* wedding. She couldn't wait a week and let me have this one day?" I hear the barb in my voice and mentally pull it out. My arms fall loose and I pick at my nonmanicured nail instead. "It's just . . . I wanted to start planning with everyone."

"I know. And you will. As soon as things calm down, you'll wish your mom would leave you alone." Bradley likes to solve things. If it were up to him, the three of us would sit down and have a mature discussion to set things right. But how can a lifetime of hurts get set right when only one side feels them?

I stand and walk to the doorway, my lips pulled up in a trying smile. "It's fine."

"Hey . . . it *is* fine."

You'd think by now men would be able to decode the word *fine*. It doesn't mean everything's okay. No, it means there's more to say, much more. As an acronym it could stand for Feelings Inside Not Expressed. And it needs a P.S., because they will be, eventually. It's just a matter of time.

I gesture toward the hall. "I'm gonna grab a water before we start, you want one?"

"No. I'm good. Listen . . ." Bradley's expression tightens and he leans forward on his desk. "I've been meaning to discuss something with you, but I don't want you to be worried."

"Discuss what?" I'm frozen in the doorway, already concerned.

He lowers his voice. "The agency's in a bit of trouble. Financially."

I step forward, surprised. "What are you talking about? How much trouble?"

"Enough that we're depending on this account to pull us through next quarter."

"Wait, what?" I'm standing rigid now, my hands on my hips. He has my complete attention. This doesn't make sense. *We've been busy.*

"Clive needs to make some cuts. A round of layoffs."

No way. Stepping closer, I stand in front of his desk, eyes wide.

"Yeah, and um . . ." His eyes soften. "It includes the creative director position, Kenz."

"Wait. My position . . . or *me*?"

"Both, I'm sorry."

My knees wobble. I lean on his desk so my hands can support me.

Bradley's talking fast. "Clive can save your position's salary and just use a few of the designers to get us through. It's the way he ran things in the beginning. He was going to talk with you after today's meeting."

"So you tell me *now*? Ten minutes before the presentation?" I push off the desk, swallowing hard. I don't know what else to say. *Did I really just hear him right?* Maybe I overchanneled Sandra's character in *Two Weeks Notice*. I *need* this job.

His hand runs over his jaw in frustration. "I didn't want to tell you at all. I've been scrambling, trying to convince Clive of other options. But this morning he mentioned he was going to talk with you and I didn't want you to hear it from him. . . . I'm sorry." He shifts, sitting straighter. "Look, worst case, we hold off the wedding a while."

Hold off the wedding.

Holding off is not an option. Holding off means pushing back starting a family. Ren's already pregnant and she's almost thirty! *I'm* almost thirty.

I can feel the tears building on my lower lids, threatening to ruin my makeup. *Shit.*

Bradley's head tilts. "Kenz, hon, it'll be okay." He stands and walks around his desk so he's directly in front of me. One hand lifts my chin. "I'm sure you'll pull off the account, you always do. Either way, we'll be fine." His voice is reassuring, although I can still see the worry around his eyes.

"Yeah, okay. We'll be fine." Only this time *fine* stands for *F**ked In Nasty Economy*. I force a small smile. "I, um . . . just need a minute. I'll see ya in there."

How can we be so busy and yet be in financial trouble? It doesn't add up. My job is on the line?

"Margaritaville tonight?" Tonya calls out as I pass by her office.

Backtracking, I peek inside. Ellie's seated in the side chair, a cup of coffee in her hands. Tonya will keep her job. She's in sales, works off commission. But Ellie's a programmer, so I'm not sure she's safe.

I give a closed-mouth smile and lean on the door. A drink with the girls does sound good. "Yeah, count me in."

"So, did your family go crazy over wedding details yesterday?" Ellie asks and takes a sip of coffee. Her words throw unintentional salt in the open wound.

"Er . . . we never really got around to it. Renson's preggo."

"Oh my God, really?" Ellie's blue eyes widen with a snort-laugh. "Can you imagine all the crapola she's going to have? Designer everything. She's going to be Pregzilla."

Pregzilla, I like that.

Tonya raises an eyebrow. "Whatever. It was bound to happen. That's what married people do, right? Have babies. Besides, Kenzi's next in line."

"Well, that's the plan; as soon as we get through the wedding stuff, we start trying." *We need to get to the wedding first. The thought stabs at my heart. I don't want to wait. I want to plan our wedding and start our family. I want to be Pregzilla. Well, not the zilla part.*

Tonya puts the cap back on her water and crinkles her nose. "Honey, it won't happen if you wait too long. And your wedding plans? Yeah, they just took a backseat to the Renson mini-me. As soon as she starts showing, the entire fam will be in hyper baby mode."

"Bitch," Ellie says to Tonya and narrows her eyes.

"Yeah, that one's deserved." She lifts her chin and looks at me. "But Kenz knows it's true, don't ya, babe?"

"Which part? About my family or you being a bitch?"

"Both!" Ellie says laughing.

Even though Tonya is competitive over everything, and I mean *everything*, she gets it. That's why I tolerate her. But if I'm being honest, she's always fallen somewhere between a friend and frenemy. I tap the door frame with my hand. "Meeting's in five. I'll see you in there."

THE CARRIAGE HOUSE IS TECHNICALLY Tonya's account, but anytime there's real money involved, Bradley and Clive basically take over. Two programmers are sitting across from Tonya at the conference table, discussing the functionality of the proposed website. Their jobs will probably be cut. My stomach sours.

"Hi." I nod, set my stuff down, then make sure all three of my concept boards are in place up front. Satisfied, I sit, leaning my forehead in my hand. I need to calm down.

I keep hearing Bradley's words, *hold off the wedding*. We haven't even locked in any plans and they're being taken away from me. And now my job? What about my bonus?

"You good?" Tonya asks, nudging my shoulder.

"Define good," I say as the Facebook chat chimes on my phone. It's Ellie. *Silent mode.* My eyes fall on the earlier chat message from Shane. I select it and hold it in front of Tonya for her to see, she's going to flip.

She squints at the screen then pops her eyes. "Oh my God! That's *Shane!*" She turns to me, excited. "You're talking with him again?"

"Shh . . . *No.* No." I look around to make sure Bradley's not lurking in the hall. He and Clive should be waiting in the lobby to escort the client to our conference room. "He contacted me," I say, then notice the programmers have taken an interest. "It's nothing, old college friend me and Tonya both know."

Tonya blows out a breath and pulls my arm closer for a better look. "*Pretty Woman?*"

"Don't *read* it." I yank it back. I just wanted her to see the photo.

All at once, there's a commotion of footsteps and voices. Clive's escorting in the Carriage House team. We stand as they file through and Clive begins casual introductions. It's like a jumbled reception line with people reaching this way and that, pumping hands and dropping names.

At this stage, I've only worked with our team, and I'm not catching anyone's name. My brain's still foggy. *Where's Bradley?* People are settling, taking seats. This is it. I'm up first. Arranging my notes, I take a sip of water then start toward the front to get things rolling.

Clive raises a finger. "Kenzi, hold on. We're still waiting on the owner of the Carriage House—" His head turns abruptly to the door. "Oh, there he is."

I whip around, catching sight of Bradley and—

"Everyone, this is Mr. Shane Bennett."

I spit my water.

I'm choking. Gagging. It's caught in my throat. *Oh my God.* I'm hacking up a lung. Everyone turns to look at me as I hunch over the table in spasm. I raise a finger in the air to signal *hold on.* I can't get it to stop.

I turn and look toward the door. *Shit.* It *is* him . . . it *is* Shane. He's watching me. I cover my mouth and wave my finger again, this time to excuse myself. I rush past him, hacking, to the restroom.

Shane Bennett's *here.*

Well, he's back there. I'm in the restroom. I clear my throat and splash some cold water on the back of my neck. This isn't a coincidence. He must've known where I worked. He totally knew everything the whole time we chatted.

Oh. My. God.

I told him I had a *big* presentation to give. My mind races through the whole conversation. *He's* the client. He's the *owner?* Why didn't he tell me? Why is he *here?*

The bathroom door opens. It's Tonya. She's shaking her head, mouth hanging open. "Oh my God, right? Shane Bennett? Quite an exit, by the way, spray the clients with spittle and run out in a crazy coughing fit." She laughs, checking her lipstick in the mirror.

"You could've warned me." My heart's still thudding hard in my chest.

Tonya's eyes narrow as she looks at me in the reflection. "I would've, had I known. Clive and Bradley went to all the meetings; I only dealt with that big guy from marketing." She spins around. "Look, boss-man sent me to retrieve your dying ass. Just take a deep breath and get it together. You got this, right?"

"Yeah." *No.* "Tell Clive I'll, um, be right in," I say and mess with my shirt collar in the mirror.

She sizes me up in the reflection.

My eyes meet hers. "*What?* I'm fine. Go. I'm right behind you." I casually finger-comb my hair until she leaves.

When the door shuts, I collapse, hands braced on the sink. *Oh my God.* Does Bradley know who he is? He can't. Tonya didn't even know. *What the hell is he doing here?* My mind scrambles trying to absorb it all. Shane Bennett's the client. The account I need approved so I don't lose my job, my bonus, or my wedding.

I straighten and shake my head to get a grip. I need to pull it together. So what if I went all Bridget Jones when I saw him. This is for everything. The whole shebang. I'm not even sure what a shebang is, but I want all of it. So, *screw this*.

Screw *him*.

I start back toward the conference room, pumping my arms with determination, but pause right outside the door to steady my heart. I take a deep breath in . . . and soothing breath out. Again. Deep breath in and . . . hold . . . hold . . . hold, and release. I exhale in a loud, raspy *whoosh*. I sound like a deranged Darth Vader. "I am your father," I say and almost laugh. It's either laugh or cry.

"So, you've traded chick flicks for *Star Wars*?"

It's cry.

I freeze and tightly close my eyes. Of course it would be him. Spinning, I face grown-up Shane holding a coffee and looking bemused.

"Hello, Kensington." The *ens* drags out a bit and the rest pops up crisp like a Pringle in his blended American Brit accent.

I'm momentarily dazed by the sound of my name on his lips.

"I wasn't sure how long you'd be, so I . . ." He holds up his cup, eyes locked on mine.

I give a forced smile. It feels plastic and strained. I can't help but notice the changes in him. He's older, filled out.

A man.

From the way his black V-neck clings across his chest I'd guess he still boxes, or at least works out. I bite my lip and try to think of something pithy and indifferent to say.

The conference room door opens with a *click.* "Oh, good, she's back. Now we can begin, *again.*" A noticeable exasperation colors Clive's tone. He widens the door and motions for us to come in. "Kensington, if you would." He points to the front.

"Yes, right." My stomach spirals.

Bradley gives me a nod of encouragement. Tonya smirks and pushes my water bottle back as I pass. I narrow my eyes.

"Right," I say again and quickly glance at Shane, who's now sitting in the back next to Clive. I turn to my design boards, remove the blank cover, and lean it against the wall.

I *can* do this. I'm Lucy Kelson, Sandra Bullock's character, cool and persuasive. "The Safia Agency has developed three complete conceptuals based on your company's unique needs in the market-place." I pull the words from muscle memory.

My heart jumps, catching Shane's eyes briefly before looking away.

"Each one focuses on a slightly different approach to reach the same goal." My hands shake as I set the first example on the lip of the huge dry erase board, then the second, leaving the third on the easel, so all three are visible. I glance around the room at everyone except Shane. "Our first concept zeros in on—"

"Can you step to the side for just a moment?" Shane asks, leaning out to see around me.

"I'm sorry?" I look at him, then Clive, confused.

Clive waves his hand to indicate I should move, so I do. Shane focuses on each board. He positions his hand under his chin as he considers the concepts. The room's quiet. Everyone's looking at Shane. This is crazy. This is *not* how it works. This wouldn't happen to Lucy Kelson.

I step forward. "I was just about to go through the plan for each—"

"Yes, right. I understand. Each one has its own agenda." His lips stretch into a hard line. "But it looks as though you weren't given mine."

"I'm sorry?"

Shane stands and walks up to the first board to take a closer look. I'm floored. This has never happened. The client listens, I give my spiel, and they pick one. There might be a few adjustments, but that's how it's done. *Why is he up here?* Clive shrugs when I give him a questioning look.

"I'm afraid some things weren't conveyed to you." There's a pause.

What the hell is he talking about?

He smiles. It's his I'm-just-being-polite smile. I've seen it hundreds of times, except now it has faint creases on either side. I'm at a complete loss. Clive is tapping his pen.

Shane continues, "The movie theater. It's a restaurant and theater in one. Maybe the theater part wasn't conveyed as being as important as the restaurant, Clive, but if this concept's successful, we plan on opening multiple locations."

"A movie theater? *Inside* the restaurant?" I say incredulously. It just slips out.

"It's unexpected, right?" Shane gives me an inquiring look.

I'd say this whole day is unexpected.

"I want the focus on the theater, not just the dinner." He nods to Clive and turns to the group. "We want to create an experience. Great food while you watch the best romantic comedies. It's the ultimate date night."

Clive is now standing and nodding his head. "Sure. Kenzi can work with you on the specifics. Shouldn't be a problem to add that in."

Shane doesn't wait for me to respond. "We'll be using well-known, classic movie moments as part of the brand and overall experience, like, say, *Pretty Woman*."

My stomach drops. I snap my eyes to him.

"Oh, I love that movie, don't you, Kenz?" Tonya smirks, then looks to one of the programmers. "The shopping scene is the best."

Oh my God.

"Yes! Great. What other movies or scenes?"

Shane spins around and motions for others to chime in. He's completely taken over my presentation.

Clive crosses his arms over his chest, eyebrows high. "I liked *When Harry Met Sally*."

"*Say Anything*'s a classic," says Rand Peterson, the Carriage House marketing director.

Tonya leans over the table so she can see him. "There's always bad karaoke in those movies and they seem to meet up in really crazy ways."

"It's called the *meet-cute* when that happens," Shane adds.

Tonya looks from Shane to me with a twisted grin. "*I* think it's pretty cute."

I spear Tonya with a glare.

Ignoring her, Shane says brightly, "We can list the top ten or so favorite scenes and movies and then incorporate them into the brand. Add in celebrity bios, movie trivia . . . What do you think?"

The room fills with an excited babble. Apparently, everyone loves this idea.

Suck-ups.

Shane's looking at me. Now everyone else is, too.

"What do I think?" I think I've completely lost control of this pitch and my Lucy Kelson character. Instead of portraying her sharp and persuasive traits, I'm twisted up as badly as her bobcat pretzel. I look Shane straight in the eye. "Well, I'm not much of a romantic movie fan, but—"

"Yes, you are," Bradley says with confidence. "You love romantic comedies. You could probably recite all the lines."

I look from Benedict Bradley to Shane. So does everyone else. It's like a tennis match.

"Oh, forgot. You're a *Star Wars* fan now, right?" Shane's smiling, clearly enjoying himself.

I really hate him.

Clive walks to the front. "Why don't we get an e-mail going with everyone's top ten movie moments, then Mr. Bennett can narrow down which ones to use in the redesign?" His brows are arched expectantly. "Sound good, Kenzi?"

I smile thinly. "Of course," I say, knowing I just need to close this deal. There's too much at stake. *Everything's* at stake.

"Unfortunately, I'm not sure that'll be enough," Shane says, looking right at me before turning to Clive. "I may need to rethink my strategy. I'm afraid another agency might be better suited."

What? My mouth drops open. We can't lose this account. *What is he doing?* It's not like he didn't know I was here. So why go to all this trouble just to walk? He's already walked on me once.

I don't need a repeat performance.

CHAPTER THREE

Truth Is Ugly

"TWO MORE SKINNY MARGARITAS please," Ellie says over the music.

We're perched at the bar at Champps; it's a great place to catch a bite and a drink after work. It's also connected to the Circle Center Mall, which is Tonya's happy place. I left the office early, but didn't have time to travel across town to Bates Art Supply, which is *my* happy place. So I borrowed hers.

I'm still not happy.

With my employment status now in question, shopping is out of the question. So, I played around in the fragrance department at Fossie's instead. At the moment, I smell of floral and musk. I wouldn't recommend this particular mixture.

I glance over at the booth where Bradley sits with Clive. When he called, I told him I was meeting the girls for drinks and he mistook it as an open invitation. *What was I going to say?*

It's fine. Whatever. That's why we're hanging out at the bar.

"I hate this." I shake my head. I've already told Ellie the whole stupid story of me and Shane and the presentation fiasco, at least the highlights. I left out how completely unraveled I am. "I mean, what are the odds? What do I say to Bradley?" I ask the bartender who is spending way too much time at our end of the bar.

He shrugs.

"And oh my God, Ellie." I palm my forehead, shaking it. "I basically required the Heimlich maneuver. So embarrassing."

Ellie nudges my shoulder. "It couldn't have been that bad."

"It actually was *that* bad, Ellie-bell," Tonya says from behind us. "What up, girlies?"

Sniffing the air, Tonya pulls her lips up in distaste. "Ick, what is that smell?"

I sigh and roll my eyes. "I was hiding out in fragrance at Fossie's."

"Jeez, Kenz, that's what they make the little sample papers for. Ugh." She waves a hand in the air.

I motion for the bartender to bring another round. "This one's on her," I say and point to Tonya. Taking a sip, I roll my shoulders, trying to loosen the tension in my neck.

I glance briefly toward Bradley and Clive. I know they're still devising a plan on how to close the deal. Truthfully, I feel responsible, like I botched things. But how was I supposed to know there was a movie theater thing? No one told me. And I can't tell Bradley how I know Shane, at least not right now.

Another sip and I turn to the door, exactly when Shane walks through. Of course. Our eyes meet. Yup, cue the music and kill me now.

I gag on my margarita.

"*Jesus*, are we going to start hacking again?" Tonya hits me on the back when I turn toward the bar.

"Slow down, tiger," Bradley says from behind me.

I didn't even see him get up.

Tonya stands and tugs on Ellie's arm. "Come with. I ordered some munchies at the table."

I drop my head in my hands, hiding my face as Bradley sits on the stool next to me. "So, is Clive angry?"

"No. Not angry. Worried."

I pull my head up and look at him. "So you think we might really lose the account?" I take a smaller sip of my drink.

"I don't know." Bradley shrugs. "It's actually my fault. I knew it was this movie thing, but every time I met with the guy, we mostly talked about the restaurant, so . . ." He shakes his head.

I peek over my shoulder to their table. Shane lifts a glass to me in a mock toast, then grins. I look away.

Definitely not telling Bradley right now.

"Bennett's not convinced we can pull off the concept. Like I said, it's my fault. I just need to convince him how there won't be any more miscommunications." Bradley turns so his legs are propped up on either side of me. "Maybe if *you* talk to him, he'd be swayed." He tips my chin and leans close.

I know he won't kiss me here; he considers us still on the clock since they're entertaining clients. But, right now, I'm tempted to plant a big one on him. Not because Shane's watching or anything. Which he is. I can see him from the corner of my eye.

"Come on, come over and be social." Bradley nudges my leg and smiles warmly.

"In a few minutes, okay? I just want to sit here for a bit and decompress."

"Well, what about just having a few words with him here, then?" He looks to the table and waves him over.

"*Bradley—*"

"Just a quick chat. It'll be fine." He gives my leg a squeeze, ignoring my glare, and heads back to their table.

Great. Tonya's laughing about something, but I turn my back to them. Bending the straw, I take a long sip.

"Hello, again," Shane says, taking the stool next to me.

I don't say anything. I analyze my drink and wonder if I'd still have the account if, by accident, it found its way into his lap?

"You're not going to talk to me?"

I catch the scent of sandalwood mixed with Shane and it registers familiar in my nose. I shake my head, exasperated. "What are you doing here?"

"Ah, she speaks."

I give him a don't-push-it glare. He chuckles.

Shane leans in close and says in a lowered voice, "So, you're dating that Bradley guy?"

Without looking at him, I hold up my left hand and wiggle my fingers so he can see the mega-rock.

"Really?"

I can still feel his eyes on me.

"Huh, I don't see it."

I snap my hand in front of his face.

"No, *that* I see. I meant I don't see you two—"

My eyes pop. "Don't," I say and point a warning finger in his direction. My heart is thumping erratically around in my chest. Hopefully I don't appear as discombobulated as I feel. I hate that he unnerves me. "Look, I'm not sure what's going on, and I don't want to fight with you, so if you want to talk about work, fine. But . . ."

Shane's eyes narrow. "Are we fighting?"

"Are you switching agencies?" I just put it on the line.

He stifles a laugh. "Huh, you didn't used to be that direct."

"A lot of things have changed," I say, with a sideways glare.

His gaze skims my outfit. "I can see that. Hardly recognize you in your corporate . . ." His hand waves toward my skirt.

Squaring my shoulders, I huff. "Are you staying or not, Shane?"

"Well, I've been thinking about that and . . ." Shane leans back on the stool. "I have a business proposition for you." A small smile hints at the corners of his mouth.

I lean an elbow on the bar and palm my chin, pretending I don't recognize the similarity to the *Pretty Woman* movie line. I mean, really, does he expect me to answer with "Yes, I'd love to be your beck-and-call girl. But you're a rich, good-looking guy. You could get a million girls."

Crap. Bradley's right, I do know all the lines. I refocus. "What's this proposition?"

"I'd like you to live the ten movie moments with me. Do *that* and I'll sign."

Heat rises up my neck and lands on my cheeks. *Is he messing with me?* "Movie moments?" I stare at him, perplexed. "*Live* the movie moments? Like act them out?" I titter with a half-smile. He's pulling my leg. "Okay, so *Confessions of a Shopaholic*, I'm going to run around speaking fake Finnish and you'll buy me a green scarf?"

"Well, in a manner of speaking, yes, but that one's not on the list. I just e-mailed you the final ten I selected."

My chin lowers. "You're serious? You're blackmailing me with movies? I'm not gonna do that. I'm not even sure I understand it. And Bradley's not going to go for that, so—"

"Wait, wait . . . hear me out." His hand lifts and hangs in midair. "The whole restaurant and movie thing, well, the movie part, was inspired by you . . . *us*, actually." He turns and meets my eyes. "The truth is—"

"*Ha,* the truth. What do you know about truth?" I mutter under my breath and take a drink.

"I was saying . . . who else would get this concept better than you, right?"

I shrug. I don't know what else to say. I try and relax the scowl that's set across my face, and round up the long-ago hurts that have been set free in order to shove them back down.

"Right." Shane scrubs his jaw. "And if you're happy with this Bradley guy—"

"Yes, *very* happy." I can't believe him. *What the hell?* I straighten, brows furrowed, feeling all prickly and vexed. "Bradley should have nothing to do with this. It's about the work. *My* work."

"You're right. And the work I saw today was good, but it was generic." Shane leans back, softening his tone. "I want something like you used to do. Like what's in your album. And if that's not something you can deliver, then, yeah, maybe a different agency can."

Wait . . . Album? *What album?* I blink, looking away. *My Facebook album.* All my abstracts and designs from my art classes. "My work from college," I say, glancing at him in acknowledgment.

"Yes. Back when you watched romantic movies excessively. Knew every line and story, and wore paint in your hai—"

"Shane, that was years ago. I'm not the same girl. *I've* grown up."

"Pity. Because the concept *I* want needs *that* girl. So maybe if you do the movie list, you'll rediscover her. And since you're so obviously happy in your relationship, it shouldn't be a problem." He opens his mouth as if he is about to say something else, but changes his mind. "Anyway, that's my deal."

"You're really serious?"

"Yes, Kensington, I'm really serious."

The air between us grows even heavier. I scoot my drink closer, and take a long sip through the straw, debating his offer, bouncing his words around in my head. I should be able to spend time with him, because I *am* happy.

"Okay, then here's *my* proposition." I sit up tall and stare him down. "I'll agree to your movie list, if you agree to my clause."

"Your clause?" His eyebrows rise.

"Yes, I've added my own little personal movie rider," I say, feeling in control finally.

"Am I going to need to buy large bags of M&M's and sort out all the brown ones?" Shane gives a crinkly smile.

I don't return it. I also pretend not to catch his reference to *The Wedding Planner*. "It's a truth clause."

"A truth clause?"

"Yup. I want the whole ugly truth." I just need to say it, put it out there. My heart's going to burst. "In college . . . tell me why you cheated."

His smile drops. "I didn't."

"Nope." I shake my head with frustration. "That isn't gonna cut it. You want participation, then I want the truth."

"You want to do this *now*? *Here?*" His jaw clenches. "I'm not getting into all of that here."

Standing, he throws the bartender a twenty, not realizing it's been taken care of, glances at me, and waits.

For what? I turn and look away. He shakes his head and walks toward the restroom. He doesn't want to get into it here? Then I don't need to be here when he gets back. Grabbing my bag, I sneak out.

I may have given up on the fairy tale, but this time, I'm not giving up without an answer. Just like Vivian in *Pretty Woman*, I want more.

LYING IN BED, I CHECK Facebook on my phone. Ren now has fifty-three likes and numerous comments of congratulations under her "Baby on board" status. I huff. I want to comment: *Baby is bored. Requests new topic. Like your sister-in-law's engagement.*

My phone rings in my hand—Mom's special ring. She never calls me late. What if something's wrong? I sit up and answer, an uneasy feeling in the pit of my stomach.

"Mom? Everything okay?"

"Kensington? It's Mom."

"Yes, I know. Is everything okay?"

"Yes, why wouldn't it be?"

I wave a hand up in the air. "It's almost eleven. You don't usually call past six."

"Oh, well, of course not, dear. But I wanted to make sure you and Bradley were aware of the family plans for the Saturday after next."

This is what she called about so late? "Er . . . what family plans?"

"Yes, well, with such big news, your father and I thought it would only be right to get everyone together to celebrate, and of course, you have to be there. Oh, hold on, I have another call. Hello?"

"Still me, Mom."

"Oh," she says. "Hello?"

"Mom, it's still me. You have to click the button that says answer."

"Oh, right," she says, then the phone goes dead.

She'll call back when she realizes she hung up on me. I bet she hung up on the other person, too. I lie back down, concentrating on her words. *A family get-together to celebrate. I have to be there?* It's too early for a baby shower.

I gasp. *An engagement party?*

Of course they're going to throw us a party, it's only natural. I mean, I'm their only daughter and they adore Bradley. I *will* get my special moment. I do get a do-over. I'm suddenly elated, floating on a happiness bubble. After the day I've had, I really needed this.

See, Shane? I *am* happy . . . about grown-up things like engagement parties. His voice keeps playing in my head. *This concept needs that girl.* What does he know? Nothing. I'm exactly the same girl I was in college, only better.

Just because I haven't picked up a brush in a while doesn't mean I'm not an artist. I still . . . well, okay, I haven't been to the art museum recently either. It used to be my weekly ritual. I do miss that. And I miss working on the pottery wheel. I loved turning sludgy brown clay into something beautiful.

And I do still watch romantic comedies. I have no problem incorporating these into the concept; I just didn't know there was a movie theme. I don't need to *live the moments* with him in order to do that. *Who does he think he is?*

I lift my phone, click on the e-mail app, and glance again at the one Shane sent. He's titled it the Love Like the Movies list.

1. Sleepless in Seattle
2. Pretty Woman
3. Bridget Jones's Diary
4. 27 Dresses
5. Dirty Dancing
6. Sixteen Candles

He hasn't specified any particular scenes. Is he going to just randomly choose one from each movie? I'm not even sure I understand what he's proposing. I roll over, hugging my pillow to my side, while my mind scrambles recalling each movie.

Pretty Woman has a multitude of great scenes. There's the shopping one. The polo match with the polka-dot dress. I *love* that dress. She looks so pretty, and the hat? The hat makes the whole look. Why don't people wear hats like that anymore? *Oh*, the opera, and the fancy dinner with the "slippery little suckers." Does Shane remember that I hate seafood?

Once when his grandparents came for a visit, they took us out for lobster. Shane tried not to laugh at my expression as I forced a few bites down. A tiny, secret excitement flitters around with the memory. Guilt quickly yanks it down with a heavy thud.

Shit. Everything's getting all mixed up between movies and memories.

I flip on the TV to force everything from my mind, then my phone rings, startling me. Bradley. *Finally.* I thought he'd call hours ago.

"Hey," I say, and immediately yawn. I can tell he's in his car. I'm on speaker and can hear myself in an echo.

"Hi, hon. I wanted to make sure you got home okay. Sorry if I woke you."

"No, I'm still up. Got home safe and sound." I turn down the volume. "You just leaving Champps?"

"Um, yeah, Clive and that Rand Peterson kept knocking 'em

back. I wanted to make sure Rand got a cab, and I just dropped off Clive."

He always looks out for everyone, always has their back. He's going to make a great dad. Mental images of Bradley coaching Little League pops to mind. All Shane knows is boxing.

"What about that Bennett guy?" I ask without thinking.

"You mean your ex?"

Oh. *Shit.*

"The one you didn't bother to tell me about? Now I get why you seemed off in the meeting." His voice is controlled, but sharp. "Here's the thing . . ."

I'm sitting in my bed, both hands clutching the phone, eyes wide.

"You could have told me, and I have to wonder why you didn't."

"Okay." I stand and flip on a light. "I didn't know until he was there today. I was completely blindsided. It was a shock. And then tonight—"

"Tonight, I sat right next to you." I'm pretty sure his hand is off the wheel and gesturing as he talks. He always does that when he's irritated. "It was just us, and you didn't say—"

"Bradley. He was *in* the bar. You guys were entertaining *his* team." I'm pacing, my stomach knotted up tight. "You told me my job depends on this account. That we might have to delay our wedding! What the hell was I supposed to do? Tell you right there . . . and then what? What if you got angry?"

Silence.

I plop back on the bed, and fall back so my head bounces on the pillow. "I'm sorry. I didn't know what to do, okay? But I was going to talk to you about it when you called." I wasn't even thinking about it, to be honest. There's a twinge of guilt.

"Guy's kind of a tool, if you ask me," he says quietly.

"Yes! He is, right? I mean, your research was dead on. And the way he just took over the meeting? What *was* that?" My shoulders drop with relief. I think he can see my dilemma in not saying anything. I think everything's okay.

"He's an ass, but we need his account." There's a slight lull. "Tonya seemed to like him."

I sit straight up again. "What?"

"Yeah, she left right after he did. You know what that usually means."

I know exactly what that means. The knot inside pulls tighter. Tonya doesn't leave early. Ever. Not when she's the only girl, the center of attention, and there are potential deals to be made.

She wouldn't. There are rules about exes, clearly stated girl-world rules. "Um, I don't think Tonya and him hooked up. We all went—"

"You all went to school together. He's your ex from college. I know. It was fun hearing *all* about it from them. And I'm still pretty sure they hooked up tonight."

His words jab. I don't know what to say. "I'm sorry, okay?" And I am. "Why don't you stay here tonight? I have on that silky boxer set you like," I lie, but I could change quickly enough. I'm actually in terry-cloth Hello Kitty pajamas that Ellie bought me for my birthday last year.

A slight pause, then he sighs with a frustrated growl. "I'm already pulling into my drive, Kenz. And since he's not committing to the contract, I ah, need to figure out another way—"

"Wait. He *said* that?" I can't believe he's taking his movie deal this far.

"He said a lot of things, but yeah. He's going to think on it.

Listen, I'm beat, just get some sleep, and I'll see you tomorrow, okay? I love you."

"Love you, too." Obviously it's not all right or he'd be on his way over. I click off the phone, then the TV, and settle in under the comforter. I should have said something to him. Tonya's *not* hooking up with Shane, he's just saying that. His ego's bruised. Can't say I blame him. He said he heard *all about it* from Shane and Tonya. He also said Shane's *thinking on it*.

What's to think about? If he can't face the truth, he shouldn't have showed up. *Ugh*. I grab my pillow and cover my face. *We need his stupid account.* That's the ugly truth.

What happened after Vivian refused Edward's offer in *Pretty Woman*? I blow out a breath. He came back in a limo with flowers and climbed the fire escape, conceding to her demands. Curling on my side, I hug the pillow and squeeze my eyes shut.

Looks like I'm the one who needs to yield. Forget *Pretty Woman*, tomorrow's feature is *Pleading Woman*. And I'm not looking forward to its premier.

CHAPTER FOUR

Sleepless in Indy

SHANE'S WORDS BOMBARDED ME all night. They continue their attack as I walk into the agency this morning. *I want something like you used to do. The concept I want needs that girl.* They're buzzing 'round my head like a swarm of angry hornets. I need repellent.

Great. Clive's waiting for me. He looks worked up. That makes two of us. He motions for me to follow, and in no time, I'm sitting across from him in his office with the door closed.

A growing panic swells inside my chest. *Did Shane really pull the account?* I swallow hard as I pull off my jacket. There may be nothing to figure out. He might just fire me on the spot. This spot. Right now.

Folding my jacket neatly across my lap, I wait, mentally preparing my case. How long I've worked here. The quality of my work. The national clients I've worked with. I knew today was about groveling, I just didn't know it was the central theme.

Clive sits on the edge of his desk facing me, and slowly exhales. "Kensington, I wanted to talk to you about the agency's financial situation and how important the Carriage House account is to us."

I straighten, the lump still wedged in my throat, and dive in. "Bradley brought me up to speed."

"We *need* this account, do you understand?" He's scowling, his voice sharp and getting louder. "We're lucky we got them at all, and now—"

"But we did get them," I blurt. My heart belongs inside a jackrabbit. I lean forward to make my point. "And it was specifically because of me. My work." My *old* college art in my Facebook album, but still my work.

"Yes. Exactly. You're right, Kensington." Clive stands and gestures my way. "And now he might be leaving because of *your* work."

Ouch. My stomach churns. This isn't fair. Sitting back, I'm at a loss for words. Shane was serious . . . How do I explain why we're losing the account? What did Shane tell him last night? Clive's going to fire me. He really is. I've never been fired.

Another sigh escapes from Clive as he walks around his desk, finding his chair. "Look, you need to play nice. Convince him to stay. Do you understand?" His eyebrows are so high they almost touch his hairline.

I can't believe it's really coming to this.

"Yes, and I can fix this. I'll get him to reconsider." I stand, determined. I already planned to agree to the movie thing. It's fine.

"I want you to make sure he does." Clive lowers his chin. "By whatever means, understand? *Whatever* means," he repeats. "It's *that* important."

My mind is whirling. Clive nods again, and just when I don't think his eyebrows can't go any higher, they do. I think I know what he's implying, but he didn't actually say it.

I narrow my eyes. "I'll get him to reconsider because of the design initiatives I can offer, Clive. That's why he'll stay. That's the *only* offer on the table."

That and the movie list, but no need to mention that.

"Of course, exactly." Clive whips his hands in the air, chortles, and pops his eyes at me.

And now he's totally playing it off.

He stands and walks to open the door. "I don't care how you do it. But do it. Bradley has his contact info; get it, call him, and convince him. Just make things right." His voice is lowered, but cutting. "Do we understand each other?"

"Yes. Perfectly," I say, but I don't. I don't understand why we need his account so desperately in the first place. How is the company all of a sudden in financial distress? It doesn't make sense. Clive's acting so weird. In the pit of my stomach, I can feel something's off.

AT MY DESK, I KNEAD my forehead, eyes locked on Bradley's office. This has already been a long work day. I glance at the clock on my computer screen. He should be wrapping up with his sales team. The door opens. Here we go, people are starting to exit. I'm up, making a direct line for his door.

Besides the contract, I just want to talk with him, some reassurance. Then I'll find Shane, swallow whatever pride I'm pretending to have, and tell him I'm on board if he's serious about the movie list. I can already taste those words and they're sour.

"Hi," I say and pull the door shut before I sit down.

"Hi, hon." Bradley looks up briefly from the papers he's going through on his desk. He seems preoccupied.

I sit on the end of the club chair. I may have interrupted something. "What are you looking for?"

He looks at his watch, then opens his desk drawer and leafs through its contents. "Proposal I was working on with Clive. If I can upsell my client into a bigger buy, it might be enough to save your job, or at least prolong things." He shoves it closed, and again starts shuffling through folders stacked in front of him.

"Wait, Bradley . . ." *He's still upset at me?* "I just talked with Clive. I'm sure I can smooth things over. I just need the Carriage House contract."

Bradley looks up. The blue in his shirt plays off the color in his eyes, making them almost translucent. He taps his fingers on his desk, his lips drawn tight. "Is there anything I need to know, Kenz? Besides that he's your ex, I mean?"

Yeah, he's still upset.

"No." It's a quick answer. Maybe too quick. Even though I haven't done anything, little jabs of guilt are stabbing my insides. I stand and brush my dress free of imaginary dust. "I don't have a clue what his problem is." Technically not a lie. "And I told you, I didn't know he was the client," I add, to remind him.

He regards me for a moment then opens his bottom drawer. Within seconds I have the Carriage House contract and info.

Bradley looks at his watch. "Damn it, I'm really running late." He stands and reaches for his coat. "I'll just have Maggie e-mail another copy over, I guess." He gives me a quick peck, pops open the door, but then spins back around. "Oh, your mom sent us an e-mail invite thing for Saturday after next. Did you see it? I guess they're having—"

"Oh, right. An engagement party for us," I say, feeling the tiniest glint of excitement.

He starts walking toward the front with me trailing behind. "Well, it's also a mini-shower for Ren and Grayson. Guess they'll do the official one closer to her due date."

Stopping, my head jerks back as the words slice through me. No slow bleed. I'm gushing.

"Your mom mentioned Ren's registered at Fosberg's. We'll need to pick up a gift. Can you do that?" When he turns back, he stops, noticing I haven't followed. "Kenz?"

"We're sharing our engagement dinner with Ren *and* she's already registered at Fossie's?" That came out a little loud.

"Really? This is what you're worried about right now?" He's stalled, half-turned, hand wrapped around the main entrance door's handle. There's a noticeable clench to his jaw. His eyebrows lift. "I, ah, I gotta go." Pulling open the door, he calls over his shoulder, "I'll meet you at the gym."

Watching him, everything goes fuzzy through pooled tears. I clutch Shane's client folder to my chest and stare blankly at the door as it closes. He's right, but . . . *damn it*, I don't want to co-star with the little scene-stealer. It's *my* engagement dinner. *My* moment. Or, at least, it was.

MY HEAD'S CRACKLING WITH STATIC and no matter which way I turn, the picture's not any clearer. Leaning on my desk, I pinch the bridge of my nose and clamp my eyes tight. I should be reviewing my team's other projects, but I can't seem to focus.

I'm appalled that Shane showed up out of nowhere, dredging up the past, screwing up my future, but if I'm being 100 percent honest with myself . . .

I'm a little flattered. More than a little confused.

Who else could pull off this concept, the whole thing was inspired by us, he said. His words are driving me crazy. The ones he said, and the ones he wouldn't. Why did he cheat? When we were together, we had that thing everyone always talks about. It was young love and bittersweet angst, and for the first time I felt appreciated just for being me. It was liberating and wonderful.

Then he cheated. And I was cheated of believing it had ever been real. At least *for him*.

I respond to some team e-mails while racking my brain for the right way to approach Shane. I can't tell him about the company's financial struggles. That's inside information. I signed a confidentiality agreement and they made a huge deal about it in a company meeting. I can't even say my job's at stake.

And it's not a matter of I *might* lose my job. Clive said it's gone *unless*. And Bradley is stressed about it.

I'll just say I overreacted, didn't mean to run off last night, and whatever, if doing a few movie-scene things helps his concept, then sure. *See?* It's not so bad. I need to just do it.

I open a chat window first and find Ellie.

KENZI SHAW: You there?
ELLIE-BELL: Snoopy.

Whenever other people are around our computers, we type "snoopy." It's our code. So much for gathering reinforcements. I guess I'm on my own.

Finding my phone, I look up his number in the file, dial, and wait through the rings. Maybe I'll get voicem—

"Hello?" It's Shane.

Of course it's Shane. I called him. My mouth opens to speak, but no sound comes out. Instead, I'm flooded with memories of his sleepy voice over the phone when we'd go home during breaks. We'd fall asleep together that way, me at my house and him up north with his grandparents.

"Hi." My voice sounds small and distant. It's a start.

"Kensington?"

"Yes." I hesitate, not sure where to begin. "Um . . . Okay. The thing is . . ."

Swallowing hard, I just spill it. "You may as well stay on, since both our companies have invested so much time in this. I mean, it'd be a waste of everyone's time and money if you didn't. Clive would be disappointed, and I guess we can talk about this movie thing if it helps the concept because we've—"

"Very heartfelt."

His dry tone stops me short. What does he expect? This is insane. *Just do it. My job, my wedding.* "Shane . . . I, um—"

"Yes. Thank you," he says to someone else before returning to me. "Why don't you meet me at Monument Circle in thirty minutes?" There's a slight hesitation. "And Kensington, bring the contract."

SKYSCRAPERS HUG THE ROAD'S ROUNDABOUT and create huge walls on all sides. That's one nice thing about downtown Indianapolis, everything's within walking distance. It has a big-city feel crammed into a few blocks.

"So, where we headed?" I ask Shane as we walk around the circle. It can't be far, because we're on foot.

"Right here." Shane steps around a group of pedestrians and rejoins me on the other side, then takes a seat on the step of the Soldiers' and Sailors' Monument. "I thought it would do us some good to be out of the office."

Cautiously, I sit beside him and pull my jacket closed against the crisp air. "So . . . my family's throwing me and Bradley an engagement party," I say, bringing Bradley back into the picture to reestablish some boundaries. I pull on my sleeve cuffs and cross my arms. "Yup, my mom called about it last night. It's going to be huge. Should be a really nice time."

He doesn't say anything. I'm rambling.

"It's set up for Saturday after nex—"

"Wanna go up?" Shane asks suddenly and stands. He motions to the monument's tower, the tower that's two hundred and eighty-four feet high.

"What? Go up there?" I've lived here my entire life. I work downtown. I now live downtown, and I have never once ventured up inside the monument's tower. Though once . . .

"Come with me to the top. It counts. It's on the list." Shane's already walking up the steps. "You brought the contract, right?"

I don't move. "Yes, but . . ."

"But what?" He disappears around the corner.

Maybe he doesn't remember about this place, *but I do.* I don't move. Instead I pull out my phone and tap the Facebook app to wait him out. I should go back to the office. But we need this account. *I* need this account. What I don't need is my past . . . *our* past, back in the present.

I suppress a laugh thinking of last night with all of us in the bar, then type a new status, "The Past, the Present, and the Future walked into a bar. It was tense."

He's really not coming back. I pocket my phone and head over, annoyed I'm even out here. He's standing near the elevator. As I take the last few steps, he notices me and smiles warmly.

"After you, I already paid." He holds an arm out, gesturing for me to step inside the elevator.

Is he kidding? "Um, no. If you want to have a meeting about the contract or talk about the movie list, fine. But this doesn't make any sense. So . . ." I'm shaking my head, arms crossed. *He doesn't remember.*

Shane moves beside me, leaning his shoulder against the wall. "Remember how you used to say you wanted to live all the moments?"

I lift my chin. *Maybe he does.* This makes things even more confusing. *What is he doing?*

His lips have the slightest upward turn as he talks. "You'd say you 'didn't want to just be in love, you wanted to be in love in a movie.' Remember?"

Locked in his gaze, I'm frozen in his words, *my* words. "It's a line from *Sleepless in Seattle*. I remember saying that and I remember *believing* it." Hell, I remember thinking I *had* it.

With *him.*

But life isn't a movie.

Shane steps closer. Too close, but I don't move.

"*Sleepless in Seattle*. It's the first one on the movie list. So come on . . ." He holds out his hand just like Tom Hanks did as his character, Sam. "Shall we?"

I reach for it without thinking, but as soon as my fingers graze his, my stomach jumps. Okay, there's no doubt he remembers. This isn't just *Sleepless in Seattle*. It's our *Sleepless in Seattle*.

I pull my hand back, angry. *He has no right.*

We were going to meet at the top of the Indianapolis monument like Sam and Annie did at the Empire State Building on Valentine's Day. Just like the movie. I thought maybe, just maybe, he was going to propose.

Instead, we broke up the week before. Right after I'd found out he cheated. I spent my Valentine's here on the steps, alone, wondering what the hell happened. Tonya actually took me out that night to cheer me up. We made a girls' night of it. *And now?*

There's a sting of pride. He can't just come back into my life and drag all this out again. I can feel the tears right on the cusp, ready to spill. I step back. "Do you seriously think that *now* we're going to have our missed Valentine's Day moment?" I'm shaking my head in disbelief. "This one's *off* the list. I've already lived it, and it's not the part I would've wanted."

It was the trying to get out of bed every morning . . . remembering to breathe in and out all day long . . . forgetting how I had it great and perfect for a while. And I didn't have a Dr. Marcia Fieldstone to help me through it, or my family . . . it was just *me*.

And it was awful.

He left for England right after graduation to work for his father. Even though we weren't together anymore, the finality of him being gone, really gone, left my chest hollow. Like the Tin Man. Only, I no longer wanted a heart.

I level my stare. "Tell me what happened in college, and I want the truth." I barely speak the words, but they're deafening.

"I screwed up, but not how you think." His voice is low. He steps closer. "I know I was a bit reckless back then—"

"Between the fights, missing class, the girls—"

"Rumors. The girls were rumors." Shane looks at me determinedly. "I adored *you*. Loved *you*." His shoulders drop and he takes another step to reclaim the distance I created.

I'm right back where I started, the back of my throat swollen with emotion.

"Kensington, between my parents' nightmare of a divorce and being sent here to the States, you were my saving grace. They were all just rumors."

"Then I don't under—"

"Except one."

Oh.

Oh.

Somehow having him admit it, changes it. Maybe I hoped . . .

Shane rakes a hand through his hair and leans his shoulder against the wall. "A girl kissed me at this party after you left. I kissed her back. Fooled around a little." His eyes search mine. "But I didn't sleep with her. We'd been drinking and . . ."

I'm more than a little confused.

That's it?

"Why didn't you just tell me?" I'm shaking my head, baffled. "All this time and it's about some stupid drunk make-out session?" I'm angry all over again, for a completely different reason.

Shane lowers his chin. His eyes close for a second, then open with a sharp breath.

"It was Tonya."

My stomach drops. I'm pressing the band of my ring hard against my finger. It pinches, but gives me something else to feel. "*Tonya?* The same Tonya who told me you cheated and then took me out drinking when—"

"Kensington, it didn't—"

My fingers held up. "No, no. Don't say it didn't mean anything. Because it did. It meant we broke up, didn't it? Regardless if you slept with her then *or* last night."

"What?"

"Bradley said she left right after you, and you guys may have . . ."

He shakes his head, but he's not saying anything. There's more. I can feel it. *Oh God*, there's more.

I look at my feet, remembering how I expected him to fight harder. "Back then, I wouldn't let you explain, but you didn't really try, did you? It made it easy to leave. Was that it?" I said the words, but I don't want to believe them. I'm holding an emotional breath, hoping . . . I glance up at him without raising my chin.

He's looking at me. There's truth in his eyes. "Yes."

Yes.

"I didn't plan it, but it did make leaving for home . . . leaving *you* easier, yes."

Wow.

This is surprisingly worse somehow and . . . *painful.*

It *really* hurts.

Stupid tears are forming. The little voice I've worked so hard to silence throughout the years is marching around, chanting triumphantly through a megaphone. *Not quite good enough. Not quite good enough.*

My lips pull into a smile that hides my teeth, but keeps back tears. "Okay . . . well, mission accomplished. I'm glad it worked out for you th—"

"I was twenty-two, Kensington." Shane steps in front of me. His eyes hold mine, intensely. "Dad was adamant I work with him. Mum was drinking again. She was a wreck from his constant affairs and neither could deal with me. It was a bloody nightmare. I didn't know what I was doing."

I can't move. Everything in me wants to run, but I can't move. *Why does he still have this effect on me?*

"Tonya said I was being selfish if I took you with me. In a lot of ways, she was right. All you talked about was starting your studio. But that still didn't stop me. You went home for a long weekend and I called. Every day, I called."

No. No, he didn't. I'm shaking my head. My heart is racing. I lift my eyes to find his. "What are you talking about?"

"Kensington, your mum . . ."

There's a dart to my chest. "My mom?" His words are fading in and out as I try to remember. Mom never liked him. She thought the relationship was too intense. That he wasn't a good influence. Wasn't on a solid path. And my studio? She never thought that was a good idea. *Oh my God*, it all makes sense.

". . . she was very resolute that I let things be. That we were too young and I had nothing to really offer you, and really, she was right."

My stomach rolls. *How could she, she knew how I felt.* Shane tries to take my hand, but I don't let him.

"If I could go back, Kensington, I would've stayed. I thought . . . I don't know." His brows pull down, and he shakes his head. "But you never even started your studio, did you? I mean, now—"

"Now?" I slowly step back. "*Now*, I'm getting married."

I start rummaging through my bag until I have the contract between my fingers, then reach in with the other hand for a pen. "You kept your end of the agreement . . ."

Shane takes both when I hold them out, and our hands touch. The sensation tangles my insides.

"Look, I wasn't really going to blackmail you, I'm not that un-scrupulous, but—"

"You think it will help in the concept development. I get it." I nod. "As long as it's kept between us and doesn't cross any lines."

"Of course." He smiles softly. "You're getting married."

"Yeah."

For now, my job's safe. Clive's going to be thrilled and Bradley should be relieved. And it's agreed . . . no crossed lines. So why am I such a mess of twisted ironies? What I want, what I wanted, what I have . . .

What I have. What I don't.

CHAPTER FIVE

27 Reasons

EVERY NOW AND THEN, when I've saved enough, I shop with Ren for a solid wardrobe investment. Something designer that will stand the test of trend. She loves lording her superior fashion know-how over me, which makes for a long afternoon, but I do end up with some great finds.

Last purchase was a tailored dress with a retro Peter Pan collar. It's form-fitting with a high waist, and I've worn it only once. But I'm wearing it today. This says I'm confident, together, and ready for business. Bring *that* girl to work. I just hope it doesn't say I'm trying too hard. It's not something I'd normally wear to the office.

Tonya's flat-out betrayal about Shane infuriates me, but I have no intention of mentioning it. I was up all night thinking about this. It only gives her ammo to use against me. If I confront her, she has two plays, denial or downplay. Either way, she'd whine to Bradley how I overreacted, and he'd question why I care when it was almost seven years ago with my ex. The same ex who is now our client. This creates more tension between Bradley and Shane, which creates a bigger issue for Bradley and me. I'm actually proud of how rational I'm being.

If your friends should be kept close and enemies closer, then a frenemy should be kept in the dark. As in blacklisted.

With a fresh cup of coffee, I'm back at my desk just as Clive's door opens. Bradley and Shane both emerge. With my back ramrod straight, I open a new document and tap away at the keys like I'm deep in a major idea storm and can't keep up with the flow.

They're walking over here. Without looking up, I type the same sentence again, and then ad lib. *Idea storm and can't keep up with the flow. Tons of ideas. Lots of ideas—*

Shane's standing right in front of my desk. "Good morning, Kensington." His floppy dark hair is pushed back off his face and a hint of growth now covers his jaw. His lips are curved slightly and my gaze falls to them.

A lost memory of them pressed to mine appears. I'm wrapped in his arms, late for class, and we're laughing. Kissing. He wouldn't let me go.

But he did.

"Hi, hon," Bradley says, striding up beside him before I can respond. He looks polished and handsome in the light-blue shirt I bought for his last birthday.

I peer over my laptop screen and smile brightly at him, ignoring Shane. "Morning, what's on the agenda today?" I keep typing random sentences, because I'm much too busy to stop. I type, *much too busy to stop.*

"I thought we could brainstorm during an outing. Maybe hash out the list," Shane says to the side of my head because I'm still smiling at Bradley. My *fiancé.* Who's still upset with me.

I pause and do my best to look apologetic. "Oh, it's Wednesday. Bradley and I have a standing lunch date." There. I looked at him.

Bradley rocks back on his heels. "Oh, yeah, sorry, can't. Tonya and I are meeting with the Indianapolis Symphony about a new print initiative." His eyes narrow. "Is that a new dress?"

I can feel my face warm. "What? No, you've seen this before." He actually *has*. I furrow my brows in a you-don't-know-what-you're-talking-about look.

"Sorry 'bout lunch, but I may be able to score symphony tickets from today's meeting."

"Great," I say and smile even brighter at Bradley. It's megawatt and directed only at him. I love the symphony. It's an excuse to get dressed up and the theater's absolutely beautiful. It also doesn't hurt that he said that in front of Shane. *See?* We're *happy*. In fact, I'm beaming.

Bradley taps my desk and smiles. "I do like that dress. You look gorgeous." He nods to Shane. No smile. "Bennett." He turns and walks toward his office.

Yay, Bradley. I'm so wearing something silky for him this weekend. I look back at my computer screen and keep ignoring Shane in case Bradley—yup, he just looked back. I smile. Having Shane here is bothering him. I just need to not aggravate the situation and stay focused on what's at stake: job, bonus, wedding, and family . . . in other words, *everything*.

Shane's still standing here.

"So, what time are you free?" He moves to my side of the desk and peers down at the screen.

What is he doing? I try to bring up the Microsoft Office calendar again, but I already closed out. I can't just close the laptop. It'll appear like I'm hiding something.

My chat window pops up. It's Ellie. Can Shane see the screen? I can't tell. The back of my neck warms as I glance at the message.

> **ELLIE-BELL:** Has your ex Mr. Britain seen you in that dress yet? Did his jaw drop?

I turn quickly, to distract him. "How 'bout noon? I'm sure that'll work." My voice is shaky, trying to play it off.

"Actually, I have a late lunch over at the mall. Can you meet me there around four? Front entrance?"

"Sure. Oh, um, would you mind if we met in front of Fossie's? I have to grab a baby gift off the registry for my sister-in-law, so I could meet you after . . . ?"

"It's Fossie's at four then." Shane turns to leave but then looks back, his gaze skimming the length of my dress. "For the record, I, ah, prefer your overalls. But I can see why Bradley likes that dress." A sly smile twists on his lips.

Without another word he turns on his heels, leaving me to slowly bleed out from embarrassment. I drop my head in my hands. *Ugh* . . . this dress. So much for confident, together, and ready for business.

My Facebook status should be a simple lol. Only it wouldn't stand for "laugh out loud"—lol looks like a little guy drowning, which sums up how I feel; and just like him, I don't think it's funny.

APPROACHING THE REGISTRY KIOSK, I type in Ren's name and wait for the printout. I haven't even thought of registering yet. With my luck, when it's time for a wedding shower, Mom will want to have Ren's big baby shower. My stomach wrenches and sours.

I'm watching the machine slowly spit out Ren's list: mahogany crib and dresser set, glider chair for the nursery, all-terrain jogging stroller . . . there's nothing under four hundred dollars. *What is she thinking?*

When I look up, I spot Shane in the main aisle walking in my direction. *Wait, he's early.* I dodge a woman who's pushing a stroller with one hand and holding on to a toddler with the other. The little girl has adorable blond curls and rounded cheeks. She waves at me with a chubby hand and I can't help smiling.

My expression drops as I near Shane. "Hi, you're early. You said four, right?" I point back toward the direction I came. "I, um, haven't even started yet."

Shane looks at his watch. "Oh, so I am. Not a problem." He motions toward the department and begins walking. "When's your sister-in-law due?"

"Oh, um, not until spring." I match his stride. *So he's coming with me?* "I guess my engagement dinner is now an engagement slash early baby shower with the family, so we're giving our gifts now." My words spill out with an unintentionally wounded tone.

Shane looks puzzled. "Wait, I thought you said your mom had everything planned? Why would they change it all of a sudden?"

My cheeks warm. I forgot I told him. "Um, I must've gotten it wrong. The phone disconnected, and I guess, well . . ." I look away and say under my breath, "Ya know, I assumed."

"Some things never change." Shane huffs and shakes his head, then looks around. "I'll, ah, be right back."

There's a warm glow in my chest from his words. Shane's spent time with my family and gets how it is for me. He always took my side.

At this point, I think my family should just forget about the engagement dinner. We can make the get-together about Ren. The whole thing feels like an obligation, anyway. Like I'm an inconvenience imposing on Ren's special day. *Not quite good enough to merit my own.*

My attention falls on a display table with little baby booties. They're knitted to imitate miniature fashion boots. As I run my fingers over the texture, a goofy grin fixes on my face. They're so stinkin' cute. When I glance up, I find Shane watching me from across the display.

"They're just so tiny." My nose wrinkles. "Can you imagine the little feet, and the itty-bitty toes that would fit in these?"

"I can imagine a lot of things."

My whole body stiffens. An unexpected tsunami of displaced emotion detonates without warning, washing over me in an instant. I look away. Anywhere. The booties. My hands. His.

Wait. "Why do you have scanner guns?"

There's an amused sparkle to his eyes. "Well, we officially have an agreement. And this is number four on our list, so I thought—"

"*What* is number four?" I ask, recoiling. Before I can get to my phone to check the e-mail, he hands me the scanner.

"Oh, and you're Ren, if that lady over there asks." He cocks his head to his right where a Fossie's employee is eyeing us curiously. A slow grin spreads across his face.

"I'm Ren? I can't register for Ren, she'd kill me. And how'd you know her name?"

"She married your brother, same last name . . ." His scanner beeps.

I eyeball what he's swiped. It's a huge stuffed pig-hippo-monster in gaudy neon pink and green. Um, *no.*

"What are you *doing?*" My upper lip pulls up in distaste as I regard it. "She won't want that." Ren's nursery will definitely not be in neon monsters. I walk over and unscan the tag.

He rescans.

I unscan.

"Shane, *stop* it. There's no way she would ever put that in her nursery." I unscan it again, and toss it out of reach. Or did I just scan it?

He's randomly swiping things. I'm frantically unscanning.

"Wait." I step between his gun and a hideous crib comforter in matching monster. "I'm not going to screw up my sister-in-law's registry. I'm pretty sure that's not on the movie list."

Although, it was in the movie . . . My eyes pop. "*27 Dresses*? That's number four, isn't it? They registered things her sister would *hate*. I'm not doing that to Ren." I couldn't. Could I? My own little monster is rearing its ugly head. I hear Ren's voice . . . *You don't want the presentation marred by unkempt cuticles. Guess what will be here next spring as well?*

No, I can't ruin her moment, regardless of how she ruined mine.

"It's either this or we hit the bar, pound back some shots, and give a rousing version of 'Bennie and the Jets.'" Shane lifts the gun and crooks an eyebrow.

"No. *That's* an absolute no." The characters end up together in the car after that little scene . . . we are *not* going there.

He swipes. The scanner beeps.

"Okay, wait. Stop." I look over Ren's registry with an idea. "How about we add a few?" My voice softens. "A few *nice* things in a reasonable price range?" I hold up the list to refer to it.

He runs a hand over his jaw in mock consideration. Narrowed eyes lock on mine. "All right. We can do that. It'll count."

I smile, relieved. "Good, 'cause I'm a really good caulker," I say holding up my scanner gun, remembering the movie line and forgetting myself for the moment.

"Girl likes caulk," Shane says through a laugh.

I try not to snort. "You're quoting *27 Dresses*? You've really watched it?" I'm actually glad he knows what I'm talking about. Otherwise, this would be awkward.

Well, it's still awkward.

"Maybe I developed more of a taste for romantic movies than I'd realized. See what you did? You've ruined me." His eyes keep flashing to mine as we walk around the product displays.

I turn away, not wanting another trip down memory lane. I'm getting married and Shane's . . . *I don't know what he's doing.*

"Aw, look." Shane holds out a tacky lamb bank.

"That's the bank that Ren will put all of the baby's money in," I say in the way James Marsden did in *27 Dresses,* without thinking.

He scans it.

"No, Shane, that was a movie line, she won't *want* that."

He scans one after another with a series of beeps: trains, giraffes, even a silver-plated turtle bank.

Walking behind him, I eye the table, but he's scanned so many things so quickly that I have no idea where to start.

"What's this?" Shane's holding up a yellow pillow in the shape of the letter C.

I smirk. It's used to support the baby during breastfeeding, among other things. I pretend with a shrug not to know. "Maybe it's a baby travel pillow?"

"Yes, because even Junior needs to travel in comfort when flying." He slips it around his neck and it hangs low over his shoulders. "How big are American babies?"

I roll my eyes and continue browsing.

"So how many?" Shane asks thumbing through baby crib sheets and blankets.

I stop with the scanner in midair and mentally debate the number of sheet sets.

"Babies. How many babies? I'm sure you and Bradley have discussed this. Let me guess, he wants the statistical two-point-five, right?" He reaches into a crib and scans the comforter set.

My stomach drops. "I want . . . well . . ." It feels wrong talking with him about this. I focus on a photo frame then turn away.

"Right. I see. So, when is the wedding? Have you and Mr. Right set a date?"

I glare at him, feeling suddenly defensive. "We just got engaged, and . . . well, yeah, spring maybe, but—"

"At least the ring is real enough," he says under his breath as his scanner beeps.

"Wait. What does *that* mean?" I eye the silver-plated bear rattle in his hands and scowl. "And unscan that."

Shane stops and turns to me. He leans the scanner against his temple, as if he's considering his words. "I think you want a wedding. Not a marriage."

"What?" I snap. *Who does he think he is?*

He's smirking with one raised eyebrow.

Wait . . .

Why is he standing there like that?

"I *said* . . . I don't think you want a marriage. And you say . . ." His head tilts and he waves a hand for me to complete the sentence. "I have the lines on index cards if you don't remember." He starts reaching into his pocket.

He's serious? Yup, he has cards. I shake my head, bewildered.

He holds them out for me to take. "Or I could feed you your lines. Let's see, I said—"

"I got it. Just . . ." I run the scene from *27 Dresses* with the main characters in my head. "Okay, you said, I think you want a wedding, blah blah blah, and I say . . . what's your problem?" I smile as I recall the dialogue. "Did you have your own fancy wedding planned, and she left you at the altar or something?" I'm speaking halfheartedly, just playing along. If trading movie lines keeps our account, then this is simple enough and shouldn't be a problem.

"Bingo," Shane says with a point of his finger. That's all he says. That was the line.

Silence.

I blank the next part because of the strange expression on his face.

I can't read it.

His lip twitches.

I think over my lines again. *Did she leave you at the altar or something . . . ?*

Oh. In the movie the character Kevin Doyle was left at the altar. Does Shane mean he was—"Shane, I'm . . . I thought we were just saying movie lines. I didn't mean to . . ."

The corners of his mouth turn up.

My eyes narrow. "You're messing with me?"

His smile widens, and I reach back and grab the supersized travel baby pillow thing that isn't a travel pillow and smack him with it.

"Ow, hey, that's not that soft," he says with a laugh, taking an elongated step to stay out of my reach in case I whack him again.

I do.

Right over his head. Then I tuck it under my arm, regain my composure, and again work my way around the table of knick-knacks. He's lucky those were just movie lines, because saying I wanted a wedding over a marriage for real would be crossing the line. I want the marriage, I do. But there's nothing wrong with wanting that big wedding moment, too. What I don't want is this hippo night-light.

I set it down, then lift a pregnancy journal. It's cream with a fabric cover and has a pretty green ribbon to close it.

"That should be your gift to your sister-in-law," Shane says and motions to the journal.

"Mm, I don't know." I start to set it back. "She'll probably hate it, it's not really her."

"No, it's *you*. That's why she should love it." He nods and moves to the next display. More beeps follow.

I glance over at the array of stuff he's adding and sigh. I'll just stop in tomorrow with Ellie and redo it all. And I'll need to call Ren and let her know I added a few more reasonably priced things. *After* I fix it, of course. I look down at the journal again. I do like it.

The giant C pillow rips from under my arm. "Hey!" I turn just as it snaps across my back. "Ow!" It really isn't that soft. From the corner of my eye I see a Fossie's employee. She's looking over.

Shane swings it again, I step and duck. "*Shane*," I whisper sternly. *Great, here she comes.*

"Excuse me, you can't be doing that in here," the Fossie's lady calls out, picking up her pace. "Sir? Sir!"

"We're very sorry," Shane says but gets one more smack in. This one doesn't miss.

Oh my God, he's twelve.

"Sir, you can't—"

"Sorry," Shane says and grins. "Last time. We're done. We just need to pay for . . ." He lifts the pillow and motions to my journal, then hands her the scanner guns.

Walking toward the cashier station, I ask, "You're getting the pillow?"

"What? You don't think I should?"

I hope he's kidding. Shane stops at another display, distracted by a silver-plated snow globe with a race car in it. He holds it so the white plastic snow swirls around the little track.

He can't buy a breastfeeding support pillow. I reach to take it.

He flinches.

The globe slips from his hands. Oh, *shit!* We both reach for it. It's a game of hot potato, bouncing first to his hands, now to mine. Shane wraps an arm around it like a football, but I have it in my fingertips. He tucks both the globe and my hands tight against his midsection.

For a moment, we're frozen, half-bent and tangled up together.

I can feel the heat off his body. His scent is in my nose. I'm looking into eyes with liquid-gold flecks. And just like the snow globe, my little world is all shook up.

"I'm afraid I'm going to have to ask you both to leave," says the same Fossie's lady from behind us in a huff.

With deliberate care we straighten. But I feel a bit unbalanced. Guilt, like a lasso, wraps around the feeling and pulls in tight. *Why should I feel guilty?* I haven't done anything.

Shane holds the globe out, satisfied, and shows the clerk. "See, not even a scratch." He turns to set it back on the display and his elbow catches a crystal bear. It falls in slow motion and shatters with a loud crash.

The Fossie's lady doesn't even blink. "Cash or credit?"

AT THE STOPLIGHT, I CHECK my phone. Three missed calls. One's from my mom, the other two from Bradley. I punch in my code and wait for the robo-voice to finish telling me the number and time through my car's Bluetooth speakers. Bradley's message is first.

"Hey, hon." He sounds worried. "It's almost six thirty and I'm at the gym."

Oh, *shit.*

"Wish you would have called if you were running late. I, ah . . . yeah, I'll hang out front for another ten minutes before starting. Call me when you get this."

A horn double beeps from behind me. Light's green. "I'm going!" I wave a hand and hit the gas.

I completely forgot about the gym. *How? How did I forget?* It's Wednesday. We always go on Wednesday and Thursday together. I look at the digital readout on my console. It's going on 7:30? Using the steering wheel control to delete the message, I wait for the next one.

"Hon, where are you?" Now he's definitely concerned.

I cringe.

"I called Clive. He said you left early, had an off-site with Shane Bennett. This isn't like you. Call me."

I delete and let the third one play. "Hello, Kensington. It's me, your mom."

I know it's you, Mom.

"I don't know why you hung up on me. I told you I would be right back after I answered the other call."

"You hung up on me, Mom," I say to the message and turn onto my street. After knowing how she kept Shane's messages from me, I'd *like* to hang up on her.

". . . I needed to tell you about the get-together. Anyway, I sent the e-mail, so I'm sure you know. But I wanted to make sure you didn't get her a diaper bag, because that's what . . ."

Mom jabbers on. She doesn't get the concept of *message.*

Come to think of it, it's not all that different from talking with her.

"It's Gucci and it's to die for, *very* Ren. She's going to love it—"

The message beeps off because it's run out of room. She probably kept talking. She got her a Gucci bag? A Gucci *diaper bag*? I pull into my apartment complex and notice Bradley's BMW parked out front.

Oh no.

Bradley's sitting on the couch, the TV's on, and his phone is to his ear when I walk in. He clicks it off. "I was just calling you, again. What happened? Everything okay?" His voice is strained.

I toss my stuff up on the counter. "I'm really sorry."

Bradley stands and moves toward the kitchen. "I was worried, I mean, you never showed up. And Clive said you were with Bennett?" His jaw is clenched.

I can hear the question he's not asking.

"Um, well, yeah . . . we hashed out the top movies and scenes to use in the conceptuals, oh, and I went over to Fossie's and picked up Ren's shower gift, like you asked." I open the bag with the pregnancy planner I found. "See?"

"With Bennett?" His face screws up, confused.

"No. Well, yes, but . . ." My heart's beating triple time. The pit of my stomach is thick in sludge, bubbling with guilt. "Shane wanted to discuss the project. He was at that coffee place at the mall for some late lunch thing, so we met there. Not a big deal. Two birds, one stone."

All true. Still guilty.

Which is stupid, because I didn't do anything wrong, nor do I intend to. I open the fridge to find something to drink, pushing some things around to stall. If only I'd remembered the gym. I grab the juice and turn.

"I should have called, but he did sign, and that means we're going to be working together . . ." I put on my best what-do-you-want-me-to-do look.

"Yeah, I know . . ." Bradley shifts his stance and folds his arms. "I just don't like you meeting him after hours. The whole thing makes me uncomfortable. So, yeah, that needs to end."

He's not asking.

I'm not sure what to say. I gaze up at him. Eyes of blue, no specks of gold. My gut twists. He's jealous. Maybe he has every right to be. How would I feel if it were reversed? "You're right, I'm sorry."

His arms drop and the tightly worn expression softens a little. Stepping close, he lifts my chin and leans down to give me a slow, soft kiss. "You want some wine?"

He's already pouring himself a glass.

"Um, sure. I'm gonna go change, be right back."

Even casual, Bradley's handsome. Cropped blond hair and clean shaven, he's always polished. I stifle a laugh. Bradley's like Jane's boss, George, in *27 Dresses*. He's perfect. And Shane? Yeah, he's definitely more like Kevin Doyle. Same hair, just add stubble and an accent.

Ren is Tess, always upstaging everyone. Tonya can be Jane's friend, what's her name? She sleeps around, actually looks a bit like Tonya. It's Judy Greer, but do they say her character's name? I don't think they do. My stomach drops.

Am I like Jane? She was afraid to say no, always trying to please everyone else. That's not me. I can say no.

"Hon? What are you doin'?"

What am I doing? Recasting *27 Dresses*. "I'll be right there," I call through the hallway and step into my sweatpants.

When I come out, Bradley's back on the couch in front of the TV. I snuggle in next to him and he leans down with a kiss. His lips are warm and move over mine with ease. I pull back and smile up at him. *He is George.*

He gives another quick peck. "Let's move the wedding up."

My expression falls. "What?"

"Yeah, let's move it up." He shifts so he's facing me. "Now that your job's safe, why wait? Grayson and Ren are expecting in the spring, so we could maybe do it in the next few months. So everything's not overlapping."

I straighten, seeing instant red. "Why are we planning everything around Ren's pregnancy?"

"We're not." A low growl of frustration rises from his chest. "We're making sure it's all about *you*. Okay?" He leans in and kisses my nose. "No overlap."

"And no time to plan, either." I pull away, leaning against the couch. I don't want to wait too long, but . . . I don't want to rush it. And I definitely don't want a Christmas wedding. "How would we get everything done, I mea—"

"We'll hire a planner." He's genuinely excited, waving his hands around as he talks. "Just think about it. I love you, Kenz, and I don't wanna wait. Do you?"

"No, but . . ." My mind's in hyperdrive thinking of everything we'd need to do. "We'd never pull it off." I want to be married, but I don't want it just thrown together. "Maybe this weekend we can talk with Mom about it, see what she thinks?" My stomach sours. *I know what she'll think.* If it's more convenient for Ren, then she'll be all for it.

"I almost forgot. I'm heading to Michigan this weekend to see a game in Lansing—box seats. It's with a client, so I gotta go. But . . ." He strokes my cheek. "I did get symphony tickets for you. Maybe take Ellie, or your mom. You can discuss wedding dates."

"Okay . . ." I shrug with an abbreviated smile. A girl's wedding day is *the* central moment. I really don't want it rushed. *He knows this, right?*

Ugh, I am Jane. I should have said no, a simple no. A surge of panic is rising up in my chest, unsettling me. That's natural, right, especially under the circumstances of Shane showing up and the movie list—*oh*, movie! I jump up and smile. "Let's watch a movie, maybe *27 Dresses?*" I'm digging around to find it.

"What about *The Bourne Supremacy?* Or *Die*—"

"*No*, come on, you'll like this one. I'll even make popcorn." See? I *can* say no. This will be great. Bradley and I can create our own movie moments. Because I already have my happily ever after, right?

CHAPTER SIX

Knocked Over

WITH ONLINE SOCIAL MEDIA, the world of marketing has changed. This means fewer designers and more programmers. Once, before my time here, there were more than twenty designers employed. Now, with fewer than half, we still have the workload of twenty.

Glancing over at my team, I notice everyone is busily working away. Checking the project log confirms we're slammed. *How are we in financial trouble?* I have two more small projects to assign but no one's open. I draft and send a quick e-mail to my team, asking who can take on extra, then prop my elbows on my desk and palm my head like a basketball.

The whole thing is screwy. There's plenty coming in. *So where's it all going?* I'd actually like to hire an additional designer.

I do a quick scroll of my Facebook feed and notice Ren's now bogging it down with round-the-clock baby updates. *Will baby Shaw be pink or blue?* Foursquare has her pinned at the

Carmel OB-GYN, and she's tagged my mom as being with her.

Of course.

I type *good luck!* even though I might be the one that needs it. I have to call her about the gift registry. I have to *fix* the registry, first. And get back to work. Having the contract is not the same as keeping it.

ELLIE AND I ARE AT a little Italian bistro in the mall. I'm always in this mall. Not only is it superb shopping, but there's fine dining and small eateries. In other words, carbs.

We're splitting a lunch plate sampler. Three different kinds of pasta: spaghetti, ravioli, and fettuccini. Plus, it comes with garlic bread to completely tip the carb scale.

"Okay, so you know the whole history with me and Shane, right?"

Ellie nods and takes a bite.

I lower my voice and change my tone to do-or-die serious. "If you mention any of this, and I mean even the tiniest minute detail . . ." I lean over for dramatic effect. "I will tell the entire office that the photocopied boobs in the picture hanging in the break room are yours."

Ellie's mouth unhinges mid-bite. "You wouldn't."

"I would and I will. That's how serious this is." I take a drink of my tea, clear my throat, and unload. "Okay, you know that Tonya was the one who told me Shane cheated in college, right? Turns out it was only a drunk-kiss thing and it was *Tonya* who he was *with*."

Ellie's mouth drops. Her hand covers it.

I nod, pausing to let it sink in.

"But wait, there's more." The words are wrapped in thorns and scrape as they come out. "Shane *called* my house the weekend after when I went home. My *mom* told him to leave well enough alone. To leave *me* alone."

Her eyes are huge and anime, peeking out over her fingertips.

I tell her how Shane signed the contract, with the added agreement of the Love Like the Movies list, then explain what the list means. "Here, look . . ." I hand her my phone so she can see.

Ellie's lips form each word as she reads.

1. Sleepless in Seattle
2. Pretty Woman
3. Bridget Jones's Diary
4. ~~27 Dresses~~
5. Dirty Dancing
6. Sixteen Candles
7. Love Actually
8. Say Anything
9. You've Got Mail
10. My Best Friend's Wedding

I watch her, my insides percolating. Somehow sharing this makes it . . . *what?* Real. Yeah, maybe too real.

Her eyebrows are arched high. "I can't believe he's doing this. Can I have him?" She giggles, glances back at the list, and lowers her head suspiciously. "*27 Dresses* is crossed out. Where'd you go yesterday? Does Bradley know about this?"

My heart skips. I shouldn't have said anything. I completely downplay it and tell her that we only registered a few things for Ren. "It's really nothing. A few movie lines said in a similar scene to get inspiration for the redesign. But it's better if it's kept quiet. I mean, it's already weird enough."

I should feel relieved. But I don't. I feel worse. I'm wading around in a thick pool of guilt. Even the carbs aren't helping.

I decide to change the subject. "Speaking of weird . . . have you noticed your workload slowing at all? There's been some talk that the agency isn't having a good quarter."

Ellie wrinkles her nose. "No. Not all. In fact, they keep piling stuff on. I'm getting behind. Where'd you hear that?"

"I'm sure it's nothing," I add, finally taking a few bites of pasta myself. *Oh, this is good.* "But . . ." I fill her in with the rest. Since we work together, it's not considered a violation of the confidentiality contract.

Ellie's eyes are wide as she listens, her fork hanging in midair, which only adds to the guilt pile. My intent wasn't to freak her out. I just wanted to see what she thought about Clive pressuring me to do whatever it takes to keep Shane's account, the threat of layoffs, and the speech on financial struggles when we're obviously swamped.

I smile, reassuringly. "Maybe Clive was just, I don't know, being *theatrical.*"

"He is a drama queen," Ellie adds.

"Right. I mean, if we're busy there's nothing to worry about."

At least there shouldn't be.

SHANE ARRIVED AT THE AGENCY about ten minutes ago, and Clive set him up in the conference room. He called and requested a meeting with the team that's working on his account. I have no idea why, I haven't designed anything yet. I'm all twitchy and nervous. The door's shut and the shades are drawn.

Do I knock? I should knock.

I rap my knuckles lightly on the door and turn the handle, but then Tonya and Bradley appear around the corner and my hand drops.

I half smile. "Hi."

"Hi, hon, you okay?"

"What? Yeah, of course." *Why? Do I look guilty?* I feel guilty.

Tonya pushes past me, opens the door, and grins. "No water for you this time."

I roll my eyes and announce I'll be right back, spin around, and walk-run down the hall. Spotting Ellie, I wave her over. "I'm recruiting you. You are now officially on the Carriage House project. I'll clear it later. Come on." I'm pulling her arm and we're speed-walking back toward the conference room.

"Kenz, what are you doing?" Ellie asks.

I shush her, open the door, and practically shove her in.

Tonya turns to Bradley. "She's not on this account."

"I invited her. I thought we needed a female technical perspective on the functionality," I say and pull out a chair up front for Ellie. It makes sense. The other programmers on this account are male.

I really just need a sounding board in all of this, a voice of reason, another set of eyes on the situation. *Is this a situation?* Maybe I just need someone here in case I lose it and punch Tonya.

Shane clicks off his phone and stashes it in his pocket. "Good, welcome." He smiles at Ellie.

She forces back a too-big smile and giggles. Shane turns to me, puzzled. I try to communicate *I don't know*, but I have no idea what my face is doing.

"I guess we just need Clive, then." Shane's eyes are still on me.

I look away, feeling the burn in my cheeks, and catch Bradley look from Shane to me. Ellie is focused on Shane, Tonya is drinking her water. And just to note, Shane and Tonya are not looking at each other. All noteworthy stuff.

"So refreshing," Tonya teases after setting down her water and fake coughs.

"Is that new?" I whisper, noticing her outfit. I've never seen it and it looks designer.

Tonya pulls down her eyebrows as if she doesn't know what I'm talking about. Whatever, she knows. That's completely new from head to toe. Sales is based on commission. You don't shop when the money's not coming in.

"All right, let's see what you're thinking, Mr. Bennett," Clive says as he walks in.

The board up front has a few spec pieces leaning on the shelf and they're covered. I fiddle with my engagement ring while we wait for Clive to get settled. He pulls the door shut behind him and sits on the edge of the conference table, because he apparently doesn't believe in chairs. My attention snaps to Shane as he pulls the cover boards, one by one.

"Right, this won't take long. I printed out some pieces I think represent what we're looking for. It's not just the design I want you to look at, but rather, the concept and feeling they evoke."

Panic. That's the feeling I'm emoting.

All three pieces are *mine*.

My mouth is hanging slightly open. He's printed out copies of my designs from college, the ones in my Facebook gallery. My eyes dart from the display to Shane. There's a knowing smile on his lips.

Two are romantic, figurative illustrations of couples in color blocks and loose line art. The third is an up-close portrait. I'm not sure how to react. Clive walks over to inspect them. Everyone else follows suit. Shane explains how these are made from online copies and the print quality isn't up to par. *What if none of it's up to par?*

This is my naked nightmare. I'm completely exposed.

Shane looks around the room. "Maybe, if the artist would be kind enough . . ."

No, no, no, no . . .

". . . she would bring in the originals for you to see." His eyes now rest on me.

Everyone turns.

Um, shit?

"These aren't Kenzi's," Bradley says, giving me a confused glance.

I shrug. "Yeah, from college, they're at Mom and Dad's." I don't tell them they're buried under my Kensington box.

"I've never seen them," Bradley says and gives me a look that matches last night's tone. He isn't on Facebook, only LinkedIn to network.

"Oh . . . they're in my Facebook album," I say quickly and instantly regret it. Now I'll have to explain to Bradley why Shane is on my Facebook account. I feel guilty, but I never intended to keep Shane friended.

My shoulders tense. Is Shane trying to start fights between us? Is that what he's up to?

"These are simple in design but produce a strong emotional response." Shane's voice is filled with energy. "One look and you feel what the image is portraying." He points to the first couple tangled in an embrace with a loose cityscape behind them. "Love."

My insides are churning. Shane has no idea when I painted these, or why. It's *us*. Well, not us literally, but the feelings of us, transferred through the paint to this couple.

He motions to the next, a couple holding hands in a park. "Romance. And this one . . ."

Tonya pulls her brows down. "No offense, Kenz, but the colors are all backwards in that last one."

It's a portrait in abstract expressionism and the color technique is intentional. Using broad strokes and opposite shades, it creates a dynamic juxtaposition. She was just a figure model in class, but her soulful eyes captivated me. Still do.

"Actually, Tonya, that's what speaks to me. Imagine this blend of colors and realistic imagery as murals across the lobby."

I look up. My work, as *murals*?

"I've purchased limited license use for the movie images and want to blend them with this treatment for the Web, our marketing materials, and the theater." He's looking around the room, but then catches my eye. "This is what I want to see the conceptuals as."

Clive stands. "Yeah, that shouldn't be a problem. Kenzi can start right away. Great. Effective and to the point, wish all my meetings wrapped as quick." Clive's up.

Everyone follows and the room fills with chatter. Shane fishes for his phone to take a call, and Ellie's quickly at my side.

"Did you really paint those?" She seems impressed.

Even Bradley's still looking at my artwork.

This is different from an online album. There's nowhere to hide. I'm sitting right here. That's *me* up on that board, stripped down, raw. I breathe deeply through my nose and hold it, trying to keep the tears back. I'm overwhelmed. I feel *seen*.

I glance at Shane. He's watching me from across the room, lips curled slightly with the phone to his ear.

"Oh, almost forgot," Tonya says loud enough to get everyone's attention. "Friday night, we're having a work get-together to celebrate Bradley and Kenzi's engagement. I'll send an e-mail."

What is she talking about?

Tonya answers my confused gaze. "It was going to be a surprise, but when Bradley told me you guys were moving the date up, I didn't have time to plan anything. And really, I don't know how you're going to plan a wedding in six weeks anyway." She snorts her disapproval.

What the hell?

"Six weeks? Holy cow. Why didn't you tell me?" Ellie's voice is an excited bubble.

Um, because I didn't know. It's like I'm in *The Proposal*, when Sandra Bullock's character announces they're engaged, but they're not.

But *I am*.

Except I didn't agree to six weeks. I give Bradley a what-is-she-talking-about look.

He's shaking Clive's hand. "Thanks. It's quick, sure—"

"Um, *quick* doesn't cover it." Clive guffaws, cocks an eyebrow, and drops his eyes to my belly.

Now everyone else is looking, too.

Wait. *What?*

I'm having a moment. Not a good moment. I'm looking at Shane across the conference room, standing in front of my college artwork. He's ended his phone conversation abruptly and is staring back. I'm confused. Embarrassed.

And *not pregnant*.

There's suspicion on everyone's faces. They're glancing at my stomach.

I suck it in.

Control-top undergarments will be a permanent wardrobe piece from now on. Maybe one pair on top of another. Maybe a full body suit.

Now, not only will I not have the time or budget to plan the wedding I really want, but it will also be forever clouded. Right after I say "I do," I *do* want to start trying to get pregnant, which will look like I was, when I *wasn't*.

I think of *My Best Friend's Wedding*, right before they pass under the bridge on the boat, when he says, "You commit to this wedding, and then there's this momentum, and you forget you chose it."

I *did* choose the wedding. But I didn't commit to six weeks. I didn't choose to have everyone think I'm knocked up.

That's a completely different movie.

This is messed up. Anger rips up my spine. What the hell is Bradley thinking? I'd like to take a chair and hit him over the head. We didn't talk specifics about *anything*.

Clive snaps a finger in front of my nose, and then does it twice more in rapid succession. "Did you hear me, Kenzi? Hell-oo?"

"Mm?" I turn my attention to him.

"We have our annual client appreciation outing at River Paint-ball next Tuesday after work, remember? Be there dressed to kill," Clive says and laughs at his joke. "Since you can't participate due to—" His eyes again drop to my midsection. His eyebrows hike.

"Clive, I'm not . . ." I wave to my belly and shake my head adamantly, looking from him to Bradley.

"Oh, right, of course." Clive clucks his tongue with a laugh, then continues discussing the game with Bradley.

Bradley seems nonchalant, as if it wasn't even implied. My eyes fall to Tonya and Shane in the back. They're talking in hushed tones, eyes darting toward me.

And that's my cue. I glower at Bradley and break for the door.

Exit, stage right, it's Runaway Bride.

CHAPTER SEVEN

Pretty Confusing

ITTING ON THE MALL bench, I watch people stroll by. The atrium ceiling is glass, and a patch of sunlight falls across my face. The tiny bit of warmth feels wonderful on my skin. My phone's been ringing nonstop, first Bradley, then Ellie, and now Mom. I sigh and answer. What can I say? I'm a glutton for punishment.

"Hi, Mom."

"Hi, Kenzi. It's Aunt Greta, actually. I'm on your mom's phone."

Oh, thank God.

"Your mom and I are with Ren talking baby crap over lunch, and she wanted me to call and confirm you got her message about the shower slash engagement get-together? I guess she sent the invites out and, well, you can imagine."

Shit. I need to fix the registry. "Oh, yeah, I got some of her message. She kinda talked beyond the limit." I tuck the phone between my shoulder and ear, jump up, and head toward Fossie's.

Aunt Greta laughs. "Doesn't surprise me . . . are you okay?"

No.

I clear my throat, surprised it was that obvious. "I'm just having an issue with a client."

"Why? What client?"

"Well . . . it's, um, the client's Shane Bennett."

"*Shane*, Shane Bennett?"

I stop walking, feeling dizzy. "Yeah, he's back. It's complicated."

"Okay. Yeah, I can see how that would be complicated. Does Bradley know about you and Shane's past?"

Where do I begin? I move closer to the wall so I'm not blocking the flow of traffic and wipe the moisture from under my eyes.

"Kenzi?"

"Yes, Bradley knows. He's less than thrilled, but we need the account. Oh, and he wants to move the wedding up to around Christmas. *This* Christmas. Like in six weeks." A few tears have broken free and race down my cheeks. "He just frickin' announced it to everyone in the office." My voice squeaks, hitching on the words.

"That just sounds like he's jealous. No big deal. If you want to wait, just tell him." My mom is calling for Aunt Greta in the background. "Kenzi, don't let choices be made for you. Your mom hardly ever approves of me, and she may not agree or get your choices, but they're yours to make, understand?"

"In theory," I mumble. I don't think she heard me.

"Just out of curiosity, how does Shane look?"

My lack of response is the only one needed.

"Yeah, thought so." She laughs. "Listen, the taskmaster's hounding me. Guess our table's ready. Call me anytime, okay? I mean it. And give yourself permission to figure things out. *Please.* Love you, sweetie."

"Love you, too, and thanks," I say and click the phone off.

Bradley's definitely getting an earful about the six-week announcement, but to tell him I want to wait? *How do I explain the shift?* Before, with the possible wedding delay, I was freaking out. And now that he wants to speed things up, I'm equally panicking?

But you *can't* pull off a storybook wedding in six weeks. Not even in the movies.

In *Bride Wars*, Liv and Emma were freaking out about the rushed time line of three and a half months. In *The Wedding Planner*, Mary's stressed over planning Steve and Fran's wedding in three. *And that's in a movie!* This isn't a movie.

I guess I just hoped that my wedding day would feel like one.

THE SCANNER BEEPS WITH EVERY unswipe and reswipe as I walk around Fossie's department store. My shoulder holds my phone in place as I talk with Bradley and fix Ren's registry. Well, he's talking, I'm ignoring him loudly.

His words have an echo, so I assume he's in his car. "Listen, I'm sorry. Honestly, I didn't think moving the wedding up would be an issue. I thought you'd be thrilled. We talked about it."

I swallow my anger, trying to bite back the slew of choice words that keep popping to mind. It was moronic, but not malicious. "Bradley, we talked about moving it up. I was thinking six or seven months. Not *six weeks*!"

I scan the elegant bath set even though I like the hooded bath towels with the tiny animal ears on them better.

"Okay, you're right. I may have gotten carried away."

That's an understatement. Holding up the animal towel, I smile. So cute. *Why am I still adding things?*

Maybe we *should* get married in six weeks. Just elope. The sooner we're married, the sooner we can start trying. Who cares what anyone thinks? It's not like Mom's been calling me to plan or anything . . . I stop myself because I can feel the tears building again. I *want* to be pregnant. I *want* to start trying. But I want the big wedding moment, too. And it feels like the timing for everything is off.

Am I living those moments?

Not if they keep being taken away from me.

"Hon?"

"It's too soon, okay? There's so much to do. We have to find a place, and order invitations, a dress, a venue. Six weeks is too fast, Bradley. I want to stay on the normal spring schedule." There, I said it. I made my choice. *See?* I'm not Jane from *27 Dresses* after all.

Why shouldn't I have a big, fancy wedding? I shouldn't have to give that up, too. A large teddy bear in the softest fuzzy material ever stares up at me with glossy button eyes.

"Well, yeah, we can talk about it. Maybe tonight? I'm meeting your dad for a quick update on his media buy, and I just pulled in. But I'll see you in a while, and I'm really sorry. Okay?"

"Yup. Okay." I click END and lift the bear. It's cream and white and begs to be hugged. Maybe I'm the one who needs one. I wrap him in my arms and squeeze.

"Kensington."

I look up to see dark jeans and a V-neck tee. Floppy hair and eyes with gold. Heartbreaker from the past and confusion of the present.

"How'd you know where—"

"Ellie thought you might be here redoing . . ." He motions to the scanner gun in my hand.

Thanks, Ellie-bell. I continue browsing the items I've already looked at with the bear still tucked under my arm. I'm not ready to put him down.

"Do you have any kids? That you know about?" That came out harsher than I meant. "Sorry, that's not how—"

"No. No kids." He loops his thumbs in his jeans pockets and walks closer.

His parents' divorce was rough, and I remember him saying how life was hard enough without dragging children into the mix. "You don't want them, do you?"

"I never said that. But I wouldn't jump into it with just anyone, no."

He thinks I'm pregnant. I can see it in his eyes. I give the bear one small secret squeeze and turn to set him on a nearby rocker.

"Excuse me!" The Fossie's woman from yesterday calls to us as she heads in our direction. She's waving to get our attention.

Shane pops his hands up in mock surrender as she approaches.

"We're going. See? Here," I say and hand her my gun. "All done."

She huffs as we leave, giving Shane the stink-eye.

"I was going to look for a dress for Saturday night," I say as we leave the baby department and head toward the up escalator. "Ellie's my date for the symphony, since Bradley will be out of town." I glance at him from the corners of my eyes then look away. I don't know why I said that. I shouldn't have said it.

Shane's voice is lowered. "Tell me why you moved the wedding up. Six weeks is . . . well, it's no time at all."

"I'm *not* pregnant, Shane."

His face registers relief. I think. Yeah, I think he's relieved.

I don't wait for him to say anything. "And I didn't move the wedding up. I don't know what Bradley's thinking. He brought it up last night after I missed our normal gym time but . . ." My insides are torn. The words feel wrong as they fall from my lips, as if I'm betraying Bradley by speaking them. "Whatever, we'll figure it out." It comes across more of a mumble as we step from the escalator.

I stop to face him. "Well, I'm gonna go . . ." I motion toward the women's department.

"Buy a dress?"

"Yup, so . . ." I rock my head from side to side.

"You realize one of the movies on the list has a shopping scene. And you do need a dress."

I wrinkle my nose with a head shake. "Oh, I don't know. Today's just been . . ."

Shane's eyes hold mine and a half-smile curls at the corners of his mouth, tempting me.

Lifting my phone, I click through my e-mails until I find the one with the Love Like the Movies list. My mind's instantly a-skitter running through the titles. My stomach dips. My eyes lift to his. "It's *Pretty Woman*."

"It is."

Aunt Greta's words whisper in the back of my mind. *Give yourself permission to figure things out.* My toes squeeze inside my shoes. I glance sideways toward the women's department, then back at him.

Roy Orbison's signature "Pretty Woman" song starts playing in my mind, and I can see the scene. Edward and Vivian walking briskly down the street while she fluffs her wild hair. Right before they enter the store, Edward turns and tells her to stop fidgeting.

It's just shopping. I was going anyway.

I give myself permission.

"We can skip the gum-spitting part, right?"

THE FOSSIE'S WOMEN'S DRESSING AREA is huge and filled with couches and chairs for the waiting husbands and guests. It's very lush and welcoming, with white marble and a crystal chandelier. Shane looks comfortable and content.

"Who are you talking to? Or are you just imitating the movie? Going all Richard Gere on me?" That's the second phone call he's taken since we walked in here. The first was in quick, hushed tones. I can't help but wonder if it was a woman on the other end. I'm sure he's dating someone, probably several women.

Shane covers his phone with his hand. "Clive. He believes we're having an off-site conceptual meeting based on the new direction." He points me toward a pile of clothes on the couch, brought over in my size by the sales ladies. "And we are. Now, back to it." He motions for me to again get moving, then says into the phone, "Yes, yes, I do think we could add in radio, but only during drive time."

Okay, so maybe it is Clive. My stomach flips but not in a good way. I promised Bradley there would be no more off-site meetings with Shane—or did he say after hours? I think it was after hours. What if Clive mentions this to Bradley? *What am I doing?*

I'm pretending to be in *Pretty Woman* and saving my job and countless others while keeping the client happy. I'm just shopping. That's all I'm doing.

My eyes catch Shane's just as he's ending his phone conversation. I quickly look away while sorting through the selection of clothing. I choose two dresses and hold each up. Shane shrugs at the first one, which is short and silky, and nods with a warm smile at the long black one with the plunging neckline.

Pocketing the phone, he stands. "Mary Kate, Mary Francis, we're going to need a lot more sucking up," Shane says to the saleswomen, whose names are not Mary anything. He's beaming. I think he's having as much fun as they are. He explained our whole *Pretty Woman* moment thing to them, even gave them lines. They're eating it up.

"Do you like this one, dear? What about red? Isn't her dress red in the movie?" asks the first Mary, who's older.

"No, I thought it was a deep purple. Wasn't it?" asks the younger woman he's been calling Mary Kate.

"Sandy," calls the first Mary. "What color was the dress in *Pretty Woman*? You know, when they went to the opera?"

I know it was red, but I secretly want a yellow dress like the one Kate Hudson's character, Andy Anderson, wore in *How to Lose a Guy in 10 Days*. When she turns and exposes her bare back, glancing coyly at Matthew McConaughey, you know she feels beautiful. I want to feel like that.

"Oh, are you going to the opera?" asks the other Mary to Shane as I step out of the changing room wearing the long black dress.

"Symphony," I say and spin for Shane to admire. I notice they brought him a coffee. This is definitely a Richard Gere moment. They're hanging on his every British word. Some things never change. I watch him curiously with the younger Mary. She's pretty and has a cute flirty laugh, but he's not flirting. *Huh*, maybe some things have changed.

"So . . . in the 'maybe' pile?" I ask and smile. I'm sucking in my tummy, just in case there are any lingering doubts.

"Definitely, maybe," Shane says and quirks a lopsided grin.

Definitely, Maybe is another romantic comedy. Very funny. Mary Kate thought so. I venture back in with a new outfit. It's a long, deep blue tank dress, with a super-high slit up the side.

"You'll like this one, honey. I set the shoes just outside the door."

I have no idea which Mary said that. I slip it on. It's pretty; the material is soft to the touch and it drapes nicely.

When I come out Shane's leaning against the chair, sipping his coffee, eyes on me. I have his absolute attention. The weight of his stare makes me nervous, so I look down and smooth the dress.

"Mercy," he says, setting his coffee down.

I laugh. He's thinking of the song, too. I bet he would've brought the soundtrack had he known we'd be doing this one today. I'm still smiling.

Shane's eyes are locked in and holding my gaze as he walks over. I'm holding my breath. Newly emerged butterflies are testing their wings, causing an inner flittering sensation. He smiles and speaks low. "This one goes in the yes pile."

Warmth shoots through me from head to toe without my permission. I step back, almost knocked over by the feeling.

Shane turns, holding up a credit card. "I have to go, but . . ." He looks at each of them. "Mary Kate, Mary Francis—"

"I'm Mary Kate, she's Mary Francis, remember?" She points to the other lady with a goofy smile plastered on her face and giggles, which makes me laugh in spite of myself.

"Of course you are," Shane says in his dry proper accent. "She needs a killer dress, shoes, and all the other intimate bits. I trust you'll take good care of her?"

They nod.

"Good, well, she has my card."

There's an awkward silence.

"I said, she has my card, and you say . . ." Shane waves as if he's cueing them. "And we'll help—"

"Oh!" They giggle and look at each other. "And we'll help her use it!"

"There we go," Shane says laughing.

Shane steps my way again, and the women busy themselves with sorting some of the dresses I had tried on, but I notice they're both still in earshot, obviously listening.

"Thank you," I say and smile, embarrassed. "The diversion was . . . nice. I can pay, though. I mean, you don't have to take it that far or—"

"I insist. I want to. But I will ask something in return."

My nose wrinkles. "I'm not really a prostitute, remember?"

I see the Marys over his shoulder share a look and a giggle. The corners of Shane's lips pull up in a mischievous smile.

"Well, then I guess I'll have to ask you for something else."

I meet his eyes, not moving a muscle, almost afraid of what he might say. *What is he going to say?* I'm getting married. This is too much. I can't—

"A tie."

My head throws back. "A tie?"

"Yes, I believe the beautiful Vivian buys Edward a tie, right?"

I laugh softly, nodding. "Okay. I will . . . find you a tie." That I can do. That's not crossing any lines.

Shane steps away, but pauses. "So I'm leaving for—"

"Wait, you're leaving?" *He's leaving again?*

"The farm. I don't live here, remember? It's about three hours out. I'm taking off from here, but I'll be back late tomorrow, just ring if you need anything."

"Oh, right. Right, well, I'm sure I won't, so . . ." I step back, creating even more distance between us. "And I should have something drafted up soon." Because that's what this is about . . . the account.

Shane nods, starts toward the exit, but then turns and says the movie line loud enough for the Marys to hear. "You're on your own, I have to go." He flashes me a smile. "And you do look great."

Mary Kate runs after him to walk him out, asking if he'll be back soon, and God knows what else, probably giving him her number. I watch him leave, in a complete daze.

Mary Francis looks at me and shakes her head. "If you let that one get away, you don't deserve him."

My stomach clenches. *He let me go.* "Oh, um . . . we're not. I mean—"

"I'll take him," says another woman from behind the dressing room door. I forgot she was back there.

We all laugh.

Okay, I admit it, I love this. The movie part. It's all about the movie moments. I'm getting completely wrapped up in it, and I need to rein myself in, at least a little. Because right now, I do feel like Vivian. I do feel special. I wanna chase after Shane and declare, *Big* mistake. *Big. Huge.* And I'm not sure how I feel about that. It's all pretty confusing.

Gathering a few more dresses, I slip back into the dressing room. But instead of trying them on, I sit on the cushioned stool. Tears completely blur my vision, so I just close my eyes and lean against the wall. I can buy my own clothes, and this movie thing is about Shane's concept, not *me*, but it strikes me personally.

In the movie we sympathize with Vivian when she says, *If people put you down enough, you start to believe it.* Her words to Edward resonate in all of us, I think.

Well, they do in me.

And it's not always obvious words that generate that feeling. Maybe it's the lack of them, and the lack of action.

Not good enough to merit a real conversation. My mom never talking to me about why she thought Shane wasn't a good influence. Never really talking to me about anything.

Not worth an apology. Tonya not caring how her actions hurt me. My mom's excuse of "Well, it all turned out fine, now didn't it?" That's not "I'm sorry," that's "What does it matter? What do *you* matter?"

An inconvenience to love. Blending my engagement party is just one example of doing what's required, instead of being excited and happy to be doing it. My moments are wrought with guilt because they mean effort and cost on someone else's part, and I'm made aware of this every time.

"You okay in there, honey? Do you need a different size?"

I sniff, wipe at my moist cheeks, then clear my throat. "Um, yeah. Do you think you could find me a yellow dress? Long?"

She says something about being right back, and I hear her call for help in locating it. In the *Pretty Woman* shopping scene, it's not really about the clothes, or how much they cost, or how great she looks. When Vivian leaves the store, she's not only a *pretty* woman, she's a *different* woman.

It gets me every time.

That's why we root for her. We *want* Vivian to feel special. We *need* her to believe this about herself.

I need to believe this about myself. *Maybe I need things to be different.*

CHAPTER EIGHT

How to Lose Your Mind in Five Days

$\mathcal{B}$RADLEY WAS OUT ON a sales call when I got back to the office. He left a note at my desk saying he'd pick me up at six for the gym. *Ugh*, I don't feel like going to the gym, but no way can I bail after missing last night, although after he pulled the whole six weeks' thing, I could. I sent him a text saying we need to make a quick stop at my parents' first.

For some reason I can't stop thinking about my original art pieces that Shane printed. I just want to see them, run my fingers against the canvas. Feel the raised texture. I don't know . . . maybe bring them home to display.

Wrapping up the last e-mails for the day, I stretch my hands and yawn, then jump up and head to the break room to fill my water bottle. I always forget to bring it to the gym. This way it will be in my bag.

Ellie and Tonya are both sitting at the table. *Great*. I'm not in the mood to deal with two-face Tonz. I notice the mystery boobs photocopy is missing again from the bulletin board and shake my head.

"They're going to put up another one, Ellie-Bell," I say, nodding to the space it usually occupies and positioning my bottle under the water cooler's nozzle.

"I don't care. I just feel sorry for whoever that poor girl is," Ellie says and takes a bite of her salad. She's trying to balance out our carb load from yesterday and is eating only green and yellow things for the next few days. "I didn't have time to finish my lunch," she says, when I notice.

Tonya snorts and narrows her eyes. "They'll never run out. One good master copy will keep us staring at copy-boobs for the rest of our lives. Who would get a tattoo there?" Tonya leans back in her chair and tips her head, "Wait, Ellie-belly, didn't you get a tattoo?"

Ellie darts her eyes to me as I sit down to join them. I've always suspected Tonya, but I could never prove it, so I've left it alone.

"How are things with Shane Bennett's account?" Ellie asks and takes another bite.

She's only changing the subject, but really? Do we need to be on *this* subject? "Fine. I'm still working on the layout, nothing worth mentioning." I tighten the cap on my bottle again.

"I was thinking of getting another tattoo. Maybe a heart," Tonya says, looking right at Ellie, and points to her own breast. "Maybe, right about . . . hmm . . . here."

"So, you and Shane Bennett used to date, huh? He still seems to like you. Don't you think?" Ellie says in a rush to me, swirling her fork in her salad.

What is she doing?

"Well, that explains the skulking around." Tonya takes a sip of her drink and raises an eyebrow. "At least that's what I heard."

"That's what you *heard*?" My heart's beating double time. My eyes narrow toward Ellie. Once you tell a secret to one person, it's no longer secret. It's like lighting the end of an extremely long fuse. You know that eventually the flame will travel the entire distance and then, with absolute certainty, blow up in your face. *What did she tell her?*

Tonya leans on her elbows. "So, you and Shane again?"

"What? No—" The words fly out in superspeed and are laced with snark. "I'm engaged, Tonya. I, unlike *some* people, don't sneak around behind people's backs and lie, *pretending* to be their friends."

Tonya's face pales. Ellie nods toward the doorway. We all look. Terry from Sales is frozen with an empty coffee mug in his hands. He blinks and holds up his cup as if he's asking permission. Ellie shrugs.

We're locked in a stare down waiting for Terry to leave. My nostrils are flared from my short breaths. It is taking everything in me not to smack her. Ellie's eyes are wide, and she keeps shoving bites of salad into her mouth, maybe so she doesn't say anything else. *Good call.* I may smack her, too.

As soon as Terry's out, I'm off. "Did you really think it wouldn't come out what you did? That he wouldn't *tell* me? How could you?"

Tonya's lips tighten into a hard line, and without a word, she gets up, opens the fridge, puts her water in the door and slams it. The whole thing rocks from the force, causing the plastic cups stacked on top to wobble. Then without a word she storms out. *Unbelievable.*

I glare sideways at Ellie.

"I only said he went looking for you and ended up helping. That you hung out yesterday." She opens her mouth and quickly fills it with a forkful of lettuce. "It's not a big deal."

Except it is. The thing about keeping a secret is you're supposed to keep it secret. Ellie may just have accidentally launched the missile sequence that starts a domino effect of destruction.

I lean over the table and speak sternly. "What if Tonya talks to Bradley about it and he gets all riled up? They're close. She might. Then, what if Bradley says something to Shane and gets him all riled up and he bails? We need his account, Ellie."

"Kenz, I'm sorry. But I only said you hung out. That's it, and it was work-related. You're being paranoid."

Am I? I'm not so sure. Maybe that's what guilt does to you. You wonder who knows what, and you become suspicious of everyone. I take a drink of my water and shake my head.

How did I even get to this point? Last Sunday, Bradley and I were excited to show off my engagement ring and start planning the wedding. Then *boom*, Ren's preggo. Shane's back, my job's at risk, and Tonya's revealed as enemy number one. Add in an insinuated shotgun wedding, shared engagement party, and Mom . . . I don't even know how to process Mom.

My head drops into my hands. It's been five days. Seriously, not even a week.

BRADLEY AND I STOPPED AT my parents' on the way to the gym. He's downstairs talking with Mom and Dad and I'm digging through the closet in my old room, looking for my work from college.

I dashed straight upstairs to avoid Mom. The Shane conversation *cannot* happen in front of Bradley, not with everything else going on.

Balanced on Mom's stool, I smack my hand around under my Kensington box on the closet shelf. I thought my paintings were underneath, but nope, there's nothing. *Where are they?*

Spinning around, I look to see where she could have stashed them. Climbing down, I push around a few more bins and boxes of scrapbook materials and supplies on the floor. Maybe they're wedged in between? I still don't see them. "Hey, Mom?" I jump up and lean into the hall. "Mom . . ."

Their voices carry up, but they don't hear me. "Mom," I say again, trekking down the stairs.

When I burst into the kitchen, I find Bradley and Dad at the table, Mom pouring Dad a refill on his coffee and Ren standing near the sink. Her long hair's pulled back neatly in a ponytail and she's casual in jeans. She nods with a soft smile.

"Hi. Um, Mom, where'd you move my paintings from college?"

"What, dear? I'm not sure what you mean." She barely looks up. "Do you want cream? I bought some of the Irish kind you like," she says to my dad, then looks to Ren. "How are you feeling?"

Dad slides his cup out as Mom opens the fridge to retrieve the cream.

"Hello?" It's Grayson calling from the foyer. I hear the door click behind him. Since Grayson and Ren live down the street, they practically live here, too.

"In here," Mom calls out and pours enough cream to completely change the color of Dad's coffee. "Ren, you should be sitting. You spend too much time—"

"Mom, really, we only stopped in for a minute. They used to be under my box in my room. Remember?" The hairs on my arms have raised.

Grayson pops in. "Hey, Bradley, saw your car. I didn't get a chance to call you back, sorry. Crazy day. What's up?"

Bradley looks at me, then him. "How about I swing by tomorrow for an early lunch?"

Grayson nods. "Great, yeah, just call me first to make sure I can break away . . ."

I'm not listening. I'm focused on my mom as she busies herself putting dishes away. "*Mom?*"

"What? Kensington . . . my word." She stops and turns to face me, exasperated, a dish in each hand.

My shoulders hike. "My *paintings?*"

Her face screws up in confusion. "Anything that was yours is in that box." She turns and places a drinking glass in the cupboard above her.

"They were *under* the box. I had like five of them. Think. Did you move them somewhere?"

Putting another glass away, she spins, a hand already on the next one in the dishwasher. "Well, if they're not there, I'm not sure what to tell you. And to be honest, I could use the room in that closet, so if you want that box, maybe take it with you? Grayson, coffee? It's a fresh pot."

"They're gone?" Something coils up inside me. I was already livid, but now this? This is too much. "*You got rid of them?*" I'm yelling, shooting daggers at her from my eyes. I look at Dad. "You let her get rid of them? Those were from school, *my* work." They were pieces of me.

Bradley looks confused. Dad lifts his hands to show he has no idea what I'm talking about, Ren glances at me and opens her mouth to say something, but then Mom starts in.

"Kensington, you can't honestly expect me to keep track of your things from college, can you?" She shakes her head. "Did you want coffee?"

That's it?

I stumble back a step, speechless. She's clueless. She doesn't get it. "Grayson's awards are still on display in the basement from high school, but my paintings? You threw out my paintings?" Forget stuffing them into a drawer, she trashed them. They're *gone*.

Just like she made Shane disappear.

Without another word, I dash upstairs, taking two at a time. She didn't even call and ask. I doubt she ever even looked at them. Hell, she doesn't even know what I'm talking about. And yet she thought she knew what was best for me and Shane? *She had no right*. Tears work their way through my lashes. Everything's blending together in one big mucky mess.

On my toes, I dig at the base of my box to knock it closer to scootch it out.

Hauling it downstairs, I pass by the kitchen. Grayson's talking about sneaking in some golf with Bradley. Dad's saying something to Ren about the nursery. I don't stop.

"I'm going." That's all I say. I'm not sure they even heard me. Right now, I don't care. The box is balanced on my hip as I work the door. I don't bother with closing it, I just storm to the car. I can hear Bradley behind me as I stomp down the walkway.

"Kenz? Kenzi!"

I'm already popping the back when he appears on the porch. He leans inside, momentarily. "Hey, Grayson, I'll call you tomorrow. 'Bye, all."

I slam the trunk and meet Bradley's confused look with one that says *Don't ask*.

He doesn't.

But he should've.

THERE ARE UNSPOKEN RULES TO working out in a gym, a code that everyone adheres to. They're not posted anywhere. But everyone knows them.

First, there are the gym-world time zones. Early morning is for everyone, newbies, fitness experts, and the in between. Afternoon is for the diehards, competitive body builders and cardio queens. And evenings are for eye candy. The in-shape A-listers.

Feel free to stare. You will be stared at. Workout optional.

Well, I'm still worked up, so this workout's necessary. Bradley and I arrive a little late because we stopped at my parents. *Great, Tonya showed*, probably because she booked a session with Troy.

I hate working out with him. The guy's muscle-on-muscle and pits us against each other in stupid competitions that I can only assume are for his pervy amusement. I mean, who really cares how many jumping jacks and burpees we can do in less than three minutes?

"Are you working out with Tonya?" Bradley asks. The conversation's been strained. I haven't felt like talking and I'm still upset with him about earlier. I'm upset with everyone.

"I think I might stick to cardio, burn off some steam," I huff, and hand him my stuff to lock up.

"All right," Bradley says, reaching over for a kiss before heading off to the weights.

Turning out of reach, I grab my earbuds. I don't want his kiss. I wanted his understanding. His support. And now I just want to zone out in my music, burn off all the extra carbs I've been sneaking, and forget everything.

Tonya's warming up on a treadmill. She's in running shorts and a yellow tank with a built-in bra. For me, these tanks are great. Tonya, however, needs to double-bra those puppies. No one seems to mind that she doesn't, especially the guy she's talking to.

Second gym-world rule, never choose cardio equipment next to someone if others are open, unless you know them and it's welcomed. I'm not sure I'm welcome, but it's the only one open.

I start up the treadmill beside Tonya, ignoring her. Setting the incline to 2, I set the warm-up speed to 3, which is a good brisk walk.

"You actually showed this time." Tonya's jaw's set.

I didn't even think about that. Yesterday, not only did I leave Bradley waiting, Tonya was expecting me at the gym, too. *Does she think I'm talking to her?*

"Troy said he'll be ready for us in ten," Tonya says, upping her incline to 3, her voice flat.

"I'm gonna pass on Troy-boy." I up my speed to 3.5. "So are you going to at least apologize?"

She reads my screen then ups her incline and speed to 4 without saying a word.

Bitch. I match her speed then pass it by half. "Really?" I take a drink of my water, feeling a fresh, raw pang. "I mean, you're the one who told me he cheated . . ." I take a few quick breaths. "And it ended up being you. *You!*"

Her chin drops. "Wait. This is about *Shane*? In college?" She's shaking her head. "*Oh my God!*"

"*Oh my God* is right, you could at least apologize."

"The Shane thing was a million years ago, Kenz." Her words are coming out in chops. "It didn't . . . mean anything—"

"It meant *everything*!" I step off the conveyer onto the side rails and stare her down. "You said *he cheated*!" My calm and cool tone is now red-hot. "I *completely* believed you!"

Tonya steps from the tread onto her rails and takes a big breath. "You were going to leave everything and follow him to the UK."

"So you *sabotaged* my life?" *I can't believe her.* My frustration with Mom, Bradley, Shane, her, it all comes out in a roar. "You know what, Tonya? You're a backstabbing *liar*!" I said that too loud. I knew it as soon as it came out of my mouth. People heard me. Bradley even looked over with a startled expression.

"Dial it back, for chrissakes!" She wipes at her forehead with her towel, then shoves it back in the console, stepping back on the tread. "Let's be honest, he could have told you it was me, *begged* you to forgive him. *But he didn't!* Yeah, that's what you're really pissed about."

Her words stab me through the heart. "Screw you." Lit up from anger and adrenaline, I jump back on and up the speed to 5. My gym shoes are clopping against the rubber tread pretty fast now. This is a serious jog.

She eyeballs me, matches my speed, and raises her incline not one level, but two. *She's on 9!*

I kick the speed to 5.5 and raise my incline to 10. Beads of sweat are forming at my hairline. My legs aren't as long, and this is a run. *Uphill.*

She's huffing, eyeing my screen, then me. *Don't you—*

Slam. She's at an incline of 12. Her hair is sticking to her face, but she can't let go of the rails to wipe it free.

The machine has an incline max of 15. I know where this is going. This is classic Tonya, always competing with me. And no way is she going to win. *Not this time.*

I drive the button down and hold, passing 12 and hitting 13. *That's right!* To keep my balance, I hold on to the handle grips in front with both hands. My feet kick out behind me in loud *clomp-clomp-clomps* as I try to keep up.

She's shooting daggers at me from the corners of her eyes. My machine beeps and flashes a warning at me. SLOW DOWN. SLOW DOWN. My heart rate's 175!

No! I've had it with everyone today. My feet pound the conveyer, the machine continues to beep, the motor whines loudly.

Tonya's pushing the button and it's rising to 14. I don't want to go to 14. *Shit!* This is ridiculous. She's bent over, gripping the handrails, trying to keep up.

Our feet stomp heavily as we full-on run uphill. We look insane. People are now watching. I can hear them gathered around to witness this display of stupidity.

Troy-boy's between us. He's grinning like an idiot and chanting. "Go, go, go!"

Other people are joining in, "Go! Go! Go!"

Tonya doesn't care. My mom doesn't care. Does Bradley? Did Shane ever care? I've had it. In *How to Lose a Guy in 10 Days*, Kate Hudson's character, Andy, asks Ben, "True or false, all's fair in love and war?" How he answers determines how badly she messes with him.

Well, I say "False." It's *not* fair! And I'm tired of people messing with me, lying to me. If Tonya wants a war . . . I lift my hand high and *slam*!

The treadmill cranks upward. Level 15!

The top level!

Ha! I win!

Cheers erupt.

Troy-boy slams on our stops, and the treadmills slow and decline.

Oh. Thank. God.

We both collapse, drenched in sweat and out of breath. *Shit*, my chest is heaving for air. I'm nauseated. Tonya covers her mouth and makes a dash for the bathroom. Bradley looks first in her direction then toward me. He mouths, *What's going on?*

This he asks about? I swear if he comes over here and says anything I'm going to completely lose my mind.

CHAPTER NINE

Ghost of Boyfriend Past

*I*T'S FRIDAY. I'VE BEEN happily painting the new conceptual for the Carriage House at my desk all morning. Not with real paint, but with digital painting software, using a tablet and pen. I'm also chatting with Ellie and watching the clock.

My co-workers are throwing Bradley and me an engagement party at Ditty's after work. And unlike my family's, it's not shared with anyone. Tonya was wrong. Ren didn't need to start showing before my family would kiss my wedding plans goodbye.

They never even said hello.

I carefully planned my wardrobe to transition from work to the party. I'm wearing a gray sleeveless tank dress I bought with Ren a while back and to-die-for pumps. I have a cardigan on now for the office and my hair is tied back in a loose pony. But as soon as it's time to go, the sweater and tail are history.

Tonya left a Starbucks on my desk this morning. She won't really apologize, but at least she knows why I'm mad. Mom still doesn't know why, but she apologized, *twice*, first in an e-mail, then in a voice message asking if I got her e-mail. Why e-mail if you're going to call?

> **ELLIE-BELL:** Did he actually call them Mary Kate and Mary Francis?
> **KENZI SHAW:** Yes, and they were completely into the whole movie thing.
> **ELLIE-BELL:** I'm dying. DYING! I want a Pretty Woman moment!

I haven't talked with Shane since yesterday. I keep eyeing the chat window on Facebook to see if the green dot is lit up next to his name. I'm sure they have Internet at the farm. Maybe not. It's gray. Or maybe he's on his way back already? I don't know. He's not online, which is good because I don't want him to know that I am. I could turn off my chat, but then how would I know if he were, or talk to Ellie about him? Very mature reasoning.

Using the movie images Shane provided as the background, I'm almost done blocking in the colors on another layer. I call it the mucky-muck layer. It's my own made-up term for the loose foundation of a painting. The detail work comes in after to give it shape and perspective.

I couldn't sleep, and we need to get the Carriage House conceptual done, so I came in a few hours early. Being lost in my process again is calming, almost therapeutic. Maybe needed.

Michelangelo is known for saying every block of stone has a statue inside. And it's the artist's job to release it. It's the same with painting. The final work already exists. It just needs to be revealed. I've tried to explain how this works to Bradley, but he doesn't really understand what I mean. I'm not sure I understand it. I just accept its truth.

Using my pen and tablet, I start to apply lines in thin strokes to define the main movie images. Right now, I'm working on the poster image of *Love Actually*.

I love the story line with Colin Firth and his housekeeper, who speaks only Portuguese. One of my favorite moments is when he marches through town with her entire family behind him. He proposes in her language only to hear the answer in his. Language doesn't prove to be a barrier at all.

Biting my lip, I'm lost in the feeling of . . . *of what?* I'm completely getting carried away in all of this. *Which was the point, right?* Isn't that what Shane wanted? For me to remember how much I loved these romantic comedies so it would transfer into my work. That's the whole point of the Love Like the Movies list. I open the e-mail and look through them again.

1. Sleepless in Seattle
2. ~~Pretty Woman~~
3. Bridget Jones's Diary
4. 27 Dresses
5. Dirty Dancing
6. Sixteen Candles
7. Love Actually
8. Say Anything
9. You've Got Mail
10. My Best Friend's Wedding

I stare at the screen, deflated.

It's about his *concept*, not me. And these are movie moments, not real life. I almost wish Shane had never come back, because the comparison is a bit depressing.

Glancing up, I catch sight of Bradley walking over. I minimize the chat window and continue to mix colors, trying to get a rich russet, but since I'm painting with the digital color wheel of RGB, my primary mix is giving me a brown-gray sludge.

"Hi, hon." Bradley glances at the monitor then leans on my desk, facing away from it.

He looks good. Clean cut and sophisticated in a fitted crisp white button down. Bradley eyes my bright pink cardigan with matching skinny belt and bunches his forehead. "You're bright today."

"Oh, yeah. Guess I am." I hadn't thought about it. This morning I just felt like wearing something colorful.

Bradley leans close and lowers his voice even though no one's around. "Look, I've been thinking about what you said, about the wedding, and if you want spring, then it's spring. I don't care. I just want you."

I stop mixing my sludge and look at him. Bright blue eyes stare back. He just wants *me*.

"But will you at least consider moving things up? Please?" His lips curl in a soft smile as he hands me a Post-it. "Yeah, I had an early lunch with Grayson and we got to talking, and he said Ren knew someone. Anyway, he just called back with her number."

I look at the note. *Bethany Chesawit. Wedding planner.* The phone number and address are scribbled below her name. I'm shaking my head. "Bradley, we didn't even pick a date."

"I know, but look . . ." He points to the Post-it. "She's supposed to be the best and she owes Ren a favor, so she fit you in on Monday. This way you can get an idea of the needed time frame to schedule everything."

"Wait, *I* can get an idea? You're not coming?"

"No. Remember, I'm leaving after the party and won't be back until Monday night, so maybe ask your mom? Or even Ren?"

ELLIE-BELL: Okay, I'm back.

He turns at the chirp, but disregards it. "Listen, we'll do it whenever you want, but the sooner we're married, the sooner we can start trying." He gives a sheepish grin. "I don't know. I'm just ready, I guess. I've really been thinking about it lately."

My heart skips. *He's been thinking about it.* I can almost hear the baby clock ticking. I'm going to be thirty. Looking at Bradley and his blond-hair, blue-eye combo, I can't help but think of the little girl I saw at the mall. Are the dad's traits responsible for hair and eye color?

I shrug with a smile. "Okay, I'll at least get an idea of the time frame needed. But . . ." I hold up a finger. "I'm not promising anything. And definitely not six weeks." This is everything I've wanted. Marriage, a family . . . and he's ready.

Bradley pushes a stray strand of hair from my cheek, leans over and sneaks a chaste kiss, then eyes the screen. "Is that for Bennett?"

"Yeah . . ." I'm actually pleased with how well it's turning out. I'm kind of proud of it. I angle the screen so he can take a better look.

He doesn't. "Sooner it's finished, sooner he's outta here."

"Hey, I was looking for you." Clive's leaning out of his office and pointing at Bradley.

"I'll see ya later." He winks before leaving.

I watch him walk away. Broad shoulders, clean cut, and golden. That's Bradley. I do love him. We have a great foundation to build on and he's ready.

Maybe it won't be a movie life, but it still can be a good one.

WHEN ELLIE AND I GOT back from our late lunch, the conference room door was closed. Not a big incident in its own right. I mean, doors do open and close. But Shane's supposed to be back and meeting with Clive and Bradley, and I'm almost positive he's in there.

A day without Shane around has cleared my head a little. I've dissected the situation from every angle and perspective, and have come to a conclusion.

He's a ghost, a boyfriend from the past whose sudden re-appearance has conjured up old, lingering feelings. And those are getting mixed up with the movie moments. It's stress from the wedding, my job, Ren's pregnancy announcement, and Tonya. It's a lot to take in.

Ellie said I should put it to a challenge. She's calling it the TFT. Tummy Flip Test.

After not seeing Shane for a day, and no new movie moments to obscure things, it shouldn't be confusing at all when I do. It should be a nonevent, really. No fireworks or firecrackers, maybe just a tiny sparkler to signify an old flame. That's all. And that's perfectly acceptable.

I'm anxious to put myself to the TFT, so I can put all this SBN, Shane Bennett Nonsense, behind me. Marriage is about stability and family with someone you can trust. Not some haunting attraction with someone you can't. The TFT will prove I'm capable of keeping the past, and its ghosts, deeply buried.

"Hey, Kenzi, are you excited for the engagement party? It's almost time," says Maggie, our receptionist, as she walks back to the front desk to grab the phone.

I smile brightly. "I can't wait. Thanks."

My smile drops with the click of the conference room door. This is it. Operation TFT is now in motion.

KENZI SHAW: It's a go. Stand by.

I close out my chat and online windows with one hand and chew on the thumbnail of the other. Immediately, I'm busy, staring at my work in progress on the screen. Through my lashes, over the screen's top, I can still see the legs of whoever comes out.

The door swings open. Dark denim. It's him. He's always in jeans. He's not moving. Nothing is. The office seems silent, still. The only sound is my thumping heart.

I lift my eyes cautiously and see him standing in the doorway, talking with Clive. He's wearing a fitted V-neck sweater over a tee, and there's scruff on his jaw. I don't remember if it's rough, or if it softens by day's end. I do remember shaving it once for him, though. I foamed up his face and slowly, carefully started to run the razor, when he jumped as if I'd nicked him. I didn't, and we ended up in a shaving cream fight.

Clive's leaving. I quickly dart my eyes back to my screen, so I can only see Shane's feet again. He isn't moving. What is he doing? I can *feel* his eyes on me. My heart drums louder.

Slowly, I glance up.

My stomach jumps.

He's looking right at me.

It's just like the first time I saw him at school. I looked across the lecture hall, and there he was, disheveled hair, wrinkled shirt, and copper-brown eyes. Staring at me. An entire conversation passed between us, unspoken but understood.

Now it's the same conversation, only this time it's forbidden.

The corners of his lips turn slightly as he holds my gaze. I should look away but I can't. There's an emotional swell in my chest. I chew on my nail and feel a smile wanting to escape behind my hand. My face contorts trying to hold it in.

Don't do it. Do *not* smile. Keep it back . . . he smiles . . . and *oh my God*, it's a great one.

Major tummy flip. It's a double.

"There's a smile I don't often see," Bradley calls out from behind Shane.

My stomach drops like a stone.

Of course, Bradley thinks the smile's because of him, because he's heading in my direction, and he's *my fiancé*. The smile *should* be for him.

Oh, God. I've failed.

I was supposed to be able to control it.

Keep the past from muddling up my future.

I'm not smiling anymore.

"Hi," I say with forced enthusiasm as Bradley nears. I bet I look guilty. *I feel guilty.* It's percolating under the surface.

He sits on the edge of my desk the way Clive usually does. I dart my eyes back toward the conference room, but Shane's turned and walked back in.

"I was thinking again, that you should call Ren about meeting with the wedding planner on Monday. It might be something you guys can connect on. It could be really good for you two."

He's solving. Helping.

I'm failing.

"Yeah, okay, she might like it. I'll call right away," I add, digging for my phone. Whatever he wants. I'm the worst fiancée. The worst human being.

"Good. All right, I need to finish up a few things before we head out." He slaps his hands on his thighs and rocks up. "So, I'll catch ya in about thirty?" He smiles and heads toward his office.

Looking around, I'm half convinced everyone witnessed the

exchange and can see right through me to all my unsupervised thoughts.

> ELLIE-BELL: Anything?
> KENZI SHAW: What's the line in *My Best Friend's Wedding*?
> After she says, "I'm pond scum"?
> ELLIE-BELL: What are you talking about?
> KENZI SHAW: It's "You're lower." And I'm lower. I'm the fungus
> that feeds on pond scum. The gunk that cruds up the stuff, that
> sits under the slime.
> ELLIE-BELL: That's a line in a movie?

Not exactly. My back is tensing. The muscles that run along the neck and shoulders are starting to spasm. I glance again at the conference room door. Forget fireworks, our TFT produced TNT. It's an epic fail. And I'm the one who's going to blow up. All my plans. Everything I want. One big kaboom, kerplowey, kersplat, and for what?

It's about the movie concept, that's *why* Shane's here. So he doesn't see me with Bradley, that doesn't *mean* anything. It's not like Julia Roberts's character, Julianne, in *My Best Friend's Wedding* when she pleaded with Michael, *Choose me. Pick me. Let me make you happy.*

No, Shane said, *It'd be fun to work together, who else would pull off this concept,* and he apologized for the past.

Okay, so old feelings still exist for me. *So what.* Relationships aren't all about fireworks. Those fade over time, right? I straighten, pen suspended in air. My heart sinks.

It's been seven years.

He's like Connor Mead . . . and I'm like Jennifer Garner's character, Jenny Perotti. *What was his line?* I quickly Google

Ghosts of Girlfriends Past to find it. Here, yes . . . *The power in all relationships lies with whoever cares less.* It's true. If I'm still muddled up in old feelings, Shane still holds this power over me.

He always did. And not just over *me.* Over all the girls. It wasn't that I didn't care that every female in college thought they had this *special* connection with him, I just got used to it. Although at Fossie's, the flirty Mary didn't seem to get his normal attention. His attention was solely on me.

Either way, I need a ghost buster.

Oh, I need to call Ren! Dialing quickly, my eyes keep darting to the conference room.

"Hello?"

"Ren, hi. It's Kenz." *Oh my God*, I'm my mother. "Well, of course you know it's me—"

"Hi."

"Well, I'm calling to ask if you'd like to maybe meet me Monday, at the wedding planner's? Bradley said she was a friend, so—"

"Oh, I planned on it. I can only be there to get you started. But at least that way someone will be around to steer you in the right direction."

Yes, because I couldn't be trusted on my own. Well, maybe I can't. Her registry pops to mind—yeah, not the time to get into that. "Okay, well, I'll meet you there on Monday, then?"

She reminds me to dress appropriately before she hurries off to meet my mom and her decorator. They're planning the nursery. Can't plan my wedding, can't save my paintings, can't understand why I'm upset, but . . .

Eloping is sounding better and better. Maybe we should just get it over with before I do something stupid and Bradley leaves me, too. Kneading my neck, I roll my shoulders to loosen the tension. I need to be working, not thinking.

"Kenzi, how are things moving along with Bennett's new concept?" It's Clive, he's walked around my desk and is leaning over my shoulder to see the screen. I didn't even hear him walk up. Everyone's in ghost mode.

I zoom out so he can see the entire collage of the movie stills Shane provided. All ten from our list can easily be identified, plus a few extras like *When Harry Met Sally* and *Pretty in Pink*. It's one wide and narrow piece, which can then be spliced where needed for individual marketing pieces.

"Has Shane seen this yet?" Clive asks, still over my shoulder. He chews his gum loudly. It smells of spearmint.

"No, not yet. I wanted to get a little further alo—"

"No, this works, he'll be thrilled. I'd save it off and make sure he knows it's almost completed."

"But it's not."

"Well, I'd like to bill him for stage two and that looks far enough along." He stands, folds his arms, and chews, while regarding my screen with his head tilted.

Since we bill in thirds we received payment with the contract sign-on. The second will be upon conceptual approval, and third is with completion. I've never seen him so anxious to bill a client before. And it's not done. *I'm not ready.*

Before I can argue, Clive has turned and is starting to leave.

"Oh." He spins and backtracks a few steps. "I invited them to the after-work thing. I'd be taking them out anyway since they made the trip."

Wait . . . "Who?" My heart's beating faster.

Clive pops his eyes. "Peterson. Bennett. The *clients*."

My I-can-handle-this bubble bursts. It's splattered all over my engagement party outfit, and there's no time to change.

Clive waves a hand dismissively. "That's not a problem, is it?"

He invited Shane to my engagement party.

Yeah, I think that *might* be a problem.

CHAPTER TEN

My Best Friend's Wedding Advice

I'VE STRIPPED THE CARDIGAN and lost the ponytail. I may have sprouted a she-devil tail, however. I'm actually surprised no one's stepped on it yet. I'm feeling unkind and undeserving.

I should be happy.

This is Bradley's and my night, and Ditty's is one of my favorite places in downtown Indy. It's a bar and restaurant that features piano music during dinner hours, with an additional piano player joining for boisterous, dueling entertainment later. By midnight, it turns into a group karaoke all-out glee concert.

My emotions are volleying from one extreme to another as we walk in, and I feel my devil tail swish like an agitated cat's.

"There they are," says Bradley, pointing to the row of tables put together along the side. His hand is at the small of my back to gently guide me toward our party.

Half the office has arrived. A waitress is passing drinks to Tonya and Ellie, and Maggie, the receptionist, is waving us over. Some of the guys from Programming are here, and most of the sales reps. I don't see Clive, Rand Peterson, or anyone in particular that usually wears jeans.

"Hey, girly, look at you," says Tonya, with her straw between her lips. She's in another expensive-looking outfit I've never seen. Guess she thinks a Starbucks makes up for everything.

Whatever. If I make a big deal about it, it will only ruin the night and drag Bradley into more of my Shane past.

The buzz of multiple conversations carries over clanking dishes and the music. There's already an unmistakable energy in the club. The man at the piano is playing "Knock on Wood." Every time he sings the chorus, people tap out the beat on their tables. I can't help but think of *Casablanca*. There's a song with this line in the chorus where they do that. Not the same song, but similar enough.

"You look gorgeous, Kenz," Ellie says over the music as I slide next to her.

"Thanks, Ellie-bell, you do too." I lean in toward Tonya with my best pasted-on smile. "Maybe we can talk sometime to-morrow?" I should have been an actress, because I keep putting in one epic performance after another. I'm not ready to just let this go. I deserve an explanation, even if I won't get an apology.

"Yeah, okay." A relieved smile forms on her face. "Tomorrow, for sure."

Within minutes, we're a group of twenty. Everyone's chatting, drinks are flowing, and appetizers have arrived. This is great. I admit it feels pretty nice to have all these people here for us. I've almost forgotten everything. I smile at Bradley and take a sip of my drink.

"Ow!" I jump and narrow my eyes at Ellie.

She kicked me. Hard. Her pointed pumps could be considered lethal.

She's nodding with a guess-who's-here expression. That's when I see Clive, Rand Peterson, and Shane, walking our way. No tummy flip. I'm on lockdown.

There are empty chairs across from Bradley and me. Right across. This means he'll be staring at us all night. The happily engaged couple. My insides twist. How am I supposed to get my footing, if he's always underfoot?

"Hi," I say when they approach, and quickly laugh at something Bradley said. I have no idea what he said.

Tonya smiles and flips her hair flirtatiously. "Hi ya, boys. Not a party without you."

"Considering I'm the one footing the bill," Clive says and takes a seat.

"Well, there's that." She looks at Shane, grins, and pops her eyes. "Hi, Shane. You look all kinds of handsome."

Bradley whips around and gives her a cool-it look. *What is that?*

Shane pulls out the seat across from me, while looking at Tonya. "Well, I didn't actually change, but thank y—"

"Don't you think, Kenz? Shane looks *hot*?" Her eyebrows are high.

Now I'm the one giving her a cool-it look. *What is she doing?* I thought we had a truce? Shane looks from her to me with a confused smile.

I pretend like I didn't hear and am suddenly fascinated by what the piano player is doing. Yup, he's playing the piano.

Bradley's arm drapes around my chair, and he leans back, looking as annoyed as I feel. He can't be thrilled my ex is here. Clive's an ass for inviting them. Actually, I'm not sure Clive really knows anything. He's been so focused on Shane's account, I doubt he's dialed in.

"What, Ellie? I didn't hear you." I turn toward her and lean in.

Ellie makes a screwed-up expression and whispers in my ear. "I didn't say anything."

I dart my eyes to the crowd and laugh. "I know? Right?" This cannot be my plan for surviving this evening.

Bradley's making small talk with Terry from Sales, sitting to his left. I lift my glass and take a drink. I'm thinking about ordering another.

Shane's looking at me.

My stomach somersaults. *Damn it.*

"You look beautiful, Kensington."

Another flip. Another TFT fail. I smile involuntarily and feel my cheeks burn. I'm sure they're a bright scarlet. Bradley turns. I'm certain he's heard and will notice my new rosy complexion. I take a sip of my drink, feeling warm and extremely thirsty all of a sudden.

"Bennett, Kenzi tells me you should have your concept wrapped soon. So, you'll be heading back to the farm? You do live on a *farm*, don't you?"

Yup, he heard.

Clive leans forward on his elbows. "Oh, it's a farm all right, but it's right off Lake Michigan, near La Porte. Big tourist town and just beautiful property . . . made a trip up there when we first pitched the Carriage House." He turns to Shane to confirm.

"Yes, that's right. Hopefully we can open within a year's time." Shane nods modestly.

"Hell of an operation, Shane. Really something else," Clive adds.

Clive's *seen* it? Shane's really doing it? I can't help but be surprised, maybe a little *impressed*. I mean, I knew, obviously, that Shane was the owner, but I guess it didn't really register as *real*. The boy I knew always had big ideas, but that's as far as they went.

"In fact, Kenzi here should go take a look." Clive is rotating his beer glass around in his fingers. "If you're putting her murals up inside, she should see the space," Clive says with a wink. It's the let's-keep-Mr.-Bennett-happy wink. He takes a drink, his eyes on me over the rim.

Tonya clasps her hands together. "Oh, that would be great! Kenz would *love* that!"

What is she doing? My assessment of the situation swings wildly between two scenarios. She's either looking out for me or stabbing me in the back. *Again.*

Shane's eyes flick to me. It's a shared don't-mention-anything exchange. There's no way I want to explain how I've already seen his farm. It was years and years ago, and now is *not* the time to bring up our past. It's weird enough he's at my engagement party.

Shane regards Clive. "I do actually think that would help." He leans back in his chair. "I was going to head back Tuesday night, after your client outing." His eyes move back my way. "If you'd like to see the restaurant and theater site, I'd be happy to take you up. You're welcome to tag along, Bradley, *of course.*"

Bradley huffs. His chin's up.

"It is a farm, though, remember?" Shane asks, his lips pressed in a tight line.

Clive doesn't let Bradley answer. "Well, we can't have the whole office gone on some field trip now, can we? Bradley, you and I have a meeting Wednesday morning with the Colts franchise anyway."

Clive's got him on a technicality. The Colts pitch is a huge deal. Bradley's pissed. I can tell by his forced smile and how he's drumming his first two fingers against his beer. I don't blame him.

Bradley's focused on Shane. "Then we can expect it done, by

what, next Friday?" He turns to me, his expression still stern. "At the absolute latest, right?"

I nod. My throat tightens. I don't dare swallow or answer.

"Good. I'm sure Shane would like to get back to his *farm life*," Bradley says, then takes a long drink. His arm is now resting around me instead of the chair back. His fingers are weaving through my hair. There's an unmistakable tension.

"I *love* work parties," Tonya says. "Ow!"

I'm certain Ellie kicked her.

"Shane, are you guys staying in town this weekend?" Ellie blurts. "Ow—what the hell?"

That kick was from me. Ellie knows Bradley's going to Lansing until Monday night. The last thing I need is for Bradley worrying about that while he's gone.

Our waitress and two other servers appear carrying trays of food. *Thank goodness.* They ordered family-style before we arrived to make it simple. Plates of everything are being set up in the table's center. Everyone's grabbing dishes, passing bowls, and commenting on the food—everyone except for me.

I'm leaning with my chin in my palm in a sudden fog. Clive just volunteered me to drive up for an overnight with Shane Bennett. I finish off my drink in one long sip and ask Bradley to order me another.

We agreed no gifts, that the dinner was more than enough. But Maggie's passing something under the table and giggling. Something's going on. I catch Clive and Maggie whispering. They feign innocence when they see me watching.

Ellie looks like she's going to burst. She laughs and looks at an index card, then Bradley. "So, how did you and Kenzi meet?" she asks loudly.

Everyone's stopped what they're doing to listen.

"Er . . . well, at work," Bradley says. He looks as confused as I feel. She already knows how we met, why is she asking? And what's with the cards? I notice everyone now has them.

"Well, that's *lame*," says Tonya.

Clive waves a hand in the air animatedly, his card clasped tightly between his fingers. "You need to spice it up. Make something up."

"Wait, I've got it," says Shane, grinning. He's talking loudly, too. No index card. "It was a mental institution."

"*What?* How much have you all been drinking?" Bradley asks, looking around, confused.

This ignites laughter all around.

Ellie reads her card then yells out, "Wasn't it because of Dionne Warwick?" It's like some badly rehearsed play and everyone has a part.

"Oh, that's me," Maggie says and stands glancing at her card. She finds her place with her index finger, then with dramatic flair she literally shouts, "Who is Dionne Warwick?"

They all yell at once, "Sacrilege!"

I'm laughing. *Holy shit*, I get it. I know what they're doing. The entire restaurant is watching a scene from *My Best Friend's Wedding* being played out. They're saying the lines from the movie. *Badly*, but those are the lines from the rehearsal dinner scene.

Everything is forgotten and I'm completely sucked in.

Shane glances around with a broad smile. "I'm sure Bradley looked at the lovely Kensington and in that moment . . . In that exact moment . . ." He's now looking right at me.

I'm transfixed with a sappy smile plastered on my face.

"He knew he could be in love . . ."

The guy at the piano starts playing and everyone turns toward the music.

Except me. Except Shane.

The first few lines of waking up and applying makeup are sung and I'm lost in them, in this moment.

The club bursts into a sing-shout, "*I say a little prayer for you!*"

I jump, startled, and laugh. This is awesome.

Another verse followed by the music kicks up! The entire restaurant is singing the chorus. "*Forever and ever, you stay in my heart . . .*"

Bradley looks completely lost. Shane is beaming. I'm flabbergasted. Everyone is in on it. *Everyone.*

"This is on the list!" I yell out over the chorus to Shane, forgetting myself. *This* is why he and Rand stuck around. It was planned. Clive knew, everyone knew! My heart is swollen with sentiment. This one isn't just about rediscovering a feeling so it transfers through my art to Shane's concept. This one's for *me.* He did this one for me, and it's the coolest thing *ever.*

"Forever and ever, you'll stay in my heart—"

"What the hell is going on?" Bradley shouts out with a laugh, which sends everyone into hysterics.

"*What?* No! No," I say, as the waitress grabs my hand. She's pulling me toward the piano. Maggie and Ellie are pointing and singing. The chorus is in full swing, and when I look back to my table, I throw my head back with a burst of laughter. Tears actually roll from my eyes. *This is too much!*

My entire work party, except for Bradley, is waving huge lobster-claw oven mitts over their heads and singing, "Forever and ever, you stay in my heart . . ."

Oh my gosh, how . . . I love *this.*

"GUESS I NEED TO SEE the movie again," Bradley's saying for what seems the hundredth time. It's late, and he's leaving for Lansing, so he's making his way around the table, thanking everyone for coming and shaking hands.

Maggie and Clive have their coats and Clive is settling the bill.

"I'll be back," I say to Ellie. "I'm gonna walk Bradley out." Grabbing his hand, I walk with him to the front lobby. Well, skip-walk. I'm still elated.

"Did you have fun?" He stops at the door and grasps my other hand.

"Yeah, of course!" It was a *really* good moment.

"I don't know what the hell this was tonight. The whole singing lobster thing," he says with a laugh. "I know you've made me watch that movie, but . . ."

"I really liked it. In fact, I adored it." I full-on grin, meaning every word.

"Well, I'm sure your family's planning a nice engagement dinner for us." He lets go of my hand and strokes my cheek.

"My family's plan is to mix it with a mini-shower for Ren. Which I don't think is necessary." I shake my head. "And there's no way it'll be as cool as this."

His head tips back. "I didn't realize you liked oven mitts and—"

"Oh, I do."

He laughs and pulls me closer. "Okay, then. I'll remember that for anniversary gifts, Christmas. You're completely covered." He leans in and kisses my nose. "Wish I didn't have to go. You're not staying, right?"

"Nope. Not long, anyway. Besides, I'm with Ellie."

He looks past me back to the table and before I know it his lips are pressed on mine. When he pulls back, he grins mischievously then pats my bottom. "I'll call ya when I get there."

Without turning, I can feel Shane's eyes on me. I know he's watching. And I know Bradley's display is for his benefit. But that's all I know. Tonight, I'm in a tug-of-war between broken logic and raw emotion.

Bradley turns and leaves. That's it. No sentimental gush of how much he loves me or what a special night this was. Nope, just a *call ya when I get there* and a pat on my backside. Well, he did say he wished he didn't have to go.

I turn and return to the table as a few others are saying their goodbyes. Most of our party has trickled out. Tonya's putting on her coat. *Wait*, Tonya's leaving? I do a mental tally of who just left. I know her game. Terry from Sales, he's married, and not her type. Rod and Patrick from Programming left a little while ago. I think they're actually a couple, so she's not *their* type.

"New guy?" I ask hopefully.

"Just tired." She zips her jacket and pulls her hair out from under the collar.

"Yeah right, don't think I haven't noticed all the new clothes."

She adjusts her purse's strap on her shoulder, looks past me, and lifts her chin. "You gonna tell me what's really up with bachelor number *two* over there?"

My stomach drops.

"Exactly," Tonya says before I can answer. "Have a good *niiight*," she sing-songs and heads for the door. "I'll call ya tomorrow," she yells out over her shoulder.

Whatever. I spin around and scan the room. Ellie's talking with Rand Peterson at the bar and everyone else has gone.

Except Shane.

He's walking toward me. I steady my nerves and start in his

direction. I'm beyond confused. Logically, I know he hasn't said one thing to make me think he wants more, but his actions, doing all of this . . .

Shane holds up a one-minute finger and turns on his heel toward the piano. Something's said, a flash of green is exchanged between their hands, and then the pianist starts to play the familiar intro of "As Time Goes By."

Really? I laugh. It's *Casablanca*. Okay, so he's still in major movie mode. He's being funny. Wasn't she married to someone else and this was their song? People begin moving onto the floor to dance. Shane steps around them on his way over.

My nose wrinkles with a smirk. "He doesn't get the girl, ya know."

"No. *He* doesn't."

My heart jumps. "What are you *doing*?" I ask, almost in a whisper.

He grabs my hand and wraps his other around my lower back, pulling me in close. "Dancing." Leaning near my ear, he whispers, "We're dancing."

I push away so I can see his face. "I only came over to say thank you for tonight and . . . and I'm *engaged*. And if I'm being honest . . ." My eyebrows are knitted, my voice is shaky. "You're making things complicated." There, I said it.

An impish grin plays across his lips. His eyes scan the length of my body and find their way to mine again. "Then you should have worn a different dress."

Wow. The smile can't be helped. "*Maid in Manhattan*? Really?"

Shane pulls me in close. "Kensington, it's not complicated. It's just a dance."

It *feels* complicated. That's a movie, too. Meryl Streep starts a secret affair with her ex.

His hand feels warm in mine. He's holding me so close I can feel the heat of his body, his breath near my ear. I squeeze my eyes shut to force out the guilt. Yeah, it's *so* complicated.

I feel myself lean in. I think I've had one drink too many. The scent of musk and sandalwood fills my nose as we move. It's familiar, comforting, but in no way safe.

"Did you like the movie scene?" He folds my arm into his, tight against his chest. I'm now completely enveloped, tucked in close, wrapped up in Shane. Surrounded by temptation.

"Mmm-hmm, so much," I mumble, still dancing. Still lost.

A soft chuckle near my ear. "I don't think Bradley did."

Still damned. "Yeah, he didn't get it, is all."

"Does he get you?"

My breath catches in my throat. My expression falls.

"Because I don't think he does. I don't think he gets you at all, Kensington."

I step back, breaking stride with the music, which now seems too loud. Shane still has my hand, his arm still has a hold around my waist, but there's now a space between us, a sudden distance of old hurts and new questions. Like is this about the concept or *me*?

Shane leans forward with a determined look on his face. "You're with Bradley because it looks good on paper. He's got the approval of your friends and your almighty family."

I pull my hand away. "You don't know—"

"I do. You have this idea of what you want and he fits the bill, right? I was in this same place. Almost married."

My chin lowers. *Almost married?*

"But, when I stepped back, I realized it wasn't really the life I intended for myself. She didn't fit. And Bradley doesn't fit you. I think you know that. You're just too scared to disappoint them or risk doing anything about it."

"Shouldn't I be scared? Wasn't I the one disappointed?" I can't believe I just said that. I step back, warnings going off in my head, my heart. Big ideals and no follow-through. He left me, too. Maybe for the same reason? *What am I doing?*

His face is doing that searching-for-the-right-words thing.

I don't wait for him to find them. My feet are already in motion. This isn't at all how I thought things would go. I don't know what I thought, or think, or anything.

I choke back frustrated tears and make my way through the crowd toward Ellie and Rand. Ellie's finishing another drink. She's no better to drive than I am. *Shit.*

"Rand, would you mind dropping Ellie and me off? Like, right now, please? I'm really sorry. I, um, just need to go." I pull my lips in and bite. That's all I'm saying.

Rand looks past me, I assume to Shane. His eyes dart back as he stands. "Yeah, of course. Sure."

I grab my bag and head for the door, not waiting for any one, not looking back. I know Shane's not following me. The scene from *My Best Friend's Wedding* pops into my head. When Julianne's chasing Michael, and George asks over the phone, "Who's chasing you? Nobody, get it? There's your answer."

The problem is I haven't asked the question.

I'm not sure I want to.

"THANKS FOR STAYING," I SAY to Ellie, rolling over under my comforter to face her. I couldn't bear to be alone tonight. I gave her a T-shirt and some sweats to sleep in, but I barely managed to change. I didn't even wash off my makeup. I'm still a bit tipsy.

"No prob. You saved me from sleeping with Rand," she says and tugs the blanket back on her. "Sleeping with you is so much better."

I laugh softly. "You like him, though, right?"

"Yeah, he's funny. Makes me laugh. He's like a giant, though. What do you think that means as far as—"

"How big are his feet?" I snort a laugh.

"Holy shit! I should be really concerned, then." Ellie giggles and props herself on an elbow. "So, you going to tell me what happened?"

"You like Bradley, right?" I don't even know where I'm going with this.

"Um, yeah. Everyone likes him. He's great, why?"

"Shane doesn't. He said Bradley doesn't get me, that he fits the bill on paper, with my family . . ." I don't finish, because a tightening has seized my chest. The back of my throat hurts from keeping it in.

Ellie sits up and places her pillow across her lap. "Your family makes you nuts. Everyone knows that."

I sit, too, and scootch myself back against the headboard, pulling my knees up tight.

"Kenz, can I say something without you throwing me out of your bed?"

I squeeze my arms tighter around my knees. "As long as it's how delightful and talented I am."

"Well, there's that." She nudges me and smiles. "Look, Bradley's great. I like him, I do. But when you and Shane are together, you're different. There's something between you guys. I haven't been around the two of you much, but even *I* can see it."

"But that's just it. He hasn't said he wants anything more, he's just said Bradley's not right for me. And he wants me to remember the girl I was in order to pull off his concept."

I take a deep, deep breath and look at the ceiling. "And then we're dancing and it's wonderful and terrible and I could die because it reminds me of what we had. Maybe what I still want." Turning, I look at Ellie. "Even his reasons for messing things up in college make sense. But he said he was almost married, so what, he still can't commit to anything or anyone. I don't know, it's just . . ."

Ellie pushes her hair from her face and leans into the pillow across her lap. "What?"

"It just felt like tonight was really for *me*, ya know?" I blow out a breath and shake my head. "I'm sure I'm just being stupid and confusing everything."

"You know Shane planned the whole restaurant song-thing." She smiles. "Yeah, he did. He had me go and find the oven mitts and e-mail everyone so it looked like I planned it. But he did it. He even called ahead to Ditty's to make sure they'd play along."

Ellie's watching me, but I don't say anything. I'm processing. He really did do this all for me.

"Okay, how about this: Tell me what you used to like about Shane when you guys were together."

"Why?"

"Just humor me."

"I don't know." I push out a breath. "He was my best friend. He loved my art, and I mean genuinely loved it." I straighten and wrap my arms around my knees again. "I always felt special when I was with him. He would hold my hand even if other guys were around. Of course, if anyone said anything he'd kick the shit out of them." I laugh. "I loved to watch him box. He was all attitude and adrenaline. His hair would curl even more from the sweat. And his voice, the way he says my name, and really listens to me."

"You mean, listened, the way he *listened* to you." Her lips turn up slightly. "You said 'listens.'"

I sink down on my back, pulling the comforter over me.

Ellie pulls it back, so my face is exposed. "Tell me about Bradley."

"He's Bradley. He's considerate and he thinks about practical, responsible things. God knows I'm not always practical." I pull my arms out from the comforter and chop them along my sides, tucking myself in. "And yes, my family loves him. So what? They're supposed to love him. Why wouldn't they? He talks politics and health care with my dad and Grayson. Mom and Ren swoon anytime he flashes his Ken smile at them. It's kind of funny."

"That's what your family likes, Kenz."

"I like those things," I say defensively.

Ellie wrinkles her nose, then slides down on her side facing me. "No, you like that your family likes them."

"What the hell are you saying, Ellie?"

"I'm just saying, that when it comes to your family, Bradley *fits*."

"And?" I turn, my eyebrows high.

"But you don't."

Screeching silence.

I'm not sure where I fit. *It's amazing the clarity that comes from psychotic jealousy.* I laugh to myself. That's the movie line, but I'm not jealous. I'm . . . *still fungus.*

Ellie scootches lower under the blankets and hugs a pillow to her side. "Hey, don't stress about it, okay? You'll figure this out." She sounds sleepy. "And tomorrow we have the symphony. I promise you'll have fun," she says through a slow yawn. "And think how gorgeous you'll look in that yellow dress."

The dress Shane bought me.

CHAPTER ELEVEN

Pretty Great

I HAVE MY STUFF OUT and have just finished straightening my hair. All I have to do is step into my dress and shoes, and I'm ready for the symphony with Ellie. She should be here in less than an hour to pick me up. *Tickets.* I grab them off the kitchen corkboard and tuck them into my bag.

Ellie skipped out early for a yoga class and left me alone with my thoughts for the day. Not entirely a good combination. Tonya never called. *Figures.* I've left two messages.

Bradley's phone keeps going to voice mail. If he's at the game, he probably can't hear it. I'm not sure what I want to say anyway. And since he's there with clients it's not like we're going to get into some big life-changing discussion. Was it going to be a life-changing conversation? I don't know. Maybe.

I keep thinking about last night. How Shane got everyone to read the lines from *My Best Friend's Wedding* and act them out. I've been replaying it over and over in my head like a selection from a DVD menu. It was the perfect moment, just like the movie, only I was the star.

Shane planned the whole thing for me. Bradley's only excited about what my family has planned. A split day with Ren. It's a little disconcerting. I mean, what about what I like?

And then there was that dance.

One dance. Extremely close. Breathtakingly slow.

Bradley didn't ask me to dance. It was our engagement party and he never asked. It's not his fault, he doesn't like dancing, but still. Shane's words keep circling around in my head like a shark.

He fits the bill, he doesn't fit you.

Has the approval of my almighty family.

I'm too scared to disappoint them.

Closing my eyes, I try to quiet my mind. The truth is, Shane's right, at least about one thing. I *am* scared.

Of making the wrong decision. Of regret. Of *him*.

At my computer, I jump on Facebook to zone out.

New status: *Some people require subtitles.*

Sighing, I focus on my news feed. It's congested by photos of Tina's new puppy. Yup, cute from every angle. And Shannon from high school has added yet another cat photo. This one's in the arms of a shirtless fireman. I click LIKE.

Surprisingly, I don't see any new updates from Ren or my mom. No links posted of cute baby stuff, or photos of the nursery's progress. Last blitz, they were considering a vintage Noah's Ark theme. Now there's nothing. The automatic baby-bot seems to have stalled.

Weird.

My phone buzzes and I grab it, grateful for a new distraction. It's Ellie. My fingers fumble with the screen slider as I glance at the clock. She'd better not bail on me.

"You're on your way, right?" I pop up from my desk, reach for my dress, and carefully remove it from the hanger.

"Yes and no. Is it all right if we meet there? I have to run to my mom's to get the dress I want. I thought it was here."

"I'll meet ya in the lobby, but only 'cause you're paying me to."

"What?"

I laugh. "It's from *Pretty Woman,* when he calls to say he'll meet her in the lobby. Then he says, *I told you not to pick up the phone*, but he calls back and of course she answers. I imitate the singsong way Julia Roberts replied to Richard Gere while shrugging my shoulders. "Then stop calling me . . . Remember?"

"Um, no." Ellie laughs.

"Yeah, okay. Sorry, still in movie mode. I'll see you there."

I'M AT THE CIRCLE THEATRE bar, a drink in front of me, and there's no sign of Ellie. The theater has been around forever. Its historic charm and ambience is dimly lit by shimmering crystal chandeliers. The only things more iridescent are the diamonds the women are wearing. My engagement mega-ring fits right in.

I love my dress. It's not an exact match to the one Kate Hudson wore in *How to Lose a Guy in 10 Days*, but it's close. It's the same long silhouette and sun-kissed yellow.

I look around again for Ellie. She should've been here by now. I'm dressed to impress, and desperate for a night lost in the orchestra's drama instead of my own. People are starting to work their way into the auditorium.

Where the hell is she?

My phone vibrates. If Ellie stands me up I swear I'll make a life-sized poster of her Xerox boobs. It's not Ellie. I don't recognize the number. I select IGNORE and start to stash it away. Again it buzzes with the same number. What if Ellie lost her phone and is borrowing someone's? What if her car broke down? The what-ifs start mounting, so I hurry to answer before it goes to voice mail.

"Hello?"

"Hi, Kensington."

My breath hitches. *Not Ellie*.

It's Shane.

I open my mouth to say something, but nothing comes out.

"Hello?"

"How'd you get my number?" Seems like a logical question. I never gave him my number. I've talked with him on Facebook. Well, I guess I did call him that once.

"Ellie, she—"

"You talked to her? She's supposed to be here." I sit up a little straighter. "Is she okay?" What if she was in an accident? Maybe they're at the hospital.

Shane chuckles softly. "I'm afraid she's otherwise engaged. Dinner date with Rand. Poor girl."

"What?" She's not dead. She's standing me up.

I'm gonna kill her.

"Yes. So, I'm afraid she can't make it. Of course, it would be a tragedy to have you sitting all alone at the symphony. Who would see you in your new yellow dress?"

I knit my brows. "I never told you what color my dress was." *I don't think.* I know I told him what I needed the dress *for*. I mean, that was the whole reason for the shopping day, but he didn't see it, and I didn't tell him. Why is he calling instead of Ellie?

"I bet you're sitting at the bar with a drink in front of you, but you haven't touched it."

I look at my full drink. My stomach hits the floor. *What the hell?* I glance around then look over my shoulder, trying not to be obvious.

"And now you're searching. Wondering . . . could it be? Is he here?"

Holy shit. He's saying Rupert Everett's lines from the end of *My Best Friend's Wedding.* He's here. He has to be here. Shane, not Rupert Everett. I stand and sweep the lobby.

"And then suddenly, the crowd parts and . . ."

I look toward the door, scanning the faces of people in suits and gowns, and then, *oh my God.* My gaze fixes on a man about twenty yards away. He's in a dark suit, with rumpled hair, and he's holding a phone to his ear. He's walking toward me. A cocky grin spread across a scruffy jaw. He's frickin' gorgeous.

"Sleek, stylish, and *radiantly* handsome." He rolls the Rs like in the movie. Our eyes are locked. "And he comes toward you, with the moves of a jungle cat."

Oh my God. The grin on my face is ear-to-ear. I can't believe he's here. In a suit. All dressed up. He stops in front of me and clicks off his phone. *God, he even smells good.*

My mind scrambles for what to say. So much for losing myself in the symphony and forgetting my drama. Instead, I'm swimming in it.

His tie catches my attention. It's the one I bought for him. I left it with his stuff in the conference room yesterday while he was in Clive's office then forgot about it.

"You can hang up now, Kensington." His smile softens.

Oh. I laugh, and slowly pull the phone down to click it off.

I swallow. This is dangerous. This time, it's not *him* I don't trust. I should run. Just turn around and make tracks, but I can't seem to move. "You're late."

"You're stunning." He's shaking his head, a soft smile on his face.

The next line is *you're forgiven*, and I have, he's apologized, he's explained, but I'm not ready to say the words, pretend or not. I feel my face flush. "It's not exactly the *Pretty Woman* dress, I switched to—"

"It's better."

My eyes narrow with a slow grin. "What are you doing here?"

"It's on the list. Number two. *Pretty Woman*."

I tilt my head. "We already did—"

"The opportunity presented itself, so who am I to argue?" He shrugs. "And I think you're missing something."

No way. That was the line, *I think you're missing something.* It's the moment where Edward and Vivian are leaving for the opera. I shift my weight to one leg, the shock of seeing him replaced by the thrill of anticipation. I know what's next.

From behind his back he produces a rectangular jewelry box. My eyes are fixed on the blue case. I look from the box to him and can't hide my smile. *I'm giddy.* This is too much.

Shane's brown eyes are beaming. He nods for me to go ahead and holds the box out in one hand, with his other positioned to open it. "Don't get too excited, it's not worth a quarter of a million like in the movie."

But I *am* excited. I lean in, my hand splayed across my collarbone as he slowly opens the lid. It's . . . it's . . . *oh my gosh.* I laugh. "It's candy? A candy necklace?" It's the kind where little colored disks are threaded along a stretchy cord.

"Symphony snack," he says with a crooked smirk. His nose crinkles. "Cost a cool quarter. We can totally keep it."

He completely played me. "I'm not wearing that," I say pointedly, still grinning. My cheeks are starting to hurt.

"You have to at least take it."

I know he's going to snap it shut as soon as I reach in. Just like in the movie. And I can't wait.

I look up and see an older couple, dressed to the nines, has stopped and taken an interest. The woman nods for me to go ahead and smiles enthusiastically. I reach in slowly, moving my hand so my fingers are hovering almost inside. I narrow my eyes with determination, glance once at Shane, and then make my—

Snap!

I jump. The woman whoops out a loud laugh, drawing curious glances from others as they pass. I smile at her. Then at him. She wraps her hands around her husband's arm, and flashes me a fresh smile before they turn for the auditorium. *This is pretty great.*

"In case I forget to tell you later . . ." My voice cracks with the sudden rise of emotion. Tears dot my lashes. "I had a really good time tonight."

"WOULD YOU RATHER GO BACK in?" Shane asks as we walk along the canal. We left at intermission and have been strolling around the man-made waterways of downtown Indy at a leisurely pace.

"No, this is nice." I glance sideways at Shane, who looks a bit chilly, since I'm in his suit coat.

We've walked down one side of the canal, crossed, and now are almost back to where we started. I've filled him in with all the *Pretty Woman* trivia I know as we circled around. Like how Richard Gere improvised the jewelry box snap. It wasn't part of the script. And Julia's infamous laugh was so captivating they had to keep it in. It was real. A movie moment that's enduring and real. It doesn't get any better.

Bridges cross over every block or so, and paddle boats tied

along the edges make a soft slapping sound as they rock against the concrete banks.

Shane bites into a disk from my candy necklace, freeing it from the elastic cord, and glances my way. We've both been quiet for a few minutes. I twist my wrist back and forth so my bracelet's charms strike my skin with a calming, repetitive jingle as we walk.

A small voice from somewhere inside whispers dark warnings. *I'm pushing things too far.* I may not be able to pull back. But, right now, I'm not the person who cares what that voice is saying. I'm not even engaged. I'm in my early twenties, in love in a movie.

And this, too, is real.

"He won't make you happy, Kensington."

Is that what he's been thinking about? I push my hair off my face and look away. I watch the flux of people now leaving the theater. The symphony must be letting out. The valets are busy collecting tickets to retrieve the patrons' cars. Taxis are lined and ready. I should go. But I'm not ready for this to end.

I wasn't ready the first time either.

We haven't mentioned our argument from my engagement party. I'm not sure you can even call it that. I've been thinking about it, though, and this time, I'm better prepared to respond.

My voice is calm and steady. "You don't get to swoop into town after forever and . . . and declare my life isn't good enough, Shane." I stop and regard him. "Just because you're the original lost boy and you don't want to settle down, doesn't give you the right to judge those that do."

"I'm not a boy." Shane's voice drops. "And I'm not lost any-more."

I start to walk again, not sure what to say.

Shane's looking at me. "What makes you think I don't want to settle down? I do. The difference is, I *won't* settle."

I meet his gaze, but only briefly. "I'm twenty-nine, almost thirty years old, and someone that my family happens to love, I love, who's never lied, and hasn't left me, wants to marry *me*. And I want a family." I look out over the water, and quietly, almost to myself, ask, "So what should I be waiting for exactly?" Swallowing hard, I wait. I can't believe I asked that.

Shane takes a step forward and turns, stopping me with his hands. Warm copper eyes level to mine with intensity. "Me. You should be waiting for me."

His words stop my heart. There's no misunderstanding that. I can't breathe.

Shane pushes the hair from my cheek and lifts my chin. He's only inches away. I'm not moving. There's no way I'm moving. He's leaning in, eyes still holding mine.

I feel my lips part in anticipation, and then I feel him. Shane's lips. On mine. So light, the sensation is a whisper. He kisses me with deliberate care. Soft. Slow. Intoxicating.

I'm reeling. My heart is beating in my ears. My hands are splayed across his chest, set to push him away, but . . . *I'm not pushing*. His hands thread through my hair and pull me in, deepening the kiss. The scratch of fresh stubble nips my cheek. His taste is both familiar and new. Tart and sweet dance on my tongue. *Oh my God*, I want . . . I . . . break away.

I gotta go.

CHAPTER TWELVE

Kenzi Shaw: The Edge of Reason

"ALL BY MYSELF" DOESN'T need to be blaring from the stereo, I'm humming it. An empty bag of chips and an almost empty bottle of wine sit next to me on the couch. Unlike the opening of *Bridget Jones's Diary*, I do have messages, six of them. Three from Ellie, two from Shane, and one from Bradley, none of which I want to listen to.

I've changed from my gorgeous yellow dress into my comfy Victoria's Secret pink. Some secret, it's just sweatpants and a hoodie. The hoodie's up with the strings cinched so tight there's only a small opening to see out of and pour wine into. I feel better in here. I have no idea why. But I plan on staying like this for a while. My phone's ringing again. I wonder why poor Bridget didn't have a single call.

"I'd call you, Bridget."

I finish my drink and head for the fridge, certain that Bradley has me well stocked with sweet wine. See, another example of

Bradley being nice. Guilt grabs me by the throat and throttles me.

Shane kissed me.

I didn't exactly stop him. Why didn't I stop him? *Me. You should be waiting for me.*

I open another bottle, pour a glass, and snatch up my phone. The one person who was supposed to call, that I *expected* a call from, didn't bother. So yeah, I'm calling Tonya. Very sound reasoning.

The recorded greeting starts. *Blah, blah, blah*, leave a message. I knew she wouldn't answer. "Hey, Tonzy. It's me, weren't we supposed to talk today? You can't call me back?"

I push off the wall, the phone wedged inside my cinched hoodie, and slip-slide across the hall in my fuzzy socks. With each word I pick up speed. "You know what? A coffee is *not* an apology." I turn and head in the opposite direction, gliding like I'm on ice skates, one hand out for a semblance of balance. "I mean, really, how could you do that to me? And not say I'm sorry? *You* messed around with my boyfriend, *lied* to me about it, and basically broke us up."

I shake my head, blinking back tears as I slide back through the living room, performing a drunken Ice Capades to the mental tune of "All by Myself." And thank God I am. All by myself, that is. I can only imagine what this looks like. "So yeah, I think I at least deserve an '*I'm sorry*,' don't you? Not that I'm going to accept it."

I'm circling the coffee table, spewing every random thought that pops to mind. Tears freely fall down my cheeks. I know the message beeped, but I keep going, doing crazy eights, blabbering into the phone, stopping only for slugs of wine before starting up again.

The *if onlys* are bursting open like kernels in an air popper.

If only I hadn't left the party that night. *If only* Tonya hadn't gone. *If only* Shane hadn't kissed her.

I stop.

If only I hadn't kissed Shane back.

My hand falls away from my ear, the phone dangles from my fingertips. My heart's heavy with grief and guilt.

My legs give way and I crumple to the floor beside my phone. Clicking it off, I let the thought settle. Tonya kissed Shane and told me he cheated with someone. That's why I broke up with him. He never told me it was her or just a stupid kiss. She never said a word.

I kissed Shane back tonight. My eyes widen. I'm no better than either of them. Was it just a stupid kiss? *Am I telling Bradley? Am I breaking up with him?* Warm tears run down my cheeks.

Oh my God, what *am* I doing?

There's a knock at the door. It's after midnight. Shane doesn't know where I live. Bradley's not home till Monday night, which is now tomorrow night.

Another knock.

Go away. I wanna be all by myself.

More banging. "Kenz? Open up."

Somehow I manage to get myself to the door. Peering out from my hoodie hole into the peep one, I make out Ellie's face.

"Ellie?" I'm actually glad to see her.

"Kenzi, are you okay? I've been calling. Let me in." She knocks again.

"She's in there."

Wait, who's with her? I'm desperately trying to angle my eye to get a better view of the hallway. "Who's with you?" I can hear her talking, but all I see is a distorted Ellie, talking on the phone. She has gigantic fish lips.

"I'm with Rand. Shane said you ran off, are you going to open?"

"You're with Rand Peterson?" I like to say his name. "*Rand* Peterson?"

It reminds me of *The Wedding Planner* scene where Jennifer Lopez is drunk and can't get into her apartment. She's reading off the names and clicking all the buttons.

"Rand Peterson? Do you know Nancy Pong? If you ever need to borrow sugar, I can't help you, because you don't know me." See? I'm doing my own movie moment. I don't need his stupid list.

"Kenz, let us in. Shane wants to know if he can come by, if you're okay."

Oh, hell no. "Is he on the phone? Tell him . . . tell him . . ." My mind scrambles for the line in *The Wedding Planner* when Matthew's character came back banging on her door. I slide my legs out in slipper splits, gripping the doorknob for balance while I think. Ellie and Rand are saying something, but it's muffled.

"*Oh!* Tell him it's simple. I love Bradley and he loves me. So, besides Shane's tux measurements, that's all I need to know. Please . . ." *Go away.*

But I don't want him to go away. I also don't want his measurements.

"Kenz, what the hell are you talking about?" More banging. "He really wants to come by. Can I give him the address? Please?"

"No. Don't!" I slide down to the floor and land with a thud. "I'm fine. I'm Fantastically Inebriated and Numb Everywhere." Thank goodness, 'cause that's gonna leave a mark.

It takes at least three more of "Yes, I'm okay," and a promise to call her in the morning before they finally leave.

After a while, I pull myself up and search through my DVDs for *Bridget Jones's Diary*. Finding it, I pop it in and curl up on the couch. My face is tear stained, my head's spinning from the wine, and my whole world is upside down.

In my mind, I see my future daughter with blond curls. She's waving a sign, firing me. Wiping my eyes, I sing quietly along to the opening credits, but change the lyrics to "I'm gonna be all by myself." The screen goes blurry from more tears. *Shit, I am all by myself.*

"I'd still call ya, Bridge."

BOTH SHANE AND BRADLEY HAVE called me again this morning. And my mom. Still haven't listened to any of the messages, but I am calling Ellie back. I mean, she did come all the way over here to make sure I was okay. I didn't even know she seriously *liked* Rand Peterson. I realize suddenly that my head's been so far up my own ass, I haven't really asked her much of anything.

I dial her number and wait. The phone's on the third ring, and I'm rubbing at my hip, which has a light purple bruise from my drunkards-on-ice debut last night. My head's fine, surprisingly. Maybe wine is the way to go.

"Kenzi?" She's whispering.

"Hey, girl, sorry."

"You're okay?" I hear her moving about her apartment. "Shane called again, wanting to know if I'd heard from you."

"Why are you whispering?" I ask in a whisper.

"What?"

"Ellie, why are we whispering?"

"Rand's here."

"What? Rand Peterson!" I shout into the phone.

She shushes me. I whisper back, "He stayed? You guys?"

"I know, I just . . . I *like* him, Kenz." I can hear the smile in her voice.

"So, any truth to the shoe-size theory?"

She giggles. "I can't talk right now." I hear rustling. "But you should really call Shane. Okay? Call him and call me later. I need to know what happened."

You and me both.

"Okay, later, Ellie-bell." I click off the phone. There's no way I'm calling Shane. There's a heavy ache in my chest. What would I even say?

Clicking the voice mail button and speaker, I decide to at least listen to the messages. Ellie's voice comes through first.

"Kenzi, Shane just called wanting to know if I talked with you. Where are you? What the hell happened? Call me back."

I delete and let it roll on to the next one. It's Ellie again.

"Kenzi, answer your phone! I'm starting to get worried. If you don't call me back soon I'm coming over there."

Mmm, guess I could've avoided that. Delete.

"Kensington."

My heart jumps at the sound of Shane's voice. I'm frozen staring at the phone, eyes wide.

"I didn't mean . . . look, can you ring me back? Please?"

I hit 9 for save. I don't know why.

"Hi, hon." Bradley's voice sounds grainy, as though he's coming down with something. "I wanted to make sure you got in okay from the symphony. Call or text me when you do. I'm surprised you're not home yet. I'll wait up." He sounds concerned.

A lump lodges in my throat as I delete it and wait for the next one. There's a gap before anyone speaks. I know it's Shane.

". . . I would've come by. Kensington, please ring me."

I hit SAVE.

"Hi, hon." Bradley again. "Ellie said you left not feeling well last night. Hope it's nothing serious. I'll be back tomorrow night and call you then. Love you."

He loves me. And now Ellie's lying to cover my lies.

Oh my God, *I hate myself.*

I delete Bradley's second message. I owe Ellie big time for playing operator. What do I tell Bradley? If I don't tell him what happened, I'm no different from Shane or Tonya. But if I do tell him, the account is as good as gone. Bradley will kill him. I'll lose my job for sure. He might even call off the engagement.

Rubbing the back of my head, I try and knead out the tension and wait for the next message.

"Hi, Kensington. It's me, your mom."

Yes, Mom, I know who you are. At least she didn't call Ellie.

"What did you think of the invites? They're wonderful, aren't they? We've already received RSVPs. Everyone's *very* excited."

Invites. I haven't checked my mailbox in a few days. If the wedding's off, what will I say to my family? My chest hurts just thinking about sitting there alone, knowing it was supposed to be my day, too.

"I want you there early to help with things. Oh, and Ren mentioned she set you up with that very exclusive wedding planner friend of hers. Be sure to thank her. She's really pulled in a favor for you. Okay, I have to go. I'm meeting the girls for lunch."

Delete. Delete and delete. Yep, she's gone.

Wish I was. I pull the hood from my sweatshirt back up and the cords snug.

He kissed me.

Okay, so he kissed me. I kissed him back and then I didn't. But I didn't want to stop. I tighten the cords even more. My Pinocchio nose is the only thing visible. I'm going to be rational and logical, and *honest.* I can be honest. It's only me in here.

I hear Shane's words, "He won't make you happy, Kensington." What does Shane know? Bradley hasn't lied to me. Bradley didn't up and leave me. No, he's here. Right now, and wants to start a family.

My eyes close as I picture my life with Bradley. We'd have a really nice house, I'm sure of it. We would start trying for kids right away. He'd hire a nanny, but I'd maybe want to stay home instead. He'd be okay with that. I'd have everything my family expects for me.

What about what I expect for me? What about being in love like in a movie? Is Bradley my knight in shining armor that I'm going to rescue right back?

Be honest.

Bradley loves me. Is stable and safe . . . but where's the spark? I'm sure I'd pass Ellie's Tummy Flip Test.

No flip. The movie's a flop.

But what about Shane? There's spark, but is there substance? Has he really changed that much from college or I am just his interest of the moment? Still no follow-through.

I cinch the hoodie's cords even tighter. *How am I going to face everyone tomorrow?* Let alone Ren? We're meeting at the wedding planner's first thing.

Should there even be a wedding?

CHAPTER THIRTEEN

Dangerous Dancing

"WHEN POSSIBLE, MAKE A U-turn. When possible, make a U-turn." The robo-lady from my GPS actually sounds annoyed. I keep missing my turn. It's not intentional.

"When possible—"

"Oh, for goodness sake, I'm turning!" I scream at it. The stupid wedding planner place needs a better sign. It's Monday, and now I'm grateful Bradley set up this appointment. This gives me a legitimate reason to take a personal day from work. I need one.

My stomach's queasy. How am I going to keep it together in front of Ren? *Oh, I see it.*

"In one hundred—"

"Shut up, already." I push the END ROUTE button. My plan to get through this is simple. Keep my promise to go and keep my mouth shut. Ren's not staying for long anyway, so I just need to keep up my façade for a little while.

A wave of regret rolls through me. This is another big moment that should be fun and exciting. And again, that's gone. This time it's entirely my own fault.

Whatever, this should be wrapped up in less than an hour—tops.

Walking through the door of the Wedding House feels like I've entered some sort of alternate universe. "I Honestly Love You" is playing over the speaker system and everything is in pink and white floral. It's like a shabby-chic monster broke in and threw up.

I've landed in Oz and somehow pissed off the great and powerful wizard.

I stifle a laugh. Ruby red slippers. Just like Cinderella: it always comes back to the shoes.

"You must be the future Mrs. Bradley Connors!" a crazy woman in ruffles says as I approach the counter. "Is the groom on his way?" she asks in singsong and wrinkles her nose.

My heart sinks. I'm not sure there will be a groom after I talk with him. "Er . . . no. My sister-in-law should be here any minute."

Her smile drops as if I said something distasteful. "Oh, well, no groom. Okay, just have a seat. I'll let Bethany know you're a single with family member assist. The other couple's here."

Other couple? It's a shared appointment? Of course it is. I give a wrinkle-nose-smile back and watch her leave the room.

Half an hour—*tops.*

The door chimes as it opens to announce Ren's presence.

Right off, I notice she's pale and her eyes are puffy. "Hi. You okay?"

"Of course I'm not okay." She plops down and blows out a breath. "I'm pregnant. If I'm not sick, I'm hungry, and Grayson doesn't understand." She sets her bag across her lap and leans back. "Whoever said this was fun was clearly never pregnant. It's *horrible.*"

My gut twists. She's complaining about being pregnant and my whole wedding may be called off, which means I'm even further from being in her shoes. At least she gets a baby at the end of all of it. What do I get?

Maybe what I deserve.

My phone rings. I'm still screening, but it's Ellie, so I answer. "Hi."

"Kenz," she says, sounding frazzled. "I tried to—"

The music's suddenly louder and the double doors from behind the receptionist's desk swing open with a *whoosh*. A tiny blond bombshell bounces out.

"I'm Bethany Chesawit, wedding planner." Her voice is helium-induced and her smile's so white, it's blinding. She has on a powder-blue sweater that reveals way too much cleavage, a flappy little skirt, and four-inch heels. "Oh, Ren, they didn't say you had arrived." She reaches for her in an air kiss-kiss hug-hug thing.

Then she turns to me and holds her hand out, expectantly.

"Kenzi?" Ellie's voice jolts me back.

"Um, Ellie? Ellie. I'll call you back in a minute." I click off the phone and reach out to shake Bethany's hand, but she has it turned funny. It's angled down as if she's royalty, and I'm expected to kiss it. I grab at her fingertips and give a little wiggle.

I'm in the wedding zone and I just met the wedding fairy.

Fifteen minutes—*tops.*

We follow her through the doors into the Land of Always-Always. I'm not making that up. It really says "The Land of Always-Always" over the door. It's stenciled with hearts and flowers around the letters. I hate Ren for setting this up. *Really-really.*

"Well, we have a full day planned. We need to choose music,

flowers, and your colors," she's squeaking on and on, leading us through a hallway decorated with pink-and-silver-striped wallpaper. "This room will serve as our headquarters."

She pulls a chair out for me at the table then retrieves a book from the shelf along the wall. "Before we can even begin, we need a theme." She flashes a too-bright smile and wrinkles her nose like the receptionist did. "Our other couple has already started, so I'll check on them and be right back."

Ren quickly has the book open and is flipping through the pages of weddings they've designed. "So what are your colors?"

"Um, we haven't decided anything yet."

Her eyebrows arch. "How do you not know your colors? That's the very first thing you need to choose." Ren's color is putrid. She's not looking good. "Kenz, you don't seem very enthusiastic about any of this. I was over the moon planning my wedding." She flips another page and turns the book to see what I think. "Aren't you excited?"

Shaking my head, I shrug, so she turns to the next page. "What if I'm confused?" I can't believe that came out of my mouth. *To Ren.*

"Well, silly, that's why I'm here. To help guide your choices. But really, you could be a bit more upbeat. Oh, this one," she says, tapping the page, not getting what I meant at all.

"Confused about Bradley." There. I said it. But why did I say it? *What am I doing?* My throat dries, and I brace myself for her reaction.

Ren snaps her eyes to mine. "What? You're confused about—" Her hand covers her mouth and she hunches forward. She's paled. She's going to . . . *oh. Oh God.* In an instant she's up and running toward the restroom in the front.

That's not the reaction I was expecting. My phone buzzes again, but I don't get the chance to answer it.

"Is Ren okay?" Bethany Chesawit asks as she saunters back in.

"She's pregnant," I say to explain. "You know what? I really appreciate you fitting me in, I do. But with Bradley not here and Ren not feeling well . . . I think we should just reschedule."

Voices are coming from the hallway. "Mrs. Chesawit, I'm sorry to interrupt. But Ms. Shaw's fiancé made it."

My heart jumps. *Really?* Bradley came back early? Maybe he really wanted to be here for this. Maybe this can be a good moment for us. She steps to the side and standing behind her is . . .

Shane.

Before I can say a word, Bethany is doing her "I'm-Bethany-Chesawit-wedding-planner-extraordinaire" intro, and her hand is out for him to kiss or shake or whatever.

Shane frowns, looking between us. "Nice to meet you, but I'm afraid there's been—"

I'm on my feet rushing toward them. "Can we have just a moment? You ladies wouldn't mind, would you?" I'm saying through a clenched smile while practically shoving them out the door.

"Oh, um, sure, I'll check on Ren." Bethany smiles but looks confused.

Pulling the door shut, I whip my head around to Shane. "What the *hell* are you doing here?"

"You didn't return my calls, and you didn't show up at your office, so—"

"So you barge into a meeting with my wedding planner? How did you even . . ." I shake my head to clear it. "You know what? I don't care. Wedding woman knows my sister-in-law, Ren. *Ren!*" I'm whisper-shouting. "And Ren is *here*. Right now." I hit him across his shoulder. "What the hell are you thinking?"

This is just too much. I'm panicking. It's a full-on freak-out.

I hit him again.

"Hey." Shane steps from my line of fire. "I just needed to talk with you."

"So, you said you were *Bradley?*"

His eyebrows push down. "No. I was going to wait out front, but I never got a word in, actually. That ruffle woman—"

"What is Ren going to think? Bradley's going to know you were *here*." I need to handle this. My breath is jagged.

There's a *knock-knock* and the door opens a crack. "Sweetie, Ren had to go. She's really not feeling well, poor thing. She said she'd call later." The door swings wider and Bethany's head pops through. "And rescheduling's really not an option, I'm *super* booked. But since your fella's here, everything's a go, right?"

"Can we just have one more minute?" My smile is wide and forced.

After a beat she closes the door.

In the grand scheme of things, this is not that bad. *Really.* It's not a hurricane, or a massive bout of twisters ripping through a defenseless town, or ravenous wildfires. Not even a flood. No. This is a temporary glitch, a string of snafus that need to be rationalized and handled.

If they think Bradley's here then they won't mention some other guy showing up, right? It would be a nonpoint. I just need to trust Shane to keep his mouth shut now, Ellie to keep hers shut in the future, and I might put a hit out on Rand since he knows about the symphony. That would shut his permanently.

Really, it's only what, ten minutes of pretend—tops.

I look at Shane and point a finger right at his chin, speaking through clenched teeth. "You're Bradley. Play along or I will kill you. And drop the accent."

"Drop the accent?" Shane asks with an amused grin on his face. His eyes are all shiny.

Another knock and the door opens. "Sorry, we're on a tight schedule." Bethany walks in. "Are we ready?"

Shane puffs his chest out. "Of course we're ready, aren't we, *hon*?" He sounds stiff and awkward.

Are you kidding me?

Bethany's smile quivers as she regards him. I give a nervous laugh and then shoot him a knock-it-off look. He shrugs with a grin.

Oh. Dear. God.

Now that I think of it, I would welcome a tornado or earthquake. What is the saying? In a hundred years from now, no one will care how clean your house is, how much money you have, *blah, blah, blah*. But they don't know my mom, or Ren. They would care. A hundred years is nothing.

BETHANY HAS BEEN BACK AND forth several times from the other couple to us. Apparently, we're taking too long and the super couple is zipping through everything. "Have you two found the color scheme that will say to your guests, this is our signature, this is us, this is who we are?"

Is there a color scheme for this-is-totally-effed-up?

I haven't really looked at the pictures. I've been mindlessly turning the pages and whispering veiled threats under my breath. Everything is dangerously close to unraveling, from one little lie to the next.

"Er . . . let's do super simple in different hues of pinks and white," I say with a nervous laugh, shutting the book with a loud *slap*. I don't even care at this point. Not really. Just throw something together and get me the hell outta here.

"Good, all rightio. Then, if you'll follow me, we need to select the music for your first dance."

"Great." I get up fast and knock my chair back. I catch it before it falls all the way over and laugh nervously again. I'm a wreck. I honestly don't think I can take much more of this. I think she knows. It will have to be a double hit, Rand Peterson and then the wedding planner. A two-for-one deal. Maybe I'll get a discount.

"You two lovebirds head on over." She motions down the hall. "And I'll go get our other couple. I'll only be a sec. It'll be *su*per." She wrinkles her nose and waits for us to leave.

Why is she doing that? Why did I just do it back?

I make a beeline for the door, through the pink-and-silver-striped hall, not even waiting for Shane. At least, if there's another couple maybe he won't need to talk.

Turning into the music room, I'm temporarily stunned. It's a mini–dance hall.

"Kensington, it'll be okay," Shane says as he steps behind me.

I wheel around and face him just as Bethany walks in with another couple beside her.

"Kenzi? Kenzi Shaw? Oh. My. God!"

It's so not okay.

"Kenzi, it's me. Liza Evans! Well, soon to be Liza Evans-Matison. This is Ryan." She's bouncing up and down excited. To her fiancé she says, "Kenzi and I went to high school together, our moms play tennis at the club. Wait till I tell her who I ran into!"

"Hi. Wow. How great is *this*?" I say, trying to match her enthusiasm. This is too many people to put hits out on.

Bethany clicks a remote and the lights dim. A mirrored ball whirls to life from the ceiling and a power ballad from Celine Dion starts. Everyone looks around in awe as the room is trans-formed into a discotheque.

"Okay, my happy wedding couples. Grab your partner, and let's dance." Bethany's voice sounds even more helium-induced as she speaks loudly over the music. "We'll play sections from all the popular first-dance songs. When one strikes you, just yell stop."

Stop!

"Dance!" She claps her hands twice, which makes me jump.

"The Power of Love" drawls out from the speakers. Liza gasps and says how this is just the best song ever. She and Ryan quickly embrace and start twirling and laughing. I'm one step away from a complete and utter breakdown. Ellie told him where I was. She's on my hit list, too.

"Dance!" Bethany claps again.

Shane holds out his hand, I grab it and fall into position. He's laughing under his breath.

"*Stop it!*" I say under mine. The music kicks up to the faster beat and we do our best to keep time with it. "This isn't funny," I say as we turn, but it almost is. "It's a disaster, an absolute disaster. And *you*! Either you're nodding like a bobble-head or you sound like a deranged John Wayne." I pull back to look at him. "And her mom knows my mom! *Are you kidding me?*" We turn.

Liza and her guy are spinning and chatting. Bethany is swaying along to the music with her eyes half closed. I think she's half baked.

"Keep going until something moves you," Bethany says over the music and then clicks the remote she's holding. Brian McKnight's "Crazy Love" begins to play.

"*This* is crazy," I mutter more softly. It's just a dance. Just go with it. I stifle a laugh. *Just Go with It.* Jennifer Aniston and Adam Sandler. She pretends to be his fiancée. My life's more like a movie than I thought. Okay, breathe, dance, everything's fine. Fine as in *Freaking Inside Needing Exit.*

We turn and Bethany looks over, so I smile on cue.

"And I didn't say I was Bradley, you did, remember, *hon*?" Shane whispers.

I'm stressed, but the sensation of his breath on my skin makes my heart pound for a different reason. "Well, how was I supposed to explain who you were?" I whisper back. "And stop calling me hon." My eyes close and I stifle a laugh. He sounds ridiculous imitating Bradley.

"You could have just said I was a work colleague. Then we could've agreed to talk after."

Huh, didn't think of that. "I just panicked," I say, feeling the burn of embarrassment hot on my cheeks.

He pulls me closer. "I'm not complaining in the least, Kensington."

I step back to create space, daring to meet his gaze. "You shouldn't have kissed me."

"I won't do it again unless you ask, and only if that is no longer on your finger." He looks pointedly at the ring.

My stomach drops. I know what he's saying, but I'm not sure what he's offering. What is he really offering? A romance? A maybe? A life?

Another click and the music abruptly changes again. It's "I've Had the Time of My Life" from *Dirty Dancing.*

I'm speechless. We both just look at each other. Shane's lips twist in a grin. The music's playing and the moment's presented itself. Another movie scene. Shane tilts his head as if to say *Why not?*

"Would you mind letting this one play through, Bethany?" he shouts over the melody, not waiting for me to respond, never taking his eyes from mine. Shane places his hands, one on top of the other, over his heart. He taps his chest in a double *thump-thump. Thump-thump.*

Everything seems to fade except for him. I'm dazed as my mind cycles through the movie scenes.

"It's a feeling. A heartbeat. Ga-gung. Ga-gung." His voice is low, hypnotizing. He reaches for my hand and tucks it under his as he continues the *thump-thump*. "Close your eyes, Kensington."

He pulls me in close and starts to move, still holding my hand to his chest, and I can feel his heart beating. *Ga-gung. Ga-gung*. Okay, calm thoughts. Ocean. Seagulls.

After a while my heart slows to match his, and I can't tell them apart. Losing myself in the melody, enfolded in Shane's arms, I sense myself wavering. Scenes from *Dirty Dancing* play in my mind, the one where Patrick Swayze teaches Jennifer Grey's character how to dance. How to listen. *Ga-gung. Ga-gung*.

Stepping back, I give a clever grin and say the movie line. "Look, spaghetti arms, you gotta hold the frame." I push his arms up and wave between us. "This is your dance space, this is my dance space."

Shane's eyes narrow with a spark of amusement. "I don't want space." He pulls me back.

"Yes! You need to lock the frame!" Bethany squeaks.

The world around us reappears.

"That's it exactly." She's heading toward us, clicking her remote in rapid succession. She stops on "Hungry Eyes." She yanks at Shane's arms then positions mine. "And it's on the two. One and two. Good." She's moving with us. "One and two. Yes. You've got it. Lock it in." She's now behind me, a hand on my hip and one between my shoulder blades.

Oh, no way.

"Yes, good. Keep your chins up."

Shane's smiling widely, looking from her over my shoulder back to me. I'm trying to hold in a giggle. This isn't exactly the movie scene I envisioned. We're dancing like Johnny and Baby did with Penny. Liza and her fiancé have stopped and are watching the three of us.

Shane laughs. "We need to do the lift."

"What?" I stop, which stops Bethany.

"Yes, the lift from the movie. Bethany can show us, right?" Shane backs away.

"No." I can't imagine we'd be able to do that. Besides, they practiced in the water and a field. *Soft places.*

"Oh, he could do it. You just have to trust him." Bethany has clicked her remote and started the song over. "Now, Kenzi, you'll just need to get some momentum and bend your knees right as you approach and jump up. He'll do the rest."

My eyes flick from her to him and back again. *They're serious?*

"Come on." Shane takes a few more steps back and holds out his hand. He curls his index finger to signal "come here" like Patrick Swayze did during the final show at the resort.

I laugh, certain we're going to end up on the floor in a pile of hurt.

"Okay." I can't believe I'm doing this. I bend over, palms to thighs for a running start. I'm off, running toward Shane with a stupid smile plastered on my face, right in front of him I spring, his hands are on my waist, mine are on his shoulders, he lifts and . . . and . . . "Oh my God!"

We didn't get high, but we didn't fall to the floor either.

"Again. This time really trust him," Bethany says.

Okay, I'm back, I'm set.

Shane's braced and ready. "Remember, you'll hurt me if you don't trust me. Isn't that the line?"

"Isn't that what happened?"

His eyes soften. "Never again, Kensington."

My heart bounces. I run. He has my waist. I spring . . . and we're . . . *Oh my gosh.* I'm up! I'm up! I'm Jennifer Grey! Ha, take that.

"Hold the position, Kenzi. You're doing it!" Bethany's yelling excited.

Well, we're kind of doing it. It's not graceful by any means. His arms aren't fully extended and I'm holding on to him instead of spreading mine out. But it's not too bad. Liza and Ryan are clapping and whooping, jumping up and down.

Oh . . . *Oh no.* "Whoa!" I'm going forward. "Whoa, *whoooa . . .*"

Shane walks quickly backward trying to hold his balance. Instinctively, my legs swing and I lean back to slide down. My arms are wrapped tight around his neck, my legs around his waist.

He has me.

"Oh my gosh." I'm laughing. "I'm sorry."

They're cheering.

Shane whispers just for me. "I'll never be sorry." It's the line from the end of the movie. The end of their romance.

But I don't think ours has ended.

CHAPTER FOURTEEN

Confessions of a Rom-com-aholic

IT'S TUESDAY. I'VE HAD all night to process. To plan. Walking into the office, I'm trying to keep things in perspective. In retrospect, the sky hasn't fallen. Ren didn't know anything when I checked on her, and Bradley seemed normal when he checked on me. So maybe the assortment of layered calamities won't escalate into anything more, at least not yet.

No one's in the office, so I flip on the first set of overhead lights and plop my stuff down on my desk. I have a change of clothes for the paintball thing after work, and a bag packed in the car, just in case Clive still expects me to visit Shane's farm. Or I, at the last minute, decide to skip out and hit Vegas.

I like that option. It has promise. My plan B is the make-myself-happy, live-on-my-own plan. So, we'll call Vegas a solid plan C.

For now, I'm dressed for a battle of confidence. Mine. I need some to get through this day. A cute orange pocket skirt, long-sleeve tee, and platform pumps is my armor of choice. It says I'm ready to take on the world.

Even if I'm not.

My puffy, red-rimmed eyes are a dead giveaway. It was a long night.

I can't believe that back in college, Mom encouraged Shane to let things be. That leaving was best. Or that Tonya thought it would be a mistake for me to go with him. Why does everyone get to decide for me? Mom, Tonya, Bradley, even Shane. His words pop to mind, *I won't do it again unless you ask, and only if that is no longer on your finger.* He's not deciding now. He's leaving it to me. But he hasn't offered anything either.

Do I need him to? Does it change anything? *No*, it really doesn't. The past has happened and *I'm* defining my future. Regardless of what anyone else does or doesn't do.

I just hope I can keep my wits about me and keep to my plan.

Opening my laptop, I log in, and check Facebook first thing. No new updates from Renson, or my mom, really weird. I know Ren's still not feeling well. I hope I don't get sick like that when I get pregnant. *If* I ever get pregnant. Plan B doesn't have that guarantee.

Running into Tonya is also playing on my mind. I know she got my whacked-out messages from the weekend, but she never called me back. Do I blame her? *Yes.* I do. *I do blame her.*

She should be apologizing to me, swearing it was a stupid thing to do. We're supposed to fight and yell. She should *want* to make it up to me, instead she doesn't even care.

Because I don't matter. *Not quite good enough.* I palm my forehead in both hands and slouch over my desk. I only need to be good enough for me. My standards. My life. My choices.

With a determined sigh, I tap out a quick, generic e-mail to

Shane requesting a review. He needs to sign off on stage two for the Carriage House. My conceptual is far enough along, even if the completion of the list isn't. Clive's already asked for it so he can bill him. Opening his earlier e-mail with the Love Like the Movies list, I copy it and paste it at the bottom.

I know what including this list implies. It says I'm still willing to go along with our agreement. That I *want* to . . .

I cross out both number 10 and number 5, and before I chicken out, hit SEND.

1. Sleepless in Seattle
2. ~~Pretty Woman~~
3. Bridget Jones's Diary
4. ~~27 Dresses~~
5. ~~Dirty Dancing~~
6. Sixteen Candles
7. Love Actually
8. Say Anything
9. You've Got Mail
10. ~~My Best Friend's Wedding~~

Opening the movie conceptual for the Carriage House, I use my pen and tablet to apply thin strokes and detail work to the poster images of *Sleepless in Seattle*. I have two I'm using in the montage, the main one with Meg Ryan and Tom Hanks looking at each other, and a single shot of the Empire State Building with the heart lit up in its windows.

An Affair to Remember is a remake of *Our Love Affair*, and the movie *Sleepless in Seattle* is loosely based on. It wasn't Valentine's Day when they agreed to meet at the top of the Empire State Building in the originals; it was just a meaningless date in January.

And in the original, the male lead, Nickie, is a painter. He's an undiscovered talent that has never really tried to make it in the art world, until inspired by Deborah Kerr's character, Terry.

This hits home on so many levels. With Shane, I'm inspired to try. Even if it means without him.

The voice mail icon pops up on my phone with a chime. With a deep breath, I wipe the tears that have built up in my lashes, and click PLAY.

It's from Aunt Greta. "Hey, kiddo. Do me a favor and give me a ring back when you get this."

That's all it says. Did the wedding planner say something to Ren? Did Ren say something to Mom, who then said something to Aunt Greta? I'm dialing her number, bracing for the worst. My pulse is racing. I wanted to control the dispensing of damage today, not be knocked over by it.

"That was quick."

"Hi, everything okay?" *Why did I ask that?*

"Yeah, I'm sure it will be."

Is there an edge to her voice? Am I imagining that? *Shit*, I don't want to explain yesterday. Yesterday is not part of today's plan. And I'm sticking to my plan.

"Have you talked to Ren?"

Oh, God. My plan is screwed. My heart thuds to the floor. "No-oo, why?" I'm imagining the hissy fit my mom must have thrown when Ren told her what the wedding planner probably said. The beans have spilled. Clean up on aisle two. Plan C is looking really good right now.

"She's been staying at your mom's. I just think—"

Wait. "What? I talked with her earlier. She never mentioned anything."

"Grayson's being his wonderfully stubborn self. Ren's being

Ren, but now with an added hormonal edge. It's a lovely combination. She walked out on him yesterday."

"*No!* The perfect Renson duo is dueling?" *Maybe she wasn't just sick.*

Aunt Greta laughs. "At war is more like it. Thought maybe she confided in you?"

"Me?" I can feel my jaw drop. "Why would she talk to me? Isn't she at Mom's? I'm sure they're—"

"Nope. Not a word. Your mom called me not knowing what to do. Ren's just sitting over there crying. Grayson's even tried, but she won't see him. Some major issues, if you ask me. And I know you probably don't see it, but I think she looks up to you. You're like the sister she never had."

We definitely bicker like sisters.

Hanging up with Aunt Greta, I dial Ren's cell. I should at least leave a message. I don't always *like* her, but I don't *hate* her. I internally rehearse what I should say. I'm concerned, hope things get better, if you need anything you can call me, *blah, blah, blah.* Yep, I know exactly what to say.

"Hello?" She answers on the first ring.

I don't know what to say.

"Hello?" Ren's voice cracks as if she's been crying.

"Oh, hey, sorry, I thought I'd get your voice mail."

Silence.

Ugh, fine. I lean back in my chair. "Are you okay?"

It was the question that broke the dam. Has no one else thought of this question? *Seriously?* Twenty minutes of Ren crytelling me how Grayson isn't being supportive, and doesn't understand her, and how she doesn't want my mom to know much because she'll get involved and might blame her for their squabble. *Wow, do I get that one.*

Twenty minutes of how sick she's been, and not just in the morning. Twenty minutes of not knowing what to expect once the baby arrives. Twenty minutes of me realizing we have more in common than I thought.

"You know the other day when you were upset with Mom about your school paintings? And you told her, well, *everyone*, how you felt?"

Uh-oh. I cringe, ready for a berating. "Yeah."

"I wish *I* could do that. Just say exactly what's on my mind, regardless of how crazy I sound or look."

"Okay . . ." I'm not sure how to take that.

"What I mean, Kenz, is . . . I always worry that if Grayson saw me *lose it*, and I mean really lose it like you do, that . . . I don't know, I'd lose *him*." Her voice cracks and she sniffs. "Maybe lose *all of you*—"

"Ren . . ." I don't know what to say.

"But you don't worry about that even with *Bradley*, and you're not even married yet. You just say it like it is and you don't even care—"

"No, I care, *they* don't." My voice takes on an instant edge. "They don't care at all! *That's* why I get so mad."

"But they do, your mom was really upset when you left. Your parents got in a fight about it."

I sit up. "Really?"

"Yeah . . ." She takes a long breath.

I'm quiet for a beat, trying to process. "You know what, Ren, *we're family*, okay?" I can't believe I'm saying this. No, I can't believe I *mean* it. "We're not going anywhere. And if I'm honest, I'd love it if you'd just lose it sometimes. You don't have to be so perfect. In fact, I'd feel less like an idiot if you did."

"Well, this whole pregnancy thing is just harder than I thought, it's all a big change and—" Ren's voice hitches again.

"It is a big change. And Grayson needs to participate and help. You need to go home right now, and just let Grayson have it. And I mean rip into him good. I promise you won't lose him. He loves you, he's just *Grayson*."

"Okay, yeah." Ren laughs. "I will. I think I really will, thanks, Kensington." She sniffs, lowers the phone, and blows her nose. "And Kenz . . ." Another sniff. "You said you were confused about Bradley yesterday?"

She has all this going on and *she remembers that*?

My stomach lunges. "Yeah." It comes out small and it's all I can manage.

"Listen, even though I'm mad at Grayson, and oh, he can make me *so* mad . . . I'm still sure he's the one. *The only one* for me. Who else is going to laugh at my dumb jokes? Or make me grilled cheese when I've had a bad day? You know what I mean? It's hard enough, all of it, so you *have* to be sure."

Now I have tears. Ren's not judging me in the least. No, Ren's just saying to be sure. That I need to be sure. *Wow.* "Thanks, Ren."

WALKING INTO THE CONFERENCE ROOM, I pull the dimmer up slightly to bathe the room in a dingy yellow haze. The three printouts of my paintings are still leaning on the board. They're really not bad. Of course, now I'll never see the originals again to be sure. *Mom felt bad.*

I pull my ring off and rotate it mindlessly between my fingers. I could maybe open my own studio. I never even tried. *Why didn't I?*

The Wedding Planner pops into my head. Not that psycho Bethany Chesawit, but the movie. When Steve, who is engaged to Fran, says to his friend about Mary, "Fran's great, but what if what I think is great, *really is great*, but not as great as something greater?"

And what if there isn't?

Can I really stand on my own?

That's what I spent all night debating. And Ren's right, *you have to be sure*. And about this, I am. I just need the courage to act on it.

"Hey, watcha doin' in here all by yourself?" Ellie's in the doorway. She looks guilty. She shouldn't have told Shane about the wedding planner's yesterday, and I *am* mad, but not at her. *Not really.*

"Hey," I say, wiping under my eyes and turning toward her.

"Kenz, I *tried* to warn you Shane was on his way." She takes a few steps inside.

"You mean after you told him where I was, right?" I slouch back in the chair.

"Well, after, yeah." She pulls out a chair and sits. "But I swear he basically beat it out of me."

I narrow my eyes. She probably Googled the address and printed out the map for him.

"Are you okay? You don't look okay."

I nod, and manage a small smile. "I'm going to be."

"So . . ." Her lips squish to the side. "What happened yesterday?"

I laugh in spite of myself, then explain about the mix-up and how they thought Shane was Bradley and his ridiculous imitation.

Ellie's staring at me in disbelief. "But *why* would they think Shane was Bradley?"

I lift my chin, then wave away the question. "It's complicated. Anyway . . ." I tell her about the *Dirty Dancing* lift, and the other couple, how I *know* them, and how *her* mom knows *my* mom.

Then I lean close and lower my voice to almost a whisper. "On Saturday, after the symphony, he *kissed me*."

Her mouth drops, but I'm going for the full oh-my-God finale. Why not, I'm on a roll so far today.

"And yesterday, Shane said it wouldn't happen again unless . . ." I tap my ring. "Unless I get rid of *this* and call off the wedding."

"You're calling off the wedding?" Tonya's standing frozen in the doorway.

"SO, WHAT ARE YOU HUNGRY for?" Bradley asks as we walk to his BMW in the parking garage for a late lunch. "Pizza?"

Maybe if it's in Italy. I'd like to be anywhere but here. Am I doing this? *You have to be sure.* I'm sure. I'm doing this. "Mm, I was hoping we could talk."

The sedan gives a *beep-beep* and unlocks. "Okay, we can talk while we eat. I'm starving."

What am I doing? I *can't* do this. But I'm going to. *Oh my God,* I'm going to. I've spent too much of my life measuring my own worth based on other people's standards, and I can't do it anymore.

I'm exhausted from trying.

It's time for plan B, which really is plan *Me*. Even if that means I don't have a plan at all. Plan B just means plan A isn't going to work any longer.

"I can't marry you."

The words just hang stagnant in the air.

Bradley's hand is wrapped around his keys in the ignition, but the motion's stalled.

"I, um . . ." My chest feels tight. I don't want to hurt him. That's *not* my intention.

He looks confused, but then tips his head back and splays his hands open. "If you're not happy with the wedding planner or whatever, hon, we can switch stuff."

He's saying the words, but his expression tells me he understood what I meant. I can hear my heart drum in my ears. I can't believe I'm doing this. *What am I doing?* But the truth is that I *know* what I'm doing.

I slip the ring off my finger and hold it out to him. Tears well up and overflow my lids. "I'm *so* sorry, Bradley." It's whispered, and it's meant.

Another sharp breath cinches his nostrils. He rubs a hand over his jaw, and exhales for a long time. "What are you doing, Kenz? Are you serious? What's your family going to say?"

"What's my family going to say?" He's proving my point. "At this moment, I don't care what they're gonna say. So why do you?" I push the ring at him again.

His blue eyes search mine. He reaches out and closes my hand around the ring, keeping his hand over the top. "You *know* I love you. You know we make sense. We can do the wedding whenever you want. Just think about what you're doing, okay? Don't make an irrational decision." He pushes my hand to me then leans back in his seat.

Bradley hasn't lied to me. He hasn't done anything wrong. He said he loves me. "I do love you, Bradley. But . . ."

Not like the movies.

And there it is. The truth. My real dark and deep secret. It's time I confessed. "I think, no, I *know* I want something *more*, I want . . ." I turn and look at him, determined to make him understand. "I want what I see in the movies, I want . . ."

"*What?*"

"No, listen. When the main characters meet, you're filled with this warm hopeful glow, ya know? And we laugh, sometimes till there's tears, because of all the little embarrassing situations they find themselves in trying to get together. And then there's this romantic confession of love, and you're elated because they're finally together. And they should be. You know this. And even though it was completely predictable, you cry. *I* cry . . ." I realize I *am* crying and smiling and probably not making sense.

He's shaking his head with his upper lip raised. "Look, I don't know what all this is, but this is the real world, and—"

"But I don't want the real world. You're *not* listening."

"Okay, let's just slow down a minute."

With the ring still in my hand, I sit back. *This is horrible.* Tears stream down my cheeks. If I know this is the right thing, *why is it so hard*? Clearing my throat, I try again. "I know this seems like it's out of nowhere, and maybe it doesn't make se—"

"It's Bennett, isn't it?"

My heart skips. I look up and meet his eyes. I'm hurting him. I shake my head. "No. It's not. It's *me.* Somewhere along the way, I just, I don't know, I lost who I am, what I wanted for myself . . . And yes, I want to get married and have babies, but I—"

"I don't get it, Kenz. I mean . . ." He's sitting rigid with a look of confusion.

Well, why wouldn't he be confused? I'm still figuring it out. "Bradley, I'm sorry. I *do* love you but it's not enough. It's not—"

"Don't." His hand is up to hold back my words. "Don't say anything else, please. Just . . . *shit, Kenzi.*" His eyes are moist, he looks gutted. He cranks the engine without looking at me. "Just think about what you're doing. I, ah . . . I need to clear my head."

Guilt devours my insides like acid. I nod, wiping at my cheeks.

"Okay." I owe him that. I owe him a chance to digest what I've said.

My hands shake as I reach for the handle.

I'M NUMB. I'M SITTING AT my desk with earbuds in, furiously painting away the last few hours of the workday. I should take off for Vegas, right now. I should. My bags are packed. I don't have a bathing suit, but I could buy one there. Ellie could come. What happens in Vegas stays in Vegas, right?

I could stay in Vegas. *That* could happen.

My mom's called again. I'm not ready to talk to her. I'm not sure if she's calling because of the wedding planner's, or if Bradley called Grayson. Because if he did, then of course Grayson would have said something to Mom.

Bradley hasn't returned. I guess I can't blame him. Ellie must be at an off-site client meeting, she's not online. I see Tonya coming down the hall. She's not looking at me. Her mouth is pinched tight and she's walking faster than necessary toward the door.

I can't believe I've called off the wedding. I'm risking everything for what? I have no guarantee from Shane. Nothing. He asks me for time and feeds me this big romantic list thing, only to pull back and say in his I'm-so-sexy British-blend accent, 'Please call off your engagement, and then maybe I'll kiss you again.'

And the fool thing is . . . *I did*. I broke off an engagement with a handsome, stable man. But I didn't do it for Shane. *I didn't.* It's part of my plan. It's the climb-the-tower-and-rescue-you-right-back plan.

And who I'm rescuing is . . .

Me.

The girl with paint in her hair who still believes in the fairy tale, only this is the grown-up version. Because maybe there's not a happy-ever-after *with* someone, maybe it's about being happy with yourself.

I should think about a new job, too. And if what Clive said is true about the financial trouble we're in, looking for a new job only makes sense.

My stomach jumps. I really could start my own studio.

So why do I still have his ring? Why haven't I called Aunt Greta or Mom and told them? Or even Ellie? I haven't called anyone, I just keep checking my phone to see if Bradley's called and watching the door for when he gets back. *Is he going to come back?*

And what about the client appreciation event after work? Shane will be there. Bradley's supposed to be. Tonya can't miss it. The tiny hairs on the back of my neck rise as I look at the clock.

It feels like the quiet before the storm.

CHAPTER FIFTEEN

Failure Launched

THE RIVER PAINTBALL FIELD looks like a crazy military obstacle course. Hay bales and tractor tires are thrown among wooden forts and stone walls. We're here for open-field play, which means our group is playing along with other groups. There are referees and rules of engagement. I have no idea what those rules are, because I'm not listening.

"Stop looking at him," Ellie whispers as I fasten my combat jumpsuit. Which is very attractive, by the way; black step-in rompers that zip up the front, with a giant insignia advertising patch on the back. It might as well be a target.

"Who?" I pop my eyes at her. I know who. Shane is standing with Clive and Rand Peterson listening to the ref's spiel. He's geared up military-style. He has black war paint streaked under each eye and is holding the paint gun on his hip, with a belt of ammunition hanging low on his hip. This would be completely hot if the gun thing wasn't bright neon blue with a see-through bubble on top.

No, it's still hot.

I keep catching him looking in our direction. Probably because I keep looking in his. I pretend not to notice.

"Here, lean over." Ellie swipes my cheeks with what looks like shoe polish.

"I don't really think that's necessary," I say but let her do it anyway.

Everyone from the office is here, except Bradley. So far, he's a no-show. Tonya's helping Maggie, our receptionist, with her jumpsuit like they're the best of friends and chatting up some of her clients. Tonya's too cool to play, but suited up for team support. She hasn't talked to me since this afternoon. I don't care. I don't have anything to say to her anyway.

For the record, Shane hasn't talked to me since yesterday either. I also haven't talked to my mom. She's called twice. I've only talked to Ellie, but when she noticed the ring was gone, I told her I didn't want to talk about it.

"There's Bradley," Ellie whispers and points across the field with a holy-shit expression.

It matches mine. My stomach thuds to the floor. *He's here.* I can't believe he's here. I really didn't expect him to show. *What do I say?*

Clive spots him and starts in his direction with extra gear. Bradley's glaring at Shane. What happened to clearing his head? He looks pissed. His jaw is jutted, and his brows are pulled down. I wonder who he's talked to. Tonya turns first to look his way, then toward me.

A horn sounds and we're set loose in the huge field of junk obstacles and bunkers. There are maybe thirty players from the

Safia Agency if you include clients and twenty or so others out on the course. When the second horn goes off, we're supposed to start. *Huh,* guess I *was* listening.

"Ellie, come on." I grab her arm with one hand and my super-soaker paint gun with the other. I'm feeling a bit renegade and rowdy. I'm mad at the world and mad at myself and ready to . . .

The second horn blasts. "Shit!" I snap my helmet down and start jogging to the side where oversized farm equipment tires are stacked. "Here's the plan. We hide."

"We hide? What kind of plan is that?" Shots zip through the air like mosquitoes.

"A good one!" I'm running now. People are screaming and darting everywhere. This is insane. The monstrous tractor tires are stacked up like stairs. We climb the first, then the double stack, and fall over into the tower of three.

The shots and screams are muffled from inside. "In *Failure to Launch*, she runs around and hides, and then at the end jumps out and gets the last one standing. That's the plan." A paint bullet splats across the top tire.

"All I remember from the movie is trigger fingers, and V for victory." Ellie holds her fingers up in the peace sign.

Another one whips overhead and splashes right near our helmets. We scream, then peek up over the top like prairie dogs, the tips of our paint shooters hanging over.

"There's Bradley," Ellie says and jabs her gun in his direction. He looks like Rambo, all rage and brawn. "There's Shane. They're firing at each other. Bradley's yelling something." Ellie turns to me. "Does Bradley blame Shane for you calling it off?"

"Maybe. Yeah, probably," I say, watching the two of them dodge each other's fire. Rand is alongside Shane. They almost hit Bradley. Clive is helping him. How is this team-building or a client appreciation event? Maggie, the receptionist, dashes across the open field, arms flailing.

She's hit! She's down. She's out. *Oh my God, people, stop hitting her!* Tonya steps from the safety zone to help her.

"Tonya!" Ellie's waving her in.

"What are you doing? Screw her, she's not even playing!" I yell, but I'm too late. Tonya's up and falls in from the top.

"Oh my God. What the fuck!" Tonya slinks down to the ground, gasping. "Those things hurt!" She's looking right at me when she says it.

"If you're not playing, why are you suited up?"

"They wouldn't let me near the field unless . . . anyways, I need to talk with you." Another splat on the tire's edge bounces and sprays Tonya on her shoulder.

All three of us drop even lower.

I huff. "Now? Now you wanna talk?"

"Look, Kenzi. I'm really sorry, okay? I don't even know what to say. I just . . . I really didn't mean for it to happen. I'm *so, so sorry*."

I look at Ellie then back at her. Why is she apologizing now when she wouldn't before?

"I just. Shit. It was before you worked here. And then when you did, well, you guys weren't serious, and then you were, and we stopped, but then it just happened again. You were broken up, well, fighting, anyway."

Wait. *What?* Another paintball zips over our heads.

All the noise outside suddenly seems to have blended together. I see Tonya and I hear what she's saying, but I'm not grasping the meaning. I look at Ellie and she's looking down. I can feel my mouth hanging open, but I can't seem to form any words.

It just happened again. You were broken up. My jaw hits the ground. *Bradley?*

She's talking about Bradley!

"Oh my God. You didn't know," Tonya says then turns to Ellie. "She didn't know? *Oh, shit.* I thought that's why you called the wedding off. Bradley said you must have found out." Tonya's standing. Panicked.

A string of paint fire zips near Tonya's chest from someone overhead. *She screams.* I look at Ellie confusedly.

Ellie's tearing up. "Kenzi, I just found out, I didn't know what to do."

She knew, too?

Tonya's hunched down again. "Kenz, don't aim that at me, what are you doing? I'm sorry, I'm—" She slowly puts her hands up in surrender.

I'm in a fog. *I can't believe this.* Tonya is messing around with Bradley? Tonya and Bradley. Tonya and Shane. I'm breathing heavily through my nose. Blinking through tears, my eyes refocus and narrow to angry slits.

I lift the supersoaker paint thingy. My finger moves to the trigger. "*Run.*"

In an instant, Tonya springs up and is over the tire's edge. I hear her scream as someone shoots at her. I can't move. Ellie has tears rolling down her cheeks.

"Just go, please." I scarcely manage to get the words out.

"Kenz, I really *just* overheard them. I swear."

A heavy ache rocks inside my chest. "I broke it off before I knew. So I . . . *just go*. Please."

Ellie climbs out and one just misses the back of her head. I wrap my knees up and sit like a ball inside the tractor tires. I didn't need the target on my back; turns out I've always had one.

I felt bad, guilty. I was worried I'd hurt Bradley when all this time, *oh* . . . The tears sting warmly on my cheeks. I swallow hard, forcing down the urge to all-out cry.

My plan B just became one of survival.

In all the romantic comedies I've seen, I can't think of one where the girl ends up sitting inside humongous tractor tires jilted by her fiancé and two best friends. Okay, so I broke it off with him first, and Ellie really didn't stab me in the back. She just found out. Tonya did, though.

Twice.

That engagement ring was like the pin in a grenade; I pulled it off and my whole world blew up.

Now what?

I didn't drive here, so I can't just leave. I could sit here and then blast anyone with paint who even dares to pop their head over the rim. That might actually feel good.

I look at the paint zapper and consider it for a moment. I haven't fired it at all. It's full and Ellie left her ammo packs. I feel a fizzy twinge of adrenaline.

Maybe.

The noise around me suddenly breaks through my mind's fog. I still hear screams and zips from flybys, although the herd has thinned. I hear Patrick Swayze's line from *Dirty Dancing*. *No one puts Baby in a corner.* And nobody puts Kenzi in a tire. Or a marriage. Or their version of what my life should be. Years of people-pleasing and frustration is bubbling up, threatening to spill over.

I let it.

Grabbing Ellie's ammo, I sling it over my shoulder. Slowly, I peek up to scan the field.

"Kenzi?" It's Ellie. She's sniffling. The voice is faint. She never left. She's crouched down on the far side of the tires. "I'm sorry. I love you. You're my best friend." Her words are jumbled together and come out fast. "I overheard Tonya on the phone and didn't know who she was talking to, but then she said Bradley's name. I would have told you, I swear."

One quick glance around and I flip myself over the tire to join her. Her eyes are puffy and red. My own tears are starting up again. I blink them away. I need to stay focused.

"It's okay. I get it. I love you, too." I place my hand on Ellie's shoulder and give it a determined shake. "You wanna make it up to me? Cover me."

Her face first reads relief, then panic. "What?" Her red eyes are rounded.

"I'm going in," I yell over my shoulder and run. I leap over a strategically placed fallen tree and head to the pile of stacked wooden skids. I hear Ellie screaming as she runs after me.

Yellow paint zings past my ear.

It splatters a little on my uniform. I turn my shooter to the guy who fired it. He's running and . . . *ha, sucker!*

"Take that!" I scream at the guy, who I don't even know. He's covered in a slew of purple blobs. *That felt good.* I keep shooting him as I make my way to the next fort.

The guy's screaming, "I'm out, *stop!*"

I don't. In fact, I zap one last blow of purple in his direction. He's lucky I'm not a good shot.

We're just on the other side of where Bradley and Clive are holed up. Rand is firing at Bradley. *Good.* Get him. I see Shane. Another round of fire, and someone ninja-rolls to another barricade.

"Kenzi!" Ellie's pushing me to move as two guys charge our way with weapons blazing. We run screaming, but then I see Tonya. She's near the sidelines, still suited up, chatting with clients. Cue the theme music, something loud and edgy, it's go time.

I stand.

"What are you *doing*?" Ellie's pulling at my sleeve to get me to crouch, but I'm not budging.

I start walking toward her.

"Kenz!"

I'm picking up speed.

I'm charging.

I *fire*.

This is where the movie would go slow-mo. Purple ammo would zip from my paint marker in streams of moving color with precision accuracy. However, this *isn't* a movie and I'm by no means accurate. I spray the ground, hit a lawn chair, then another, and almost hit the client near it.

"Kenzi, stop!" Bradley's yelling, frantically waving his arms.

I don't. I'm focused on the backside of the scheming, two-faced target running away from me. Tent pole, someone's duffel, *ha! Got her leg! Ha! Got her other leg!*

"Wait! Kenz, *stop!*"

Tonya darts behind a tree. I close in. I blast a purple reign of terror.

"Kenz, stop, she might be *pregnant!*"

I stop.

The whole world does.

My arm goes limp. The paint gun hangs heavy from my fingertips.

Tonya peeks out, half hidden by the tree. She's lightly spattered in purple dye and saying something, but I don't understand her words.

"You're *pregnant*?" I don't say it loud enough for anyone to hear.

She might be pregnant?

Bradley's baby.

When I turn, everyone is staring at me. Clive. Clients. My design team. People I don't know. I see Maggie. Then I hear Ellie say something. And Shane. I see Shane. He's walking over to me.

Oh, *God*.

He *saw*. He heard. *He knows*.

I run.

I DON'T HAVE A CAR. *Oh my God*, I don't have . . . I'm running through the parking lot. I need to get out of here. *What do I do?* Think. My adrenaline is really pumping now. It rockets through my veins. Forget fight or flight. It screams, GET THE HELL OUT!

My breath is jagged. I'm trying doors. I think that's Clive's car. It's locked. I set off the alarm. *Shit!* I hear them calling me. I see them. I spin back and look for something, anything. There's a River Paintball promo van. Some punk kid is unloading stuff from its side door.

"You wanna make a hundred dollars?" I scream, running at him. I sound crazy. I look insane.

"What?" His eyes are wide. *Is he wearing eyeliner?*

"Two hundred. Just get me the hell outta here!" I look over my shoulder. They're coming.

He follows my gaze, "Um . . ."

"Good. Let's go. Come on." I'm already in the passenger seat. "Come *on*!"

He runs around and jumps in while I scream, "Go, just go. Move!" The van pulls out, and I watch Shane and Ellie run into the parking lot, followed by Bradley and Clive. They're going to their cars. I guess that *was* Clive's car.

I look at the kid behind the wheel. He has a faux-hawk and those earrings that look like mini-doughnuts stretched in each ear. A hoop is hanging from his bottom lip. His eyes are wide and he keeps looking over at me. Looking down, I realize I still have the paint blaster. It drops.

"I'm not kidnapping you," I say, my hand on my chest, practically hyperventilating.

"Whatever, you said two hundred, right?"

I nod. We need to go to my apartment for money. I don't have my bag, or my bank card. At least I have a spare key so I can get in. My phone rings from the coverall's inside pocket. A horn is honking from behind us. *Really?*

"Go! Move!" I yell, spinning around to see who it is. Clive. And he's with Bradley. It's stupid Bradley. "Go! There. Get on 465!"

"What? Shit, lady." But he does it. We're on the expressway.

My phone's still ringing. I grab it and without looking just click it on and scream, "*What?*"

"Kensington, it's me, Mom. I hope you don't always answer the phone that way. My word. That is not how I raised you at all—"

I lower the phone and point to the sign. "Take it north. Stay north," I say then wheel around in my seat. My mom is still talking away. Clive and Bradley are still coming. His horn is blaring and now Ellie and Shane are behind them in his Range Rover. Mom's still talking.

"Mom, Mom. Now is *not* a good time."

"What are you doing? Did you hear what I said? How do you explain Trish Evans saying her daughter met your British fiancé at the wedding planner's? British? Bradley was out of town. Do you know how this looks?"

We swerve into the next lane. They're still honking. From the phone I hear, "What is going on, Kensington?"

Hearing my name snaps me back. "Mom! You wanna know what's going on? Yeah, okay. I'm in a paintball van with some teenage Goth mutant." I look at the kid. "Sorry."

He shrugs.

"I'm trying to outrun my boss and Bradley, who are right now following us on 465. *Oh*, I called off the wedding. I did. He's *not* the one for me, okay, Mom? And guess who's back in town? Guess? I'll give you a hint. He's *British*. And you chased him away years ago. Can't you go any faster?"

They're now beside us, honking and yelling. My teen driver's eyes are wide listening to my rant. I'm looking behind us to see if we can change lanes.

My mom is saying something again, but I interrupt her and continue my outburst. "So, I called it off. Then I found out he was messing around with Tonya. *He was screwing Tonya!*"

"The British guy?" the teenager asks.

"No. My fiancé, Bradley. Although she says it happened when we were fighting and broken up. Like that matters." I turn back around and continue into the phone. "Oh, and guess what, Mom? Your darling Bradley might've knocked her ass up! Tonya might be pregnant. *Pregnant!*"

"Bitch," says the teenager.

"I know, right?" I say looking at him. "So, *no*, this is not a good time, and I don't care how it looks to Liza Evans's fucking mom or if you *approve!*" My mom's quiet on the phone. I can't believe I just said that.

There's a cop behind us.

"I gotta go."

"I'M SORRY," I SAY TO the teenager for maybe the fifth time. It's his first ticket. "I'll pay the fine, too."

He's looking straight ahead, both hands on the wheel, because that's what he was taught to do in driver's ed if he's pulled over. He's told me this twice. He also turns seventeen next week. The police officer commented on it when he collected his license and registration.

Clive and Bradley are parked behind us. Shane and Ellie are behind them. The officer has gone to all three cars and is making his way back. We have been here awhile. The teenager looks tense.

"Think of all the money you'll have for your birthday," I say, in my best encouraging voice. I've already upped my earlier two hundred to two fifty.

He sulks. His eyeliner's smudged.

The police officer stops at his window and hands back the kid's stuff. "You." He's pointing to the kid. "I will let off with a warning." Now he's pointing to me. "You. Out."

"Out?" *Shit, is he arresting me?* Am I going to jail? I don't have my wallet, or any ID. I open the door and look back to Teen McQueen. "I will mail you the cash. I promise. I'll send it to you at River Paintball."

"Let's go, follow me." The officer is walking past the police car and approaching Clive's. What is he doing? I slow down to watch where he's headed. He keeps going, so I keep following.

When I start to pass Clive's car, I notice his window's down. I lean over so I can see Bradley in the passenger seat. "You're an *ass*." Then I look at Clive. "Um, I'm using my vacation days for the rest of the week."

Clive nods, so I leave.

"Kenzi," Bradley calls out, but I keep walking until I meet up with the officer. He's standing next to Shane's Range Rover. I can't look at him. I don't want to know what he thinks of me or this whole mess. I'm mortified.

The police officer looks at Shane and Ellie. "Get her home. I've heard enough of this." He looks at me. "And you're right, he is an ass."

I don't know what they told him, but right now, I think he's the coolest cop I've ever met. I half smile and open the back door. Clive and Bradley are pulling away, the officer returns to his vehicle, and Shane is looking at me in the rearview mirror like he wants to say something.

"Don't," Ellie says to Shane, and crawls over the middle console to sit next to me.

Shane pulls from the side of the road without a word and takes the next exit. We need to go back to the paintball place so I can get my stuff.

My head drops to Ellie's shoulder with a sigh. All the adrenaline from before has fallen away to leave a vast wasteland of nothing in its place. I'm abandoned, betrayed . . . and lost. I have no inner compass.

Today's plan was V for victory. Instead my plan B, plan *Me*, blew up in my face. The only thing launched was failure.

THE PAINTBALL PROMO VAN IS back in the lot. The teenager is talking with what appears to be his manager. I still haven't said a word. Ellie hasn't left my side. I can see Clive and Bradley waiting for us in the staging area when we pull up. He has my bag from the locker.

"I'll get it, you guys stay here." Ellie's gone before I can say a word.

Shane steps out as soon as Ellie leaves. My handle clicks and he's standing in front of the open door. I can't look up. I'm frozen.

"I'd still like to take you to the farm. It'll be quiet there and I'll give you your space, okay?" His hand moves to mine. He has nice hands. "Come on." He guides me from the backseat and into the passenger side. Without another word, he fastens my belt and closes the door.

Ellie's walked back with my stuff, she hands the bags off to Shane. Before she leaves she knocks on my window. I glance up and she mouths the words *Love you*.

Love you, too, girl.

Shane slides into the driver's side and starts the ignition. My shoulders sag and I lean into the door, forehead to glass. My distorted image looks back.

Figures, I have paint in my hair.

CHAPTER SIXTEEN

While You Were Cheating

*I*T'S DARK. WE'RE OFF the main highway and are now traveling a rural one. Headlights passing in the opposite direction brighten the SUV's interior in brief flashes. Shane's been quiet, although I notice him glancing at me as he periodically changes the station or adjusts the heat.

I don't know what to say, so I haven't said a word. Not one. I mean, where do I start? Today has been a string of cataclysmic events. My life's plan didn't just spiral in a new direction. It unraveled, looped around my ankle, and hung me out to dry.

I stifle a laugh, wipe the moisture from under my eyes, and rub my forehead. Shane looks over quizzically.

"I've had a really busy day," I say in his direction. I guess I'm talking again. I'm rewarded with a warm smile.

He nods and says softly, "You have. Yes."

I'm sure he thinks the choice was made for me. The thought squeezes all the remaining air from my lungs. "I broke it off with

Bradley at lunch, before I knew anything. Tonya thought she was the reason why and outed herself." I glance at him, then look at my hands.

My empty finger.

He suddenly pulls onto the shoulder.

I look up. "What are you doing?"

"You haven't said one word for two and a half hours, Kensington. So, if you're talking, I'm listening." He says this in the way of *I'm interested*, not *I'm waiting for an explanation*.

Biting my nail, I search for the right words. "I broke it off after I talked with you. *But* I made my decision last night." I add the last part to assure him it was *my* decision, and not because of anything he had said.

Light brightens the interior momentarily as a car passes. It chases the shadows from Shane's features and catches the gold specks of color in his eyes.

Tears surge, they hold on the lower lid, ready to spill. I made the choice to leave Bradley. I did. I somehow found the courage to admit he wasn't what I wanted. But I still feel heavy with grief over walking away from the parts I *did* want.

"I really wanted to start a family. Have a baby . . ." I wipe at my eyes. "And I didn't know about Tonya. I mean, I thought she was seeing someone. She's been wearing lots of new designer clothes lately, but I didn't know she was . . . not until, well, you saw." I flush, feeling stupid.

Shane shifts in his seat, reaches over, and takes my hand.

I'm focused on it. How it completely covers mine. When I find my voice again it's quivering. "My family won't understand . . . it won't be about if I'm okay." I sniff. "Or how I feel. Or if I'm hurt. It will be about how it affects them."

Shane shakes his head. "They've got it backwards. They always have."

"I know. But the thing is . . . I know it's never really going to change. Logically, I know this, but it still surprises me." *It still hurts.* I shrug. "I'm just embarrassed by it all."

"You shouldn't feel embarrassed. You should be angry."

Tears. More tears. I'm a faucet. This is beyond humiliating. He's right, though. I should be angry. The whole time Bradley was cheating, and who knows how long it really went on. And while he was cheating, I was trying to convince myself how perfect we were together, how lucky I was that he wanted me, so happy my family loved him.

Shane reaches into the console and pulls out a small travel pack of tissues. I blow my nose then grab another.

I look up but can't quite meet his eyes. "Bradley lied to me. Tonya lied to me. *Twice.*" I lean my head against the seat. "But really, it doesn't matter that he was cheating, because I was cheating myself, lying to myself. That's the worst part. I think, deep inside I *knew.*"

Shane shifts and meets my gaze head on. For a moment, we're just looking at each other, blinking. The truth stripped down and on display between us like a bridge.

THERE'S A CHATTERING. *WHAT IS that noise?* I blink. A hazy beam of light filters through the room's double window onto the bed. I yawn and open my eyes wide to focus. I'm at Shane's. The quilt is tucked up around me tight. I stretch underneath it. More chattering—*birds*—that's what the noise is. It sounds like there are hundreds of them right outside. I peek over the quilt and look at the couch.

No Shane.

I sit up to listen. I don't hear him walking around, so I get up and peer over the loft railing. No one's here. When we pulled in last night, I couldn't really see the house in the dark. It's more like a cottage, the inside's so small. This isn't the main house I visited with him years ago.

Grabbing my phone from the nightstand, I crawl back in bed and scooch under the quilt. It feels like I'm a million miles away, except I'm not. I'm only a phone call away. Yesterday's reality seeps back in and settles in the pit of my stomach.

Pushing my hair from my face, I blink my phone into focus and click voice mail. Robo-lady announces I have thirteen new messages. *Thirteen?* My gut wrenches. That's not counting the missed calls that didn't leave one.

It's Bradley. "Kenzi, I need to talk to you. *Please.*"

Just the sound of his voice has me tearing up.

"You can't take off and not hear me out. You've got this wrong. We need to talk. Please."

Delete. In fact, the next eight messages are from him. *Why does he even care?* Tonya might be *pregnant.* Each message, Bradley sounds more desperate, and I think he's been drinking. He's talking loudly and there's a definite slur.

There's one from my mom. I don't listen to hers. I instantly delete. And I have a message from my brother.

Grayson called?

"Kensington, I don't know exactly what's going on. Bradley called and said you two had a fight. There was a misunderstanding and you took off with another guy? Really, Kenz? You're *engaged*, for Christ's sake."

Was engaged. *Was* getting married. The tears are a steady stream now.

"Mom's called a few times and is really upset by this. She's in tears, said you called her drunk or something. Can you please call her? And Bradley? Get this straightened out already. It doesn't look good."

I delete. My heart is in my stomach, and my stomach's in a double knot around it. Everything's all balled up inside. Why does Grayson never talk to me? *There's two sides, Grayson.* My family's upset.

The next message starts. Ren's voice snaps my attention. "Hi. Kensington . . . *oh my God.* Are you okay?" She's almost whispering. "Grayson's, well, he's just worried." Did she let him have it? *Did they make up?* "Bradley's been on the phone with him nonstop. Call me back."

She asked if I was okay. I delete and wipe at my eyes. I might actually call Ren back. The last message is from Ellie.

"Hey, girlie, I wanted to check in on you. Bradley's a mess. He's been drinking and came over last night. I've never seen him like this. He says Tonya was trying to trap him and he didn't know what to do. I told him he should have kept it in his pants. Hope that's okay."

"More than okay, Ellie-bell," I mumble to myself.

"And he said he doesn't know if he believes her about the pregnancy, like that changes anything. Did you know Bradley and Tonya used to be a thing before you worked here?"

No. I knew they were good friends, but I never put it together.

"I'm sure you did, but that's still no excuse. And then to hook up again? I don't care if it was when you guys were fighting. She's a bitch. Oh, your mom called here, too, very ups—"

The message ran out of time and cut her off. My heart beats wildly as I'm face-to-face, again, with my so-called life. I wipe my falling tears and click off my phone.

A baby.

Sliding completely under the quilt, I cover my face with my hands. In *While You Were Sleeping*, Peter Gallagher's character asked Lucy to marry him by saying, *My family loves you. I may as well love you.* Ridiculous reasoning, and yet isn't that what I kinda did? Wasn't that part of why I accepted Bradley's proposal? The back of my throat tightens and the dam bursts from the pressure. Tears wet the insides of my palms, and I gasp for air in uncontrollable sobs.

Peter in *While You Were Sleeping* says, *It took a coma to wake me up.* He meant to what was important, what was missing in his life. I wonder if one can help me forget. I just want to sleep and forget everything.

"KENSINGTON?"

I feel a hand on my shoulder, gently rocking me.

"Kensington. Come on, sleepyhead." It's Shane. "You can't sleep all day."

I fell back asleep? I didn't even hear him come back. Pushing the stuck strands of hair from my cheeks, I open my eyes and squint. It's bright, even under the quilt.

"Sorry." My voice is crackly. I clear it and try again. "What time is it?"

"It's afternoon." The mattress sinks as he sits beside me. "Are you going to just stay under there all day?" he asks, tugging at the quilt so it pulls down an inch.

Quickly, I yank it back and hold it secure. "Yes. Maybe." That actually sounds like a good plan. One, I feel safer in here, and two, I can only imagine what I look like. So my hiding is as much for his benefit as my own.

I hear him let out a breath. "Are you okay?"

My thoughts are racing. "No . . ." I feel for my phone and push my hand out the top of the quilt, holding it. "I listened. I shouldn't have."

I tell him everything from under my makeshift blanket shield. "I guess Bradley's been over to Ellie's place and even called my brother, who then called me. My mom's crying. Bradley's left a million messages and has been drinking. He's now wondering if Tonya lied, if she's really pregnant after all, and . . . I don't know. It's all a mess."

Such a mess.

Shane shifts, causing me to roll slightly toward him.

"Kensington, I can take you home. I'd understand if you want to deal with things. Originally, you were only going to stay for a day, but I had hoped . . ."

I shouldn't have listened. I should have just kept the world far and away, instead of shortening the distance with my stupid phone.

I don't want to go back. Everything's waiting for me there, and it's nothing good. I'm not ready. "I'd like to stay . . . unless . . ." My gut wrenches. Maybe he doesn't want to deal with this. *Why would he?* All my insecurities bubble to the surface. "I mean, I understand . . . if you don't want to deal—"

"I want you here, Kensington." His voice is low. "I want you to stay."

Closing my eyes, I release my shoulders. *He wants me here.*

"I was just out for a run, so let me grab a shower, and we can head over to the Carriage House, okay?" He stands and the mattress rises from the loss of pressure. "Oh, I picked you up a few things for later. I, ah, put them by the window. It's actually quite a view, you should have a look. It's the whole reason I chose this cottage."

I manage a thank you and stay covered until I hear running water. Pushing the quilt back, I look toward the bathroom. The door's shut, so I sit up and finger-comb my hair. By the window is a small plastic bag with red lettering printed on the side. *Video Max.* He rented me movies. Bet he doesn't have digital cable here.

Wrapping the quilt around my shoulders, I pad over to investigate. *When Harry Met Sally* and *Never Been Kissed*. Some of the best romantic comedies are less about the movie boyfriend you swoon over, and more about the heroine you relate to. A small smile creeps across my lips. A night hanging with Meg Ryan, and Drew Barrymore as Josie Grossie, is *perfect*.

I glance toward the huge double window, curious. Instead of curtains it has two wooden shutters that swing to the inside. I unlatch the metal hook and pull them open.

Oh. This is a view.

Sunflowers for as far as you can see. Their yellow faces, smiling, turned toward the sun. We must be on a slight incline, because the drive curves down and around. The horizon is a blast of gold and green framed by rolling hills of tilled-up tan. It's breathtaking.

I wipe the dust at the window to see better, then fiddle with the windows to open them, but they're swollen in the frames. I push harder until they pop free. The air bites, and I'm scolded by the birds as I swivel the windows out.

I wrap myself tighter in the quilt and take a seat on the ledge. There's a pair of ladybugs crawling toward me. It makes me think of *Under the Tuscan Sun*. When she says she was looking for ladybugs, but she could never find them. When she finally gave up looking, they were everywhere.

Maybe I've been looking too hard. *Trying too hard.*

Readjusting the quilt over my shoulders, I lean into the frame and look across the field of yellow. This would be the perfect spot to paint. I fill my lungs with crisp air and spot more ladybugs. Then I feel a tickle.

What the . . .

Something's . . . *oh!* It's crawling on me! I jump up, flinging the quilt and shaking out my cami top. It falls inside. The creepy little bug is inside! *On* me. Against my skin. I scream and try and knock him off so he'll fall, but his little sticky legs are now gripped into my top. *He won't fall.*

Get the hell out! I'm shaking it violently. I yank off the cami and whip it across the room. I extend my arms in a mad inspection. I survey my front for any other intruders, then twist around to see my shoulders, my back, and—

Shane's leaning in the doorway.

Embarrassed, I smile and draw my arms to cover my bare chest. He's in only a towel and his hair is drenched and clinging to his neck and forehead in wet curls. I can't help but notice the tattoo across his left shoulder and arm. That's new. It's black and tribal and dips in and out over each muscle.

"Um, ladybug . . . it went down my shirt."

His grin is boyish, mischievous. "Lucky ladybug."

CHAPTER SEVENTEEN

Seven Candles

$\mathcal{T}$HE CARRIAGE HOUSE IS built into the side of a hill and is white on white with gray Indiana fieldstone on the lower level. The old barn has been completely refinished. It's amazing. I'm really impressed, no, more than impressed.

I'm gobsmacked.

"Shane, this is . . . I mean, *wow*," I say, as we climb the last few steps to the upper deck along the back. Twinkle lights hang from the pergola, giving the tables below a guaranteed starry night.

Shane's walking ahead of me with a wide grin that reaches his eyes and causes crinkles along their sides. "We'll have enough seating for regular dining inside and out. But the best part . . ." Shane unlocks the huge double barn doors and slides them open on their tracks. "Is in here."

The space is still under construction and huge with exposed post-and-beam throughout. We're level with a partial loft and a full two-story screen resides along the back wall.

"The kitchen is below us and the murals—your murals—" Shane's pointing to the bare walls along either side "—will be hung throughout. Come on."

I follow Shane downstairs. My eyes are still puffy from all the waterworks, and I wasn't able to get much breakfast down. I'm still not sure what I'm doing here or really in general, but I'm grateful for the distraction and in awe of his accomplishment. He always had big ideas, and I knew, of course about the Carriage House, but to see it actually in development is amazing. *He's really doing it.* Maybe he has grown up.

Shane lights up while he shows me the kitchen, adjoining dining area, and theater. I like seeing him like this. Even though his jeans are well worn and his hair's a glorious mess, he's never looked better. Well, maybe in the towel earlier.

My eyes fall to the empty spaces designed to house the murals. My work, *my murals*, will be . . . everywhere. A small flitter of excitement finds its way to the surface. Then it slams my heart. My mouth hangs open and I blink, not believing my eyes.

"No way. No frickin' way!"

In the hallway three stretched canvas paintings hang. *They're mine.*

The same ones Shane printed from my Facebook gallery and that hang in the conference room at work. The two figurative illustrations of couples and the close-up portrait in reversed color blocking, the same ones missing from under my Kensington box.

Mom *didn't* throw them away.

I had them flat for storage. He had them stretched? They're hung at eye level with a single light illuminating each one. They look . . . *beautiful.*

I glance at Shane. He loops his thumbs in his jeans pockets and leans against the wall; a small twinkly smile plays on his lips. I'm floored.

"But *how*? How did you get them? *When?*" My mind spins around the implications. My chin lowers to a slight angle, eyes darting between my work and him.

"I stopped at your parents, about a month or so before the agency meeting. Had lunch with your dad, actually."

My head kicks back. "What?"

"I popped by and, well, we started talking."

"You 'popped by,' *why?*"

He smiles and shakes his head, as if the question didn't make sense. "To see you. It was never my intention to show up out of the blue at your office. And I told you, when I started developing the Carriage House concept, it was largely in part because of you. So I came by to see if you'd be interested in developing the concept with me." A soft smile turns at the corners of Shane's lips. "And it was a legitimate reason to see you."

"And then what? One lunch with Dad and you changed your mind?" The thought steals my breath. "Don't tell me *he* told—"

"No. No, quite the opposite. He was a gracious host and we enjoyed a long conversation. I told him my business plans, he told me where you worked, I was considering hiring your agency, and how my concept was based on your paintings, your love of cinema . . . and well, when I dropped him back he found them for me."

"He *gave* them to you?"

He laughs. "I didn't intend to *keep* them, only use them to demonstrate what I was looking for in the first concept meeting, but well, I rather like them here . . ."

I'm confused. "You used printouts from my Facebook album."

"I know."

"And you never contacted me—well, on Facebook—but you never said anything about—"

"I know."

My hands are raised, he's not explaining. "*Shane . . . ?*"

"Your father told me you were engaged, so . . ." He shifts position, leaning his shoulder on the wall. "I, I don't know. Didn't want to overstep."

I laugh softly, wrinkling my nose. "I'd say you kinda—"

"That was after I saw you with him, and . . ." His lips press into a hard line, his entire expression falling cold. "He didn't deserve you. Gloves came off."

I step back, soaking in his words and remembering Ren's. *Your mom was really upset when you left. Your parents got into a fight.* That's why Mom was ignoring me, and they didn't say anything because Bradley was there. She must've been angry at Dad and *oh,* guilt drops heavy in my heart. And she probably didn't bring it up on the phone because, well, she didn't really want Shane back in the picture. Mom's firmly in Bradley's corner. *Is she still?*

"So yes, I still have your paintings. Really love them. I hadn't found the right time to—"

I walk over and surprise him with a kiss on his cheek, and smile. "You bought my chairs."

"I have no idea what you mean, but if it makes you happy, then yes, okay, I bought your chairs."

My smile widens. "The movie *Phenomenon,* remember that one?"

His eyes narrow a smidgen in thought. I don't wait for an answer.

"Lace, Kyra Sedgwick's character, makes these chairs, all kinds, and tries to sell them. And all at once, they start to sell, so she makes more." I'm not sure he remembers the movie, but I keep going. "It was John Travolta's character, George. He bought them all. In fact, his whole yard was full of them." I shrug, my movie-spiel recap winding down, and nod to my paintings hanging on display. "You bought my chairs."

"So I did." Shane smiles warmly, then straightens. "I'll be right back, why don't you have a seat," he says, motioning to a large booth. He disappears into the kitchen.

From speakers tucked along the walls, music kicks on and Shane appears with . . . I puzzle my brows. "What is that?" Flowers. *A circle of flowers?*

"This is for you," he says, placing it on my head with exacting care.

With him standing so close, the scent of his aftershave fills my nose. It's a familiar mix of woodsy and Shane. My hands immediately pull the flowers from my head so I can see them. They're wild and wound loosely to form a wreath of pink and white. I smile, brows knitted. *What is he doing now?*

"Nope." Shane takes it back, replaces it on my head, and pulls down securely. With a final adjustment, his hands fall. But his gaze still lingers. "That needs to stay there, and hang on . . ." He disappears again to the back.

My fingers touch the flower wreath on my head. A small smile forms on my lips as my eyes again rest on my paintings illuminated by soft light in the hall. On display. Not in a drawer, but up for everyone to see. Tears pool on my lower lashes.

Music starts playing through the sound system. It's . . . "If You Leave" by OMD. Fiddling with my jacket's cuffs, I hum along to the song. I haven't heard it in years. *Seven years went under the bridge, like time was standing still . . .*

It *has* been seven years . . . *Funny*, and the next line asks what will happen now? That's the million-dollar question, isn't it?

My phone vibrates again from my pocket. It's been buzzing all day. Fishing it out, I'm firmly restating the rules in my head. I *can't* listen to any messages. I will *only* look at the screen.

Three missed calls.

I scroll and see two from Ellie and one from Bradley. Instead of listening, I open my e-mails to view the Love Like the Movies list. I know he's up to something.

1. Sleepless in Seattle
2. ~~Pretty Woman~~
3. Bridget Jones's Diary
4. ~~27 Dresses~~
5. ~~Dirty Dancing~~
6. Sixteen Candles
7. Love Actually
8. Say Anything
9. You've Got Mail
10. ~~My Best Friend's Wedding~~

It's number 6. When I see Shane round the corner from the kitchen, it confirms it. I'm wearing a flower wreath, "If You Leave" is playing, and . . . He's walking in with a birthday cake. My heart floats high in my chest like a balloon.

This is *Sixteen Candles*.

And it's surreal.

Shane smiles. "You need to be sitting up there, I believe." He nods to the wooden table. "Legs crisscrossed."

My throat tightens, and I already have tears as I climb up. Folding my legs, I adjust my skirt over them. In the movie, Samantha's birthday is eclipsed by her sister's wedding. I feel like *my* wedding was overshadowed by Ren's baby announcement. I'm *invisible*. No one cares, and my big moments don't matter. And here's Shane, just like the handsome Jake Ryan, doing all of this for me. *Just for me.*

Placing the cake in front of me, he steps up on the booth then slowly lowers his weight onto the table. "Okay. Good. Wasn't sure it would actually hold me."

I laugh through my tears and gaze at him across from me.

Shane smiles crooked. "Thanks for coming over."

"Thanks for . . . *coming to get me.*" The movie lines are swallowed by my breath. I give a closed-mouth smile, choked by emotion.

Wiping under my eyes, I clear my throat and watch Shane light the candles. There's . . . two, four, six . . . "Seven? You have only seven candles."

Honey-gold eyes flick to mine. He leans in close and says softly, "I only missed seven birthdays."

My stomach flutters. I was twenty-three when he left. Seven years ago. Seven birthdays. A lifetime between then and now. But like the song says, it's like time has stood still.

"Happy birthday, Kensington. Make a wish."

My gaze drops from his to the cake because I remember the line. The scene.

The kiss.

I'm glowing from within. Little nervous butterflies are attracted to the inner light. They may be too close. They could get singed.

Gazing up through my lashes, I bite my lip and debate if I should say the line, knowing what follows. Knowing I'm not quite ready. Not knowing what he expects.

But he doesn't give me the chance.

Placing a hand in front of him for support, he leans over and delivers it. "Mine already came true." It comes out low, in a breath, his lips a whisper away.

After a beat, he places a slow, lingering kiss on my cheek that causes a frenzy of flutters. Anything more would have been too much. Anything less wouldn't have completed the scene.

There are no more lines.

The credits simply roll over the still frame of Samantha and Jake, frozen in a kiss. The song's hypnotic melody drones on in the movie, just as it is now. The viewer knows everything will be all right. That Samantha is fine. Someone finally sees her.

Sees *me*.

Shane always has.

"FAVORITE COLOR?" IT USED TO be blue. I want to know everything, if only to distract myself from my phone. My thoughts. My nerves.

We're situated in rockers on the upstairs balcony of the main house. It's peaceful with the temperate breeze and backyard view. I remember sitting here with his grandparents years ago having iced tea.

"Um, I will say blue," Shane says, finally.

"Still blue? Just blue? Not sky blue or ocean blue?" I push off the deck with my toes to get my chair rocking steadily again. "There are actually fifty-nine shades of blue, and that's only if you don't count the made-up ones like toilet water blue."

"Toilet water blue? Yes, perfect for a paint swatch." He smiles. "I'm sticking to plain blue."

"Okay, fine, blue." I wrinkle my nose. "Moving on. Favorite number?"

"Mm, I'd say number two. And five, yes, I'm quite fond of number five."

I knit my brows together as his meaning registers. "Number

five was *Dirty Dancing* and two was *Pretty Woman*. You liked shopping?"

"I liked watching you."

I smile. "I think you enjoyed the Marys fawning all over you."

He shrugs. "I liked seeing you happy, Kensington."

I can feel the burn creep across my cheeks as I turn and look at him. There's a beat, a pause, an understanding. Maybe the tiniest glint of happy.

"I needed this," I half whisper. "Thank you, Shane."

"You are very welcome." He tips his head back and closes his eyes. His lips are curled in a contented smile.

Trees rustle like paper in the light breeze while sparrows squabble over a feeder that hangs from a low branch. I shift my weight to set the rocker in motion again.

This *is* nice.

"I think your grandfather would have liked the Carriage House plans. What you're doing, I'm sure he'd have been proud." Shane hasn't mentioned much about his passing. Only that he left him everything and that included looking after Gram.

His rocker stops, and he looks to me. "Have you considered leaving Safia for real? Finally having your own studio?"

I look back at the horizon. The shades of yellow are now a deep grainy tan with dusk. "Oh, I don't know."

"You could do it." Shane's sitting up, leaning over the chair's arm. "I'd hire you. You wouldn't need to go back to Safia."

"What?" My brows pull down. "You mean, *work for you?*"

He laughs. "No, you'd work for yourself, and we would be your first client, or your only client, and then you could . . . I don't know, *paint*."

My heart is beating loudly in my ears. That's what I'd always wanted to do. Life somehow pushed forward and I never got around to it. I'm lost in thoughts of what is, what isn't, and what I've left behind. I want the same things I wanted yesterday. I want to be married. I want a baby. And today, right now, I'm further away from both.

But maybe I'm somehow closer to *me*.

"You like the cottage?" Shane asks with obvious excitement in his voice.

"Of course. And you were right, the view's beautiful."

"What if we change it around to be a studio? Your studio."

"Why would—"

"It's just something to think about. You could set up here, if you wanted. The whole town is crawling with tourists in the summer. You could use it to build your name." He leans over and lowers his voice. "I know I'd like you around."

He wants me around.

I sit back to juggle his words. Closing my eyes, I try and picture the cottage and me in it. I'm painting. The windows are open and an afternoon breeze blows through, clearing the fumes out. I could be messy. God knows I'm messy when I paint. It ends up everywhere.

Shane likes my work. He wants me here. Why am I thinking of *Pretty Woman* again? Edward offered Vivian an apartment, a car, unlimited shopping, whatever she wanted. What she wanted was him. *It's all I'm capable of right now*, he says.

Shane's offering me a place to live, my own studio, him? But right now, at this moment . . . It's *more* than *I'm* capable of.

Leaning back in the rocker, I turn toward him. "I think that sounds fast . . . I think having my own studio and really trying is exactly what I need to do, but . . ."

Shane pushes out a breath. His smile is hesitant. "But, not *here*—"

"Not *yet*." Wetting my lips, I swallow and sit up. "I think I need to do it on my own first. Be on my own for a while. Does that make sense? I mean, up until yesterday I was engaged, and only last week I believed that was the right direction for my life, and then you showed up and . . ."

Shane searches my eyes. "You are not the impulsive girl I once knew. Not as quick to jump, a bit more reserved." His lips lift slightly at the corners. "She's all grown up, isn't she?"

I smile with a sigh from somewhere deep. After seeing this place and what Shane's accomplished, I can't help but think maybe we both have.

The sound of tires and kicked-up gravel from the front drive interrupts the country quiet. Gram must be here.

Shane looks confused. "Be right back." He's up and off.

I'm up, too. Smoothing my dress and fixing my hair. I'm nervous to see her after all this time. I shouldn't be, though. She always liked me. Everything will be—

Shane comes bounding back onto the balcony, he's leaning in the doorway, jaw clenched.

I feel my eyes go wide. "What? What is it?"

"It's Bradley."

CHAPTER EIGHTEEN

Crazy Stupid Bradley

$\mathcal{S}$HANE SPRINTS TOWARD THE stairs. I run to the window and peer out. *Shit,* Bradley *is* here. His BMW's parked next to Shane's SUV. *What the hell is he doing here?* My heart beats in triple time. I race to the bedroom door but then stop, only to turn and run back to the window. I don't see anyone.

Voices from downstairs. It's not a friendly exchange. Oh! Oh *no*, no, no no . . . without thinking, I fly through the hall. I'm halfway down the stairs when I see them. And Bradley sees me. Coming from upstairs. At Shane's. I know how this looks. I'm sure he thinks . . . Bradley's eyes are narrowed. Yeah, he does.

Motionless, I stand on the bottom step, mute. I shouldn't care. Or feel guilty for being here. But *I do*. I'm cloaked in it.

"Can we have a few minutes, Bennett?"

Shane's eyes are fixed on Bradley. "If Kensington wants me to go I will." One wrong word, one quick move, and he'll pounce. I can feel it.

Shane and Bradley both look at me.

My fingers tighten on the wooden stair handrail. "Whatever you need to say, Bradley, just say it." My voice sounds strained.

Bradley takes a step around him. "The baby's not mine, Kenz. Truthfully, I'm not even sure she's really pregnant."

Does it matter? I swallow hard. He still cheated. I still broke it off before.

"I was *not* screwing around on you." His voice is filled with emotion. "We had a thing before you and I even met, but it was never serious." His head drops. "And then, okay . . . once. It just happened. We had that fight, remember? I had been drinking and I . . ." His hand runs over his jaw. "I screwed up. I know I screwed up."

My stomach's on the floor. This is just like Tonya with Shane. *Drinking. Didn't mean anything.* Hurricane Tonya is whipping around my insides with gale-force winds, tearing away any scrap of truth. I don't feel well.

"Kenz, it was a mistake." Bradley's voice lowers. He's at the base of the stairs now.

I haven't moved.

He talks faster, inching closer. "I didn't know what to do. I screwed up everything. Come on, Kenz, I love you. It was a mistake, and we just need to work through it."

My eyes move from Bradley to Shane. Bradley's follow.

"No, don't even tell me this is about *him*." Turning back to me, Bradley tilts his head. His blue eyes soften. "He's using this to get to you. Hon, don't . . . don't throw everything away. *Please.* It can all be worked out."

He still slept with her . . . I still broke it off before I knew . . . Tonya may or may not be pregnant . . . My family's upset. I slowly sink onto the step, now grabbing hold of the rail with both hands.

Bradley starts to climb the first step toward me, but Shane steps up behind him, his voice low and sharp. "Tell her the truth. *Now.* Or I will."

Shock slams my chest. *There's more truth?* I don't think I can take any more truth today.

Bradley spins and steps down to face him. "Fuck you."

Shane's eyes narrow, his jaw sets. Every muscle is flexed. "Tell her where you were last—"

"Careful, Bennett." It's said in a growl, his voice an octave deeper.

Now the room is definitely turning. I lean into the rail. I may hurl.

"Then get in your fucking car and go home." Shane's voice is strained, his temper barely contained. "She broke it off. I think she's made that clear."

Bradley moves in front of Shane so they're eye-to-eye. "She broke it off? Then why does she still have the ring? *Asshole.*"

Oh, shit.

They're deadlocked in a stare. Then Shane turns to me. His head is cocked. "You still have his ring?"

"Hell yea—"

"Shut the fuck up." Shane shoves Bradley hard with one hand.

Bradley backs up with his hands up, palms open. A smirk.

I sit up, trying to compose myself and process. "He wouldn't . . . he *wouldn't take it.*" My voice sounds small, lost. My heart is bleeding out. I can't get enough air.

"Because we decided to think on it, take some time," Bradley says, arms now folded, still looking smug.

Shane runs a hand through his unruly hair. He looks frustrated, angry. "Do you have his ring, Kensington?"

This time I don't like how my name sounds from his lips. "I . . . I called it off bef—"

"Yes or no?" His voice is sharp.

My heart jumps.

I remember to blink.

I nod.

He looks to Bradley. "Tell your *fiancée* how I ran into you at the Canterbury Hotel with Tonya. Maybe you should have done your homework on where Clive sets his clients up. First at Champps, then I find them in my hotel lobby last week."

My stomach rolls, so I cover my mouth. I can't breathe.

Bradley whips his head back to me. "We met to discuss the possible preg—"

"They weren't talking."

Bradley lunges.

He has Shane by the shirt, shoving him back. Bradley's bigger. He's all brawn and brute strength. He pushes Shane against the wall. *Hard.* Hanging picture frames jostle. One falls and shatters.

Shane bucks under his grip, causing Bradley's hold to loosen. Shane's a boxer. He's quick, and Bradley doesn't know what hit him.

The first, the second, or the third time.

Bradley muscles another hold and gets a clean shot to Shane's jaw. There's blood, but I don't know whose.

This is crazy.

My eyes are covered. I can't watch.

"Stop," a small voice calls out. "Stop it, right now!" A tiny woman storms through the wide-open door.

It's Gram. She has the same steely, honey-brown eyes and no-nonsense tone I remember.

"Stop it! What in the *hell* is the matter with you both? You, I don't know you, but get over there. And you." She gives Shane a stern look and finger wag. "Over there."

Shane steps back and wipes at his nose. There's blood under it. Bradley looks at me and straightens. Gram follows his gaze.

"Oh, well now, I didn't even see . . ." She tilts her head and squints for focus. "Kensington? Kensington Shaw? Shane said we had a special guest for dinner, someone I'd remember . . ."

I don't think a *hey-how-are-ya* is going to fly at the moment, so I don't say anything. Her eyes sweep me from head to toe. Between the tears and shocked expression, I'm sure I'm quite the sight.

"Why don't you take a minute, then meet me in the kitchen, Kensington?" Gram's eyes stay on mine for a beat. It's not really an invitation, and I know better than to argue or protest.

I stand on wobbly legs, glance at stupid Bradley, then Shane. His lips are pulled in a grim line.

With my last bit of reserve, I mutter, "*You knew?*"

Shane's expression falls.

I don't wait to hear his reasons. I don't remember walking up the stairs or going into the bedroom. He knew about Bradley and Tonya and never said a word. Even when I found out, he didn't say anything.

Tonya *may* be pregnant. She *may not*. And none of it matters, right? Except that Shane *knew*. And it had to do with Tonya. Again.

The question of trust has been answered loud and clear. Again.

My world has catastrophically turned upside down.

Again.

UPSTAIRS ON THE BALCONY, I sit in the rocker, dazed, and wait. I find my phone and dial Ellie. *Please answer. Please pick—*

"Hello? Kenzi?"

Oh, thank God.

"Hi. I, um—" But that's all I get to say.

She's launched into a word fury. ". . . and I tried to call, but you never answered . . ."

". . . Bradley, shit, and then he said he was going up there . . ."

". . . I'm about thirty minutes out. Wouldn't you say? Yeah, Ran—"

I stand up, promptly revived. "Wait! *Wait*, Ellie? You're coming here? Now?"

"Yes! That's what I've been saying. Rand drove to Indy with Shane, but Shane left with you at the paintball thing, so he was stranded . . . I thought you could come back with me, if you want. If you'd rather stay with Shane, that's fine, I can get back—"

"You're the best, oh my God. *Yes*, I need to get out of here. Tell Rand I'm at the main house, okay?" I hear her repeat what I said. A heavy sigh escapes from my very soul.

She begins to ask about what's happening, but I just can't. Not right now. Hanging up, I still don't move. I can't bring myself to go downstairs to face Gram, or either of them. *I just want to go home.*

I look to the window. I'm sure there's a trellis. You always see that in movies. I could wait by the road.

Am I really considering this? Yes, this is how bad my life has gotten. And of course there's a trellis. I lean out from the balcony's side and shake the wooden makeshift ladder against the house. It feels secure. I try to rip it away from the house and it doesn't budge.

Taking a breath, I swing one leg over and secure my boot tip in the crossing of the lattice. Okay, another breath and the other leg. Holding on tight, I shift so all my weight is on it. It holds. I bounce a little to be sure. I shake around to be double sure. Good. I've got this.

It's surprisingly easier than it looks in the movies. With ease, I make my way down. I cannot believe I'm sneaking out. This qualifies as a new all-time low. One more step and . . . I land with a *thump*, but unharmed. I take a step and smooth out my skirt.

"I thought you might want your purse." It's Gram.

I stand corrected. *This* is my new all-time low.

She's standing on the back walk, purse in hand, with a nonplussed expression. Had she been there the whole time? I feel like someone is wringing my stomach like a towel, trying to squeeze out every last sour drop. I clear my throat, walk over, and take my purse from her hand, feeling ridiculous.

"You never were one for doors, if I recall." I'm quickly reminded of climbing *into* Shane's dorm room more than once, and the time when she surprised him and stayed late for a visit. She wasn't the only one surprised when I popped up in the window.

Gram spins on her heels and heads back in. "Let's go, I'll put the tea on."

With lowered head, I follow in silence.

"Well, coffee will have to do. Shane never has anything stocked here." She's opening a cupboard and pulling out mugs. "I stay over at the back cottage now. There are three units, all together."

There's no sign of Bradley or Shane. I stand in the doorway, not really sure what to say. *I should say something.* Instead, I fiddle with my dress.

"Well . . . sit down," she says and sets a cup in front of me on the thick wooden table.

I take a seat, lacing my fingers around the cup's handle. "This isn't how I imagined seeing you again."

"No, I wouldn't think it is. Do you want sugar?" she asks as she fills the cup.

"Yes, please." I take a spoonful and stir, making it clink along its side. What if she tells me I'm not right for Shane? Isn't that what my mom did to him?

Gram pulls a chair out and sits across from me. "There's no cream or milk either, I'm afraid." She draws her thin hands in, folding them in front of her, and looks at me seriously. "This guy who showed up here, tell me about him."

I look up. She reads my mind before the thoughts clearly registered.

"Oh, I sent him home, dear. And Shane, I sent to the cottage for your bags."

My bags. My heart drops. They want me to leave. Well, I am. Ellie's on her way.

"We were engaged until, well . . . yesterday." *That sounds horrible.* Was it only yesterday? God, this *is* horrible. I fidget with the mug's handle. "My family loves him. But after a while I realized I didn't, at least, not enough. Not in the way I should. And then . . ." My eyes glance up to her. *Do I tell her about Tonya?* "Um, it turns out he was cheating . . . and she may be pregnant." There, I said it. Yes, I'm pathetic. "It was with . . . someone I thought was a friend."

Her eyes narrow. "And how exactly does Shane fit into all of this?" she asks, drawing the cup to her lips. Perceptive eyes peer over the rim at me.

I've forgotten how direct she is. I adjust my cup, turning the handle so it's facing in the other direction for no reason whatsoever. *How does Shane fit into all of this?* I start thinking about him friending me online, the first day he showed up at Safia, the Love Like the Movies list, and all the movie moments.

I meet Gram's eyes. She's patiently waiting for me to formulate an answer.

"He, um. Well, he showed up at my work, as a client, and we're working together. And there's this list . . . and he . . ." I half smile, glance at Gram, and look down.

"I see." Gram holds her cup with both hands, elbows propped on the table. "I remember when he left for home, without you." She pulls her brows down as if in thought. "Wasn't easy on him. The next couple of years weren't much better." Gram leans back.

My ears are pricked, I'm listening intently.

"When my Charles passed away last year, he left Shane everything, with provisions for me, of course. Shane's father, my son, felt it all should have been left to him. There was also a girl Shane had been seeing."

I'm not sure I want to hear about this. I take a sip. *Please don't say he still loves her.*

"Shane was on track for a very promising career with his father, she was on track to bag a promising husband." Her eyes narrow. "But when my Charles left Shane the family trust and farm in America . . . well, it promised to throw a wrench into everything if he moved here." She reaches out and places her hand on mine, her nose wrinkles with a smile. "I'm rather glad it did."

He never told me any of this. *He doesn't tell me lots of things.*

"She wanted him to sell it, so they could start a life from the profits. His father agreed with her. Together, they tried to convince him it was the right way to go. Nearly did."

She takes a drink. I don't know what to say. *Should I say something?*

"Shane had a choice. He could sell, profit, and leave me to my own. Or he could move back to the States and look after little ol' me. Maybe start again." She narrows her eyes. "Choosing is the act of living with purpose. And I think he made the right choice. Maybe you have, too."

I lean back and give her a small smile.

She smiles back, then turns to the doorway. "Shane, you may as well come in, I can hear you sitting out there." She winks at me. "I hear everything, drives him crazy."

Shane heard? I hear movement, but I'm focused on the coffee cup, the death grip I have on the handle.

"You need some food in here, at least some cream for coffee." She stands. "Kensington, it was nice to see your pretty face again. I expect to see more of it."

I look up and catch her smile as she heads for the door. Then I see Shane. He's leaning in the doorway, his thumb hanging from his jeans loop, his head tilted back warily. The lips that pressed to my cheek less than three hours ago now have a slight swell and split along the bottom. His eyes are locked on to mine. Right now he looks more like the boy I remember than the man I was hoping to know.

He takes a breath, as if he's about to break the silence, but the doorbell does instead. He straightens and considers it. My eyes fall on my bags behind him.

Packed. Ready. Decided.

"It's my ride," I say in a whisper. In an instant, I'm up. My shoulder brushes against him as I pass to grab my bags.

"Kensington. Wait." He turns, placing an arm in the doorframe to block me. His chin's lowered, his eyes are soft.

I would like nothing more than to hear him say I misheard him. That he hadn't known about Bradley and Tonya. That I can trust him. But I did hear him. He knew. *Everyone knew.*

I'm shaking my head. "I, um . . . I need to sort everything out." My hands shake as I snatch up my bags and sprint under his arm back to the door.

Shane's right at my heels. "Kensington, *please.*"

I don't stop. In fact, *I run.*

But what am I running to?

I wipe at the flux of fresh tears, avoiding Rand Peterson's stare as I pass. Ellie's eyes widen when she sees me. I'm visibly upset and stumbling toward her car.

"Here. *Here*, I got it." She reaches for my bags and quickly throws them in the trunk.

I jump into the passenger seat with a slam. Locking my door, I sink down, buckle up, and mentally check out. Ellie gets behind the wheel and pauses with her hand on the ignition. I'm aware of Shane standing just outside my door.

"Please, just take me home, Ellie." I'm assaulted by the truth, and it hurts. *God, does this hurt.* But at this moment, the tears have stopped. Maybe I've finally reached my limit. *With everyone.*

Stupid Bradley's had his say. And Shane's said plenty by not saying much. He didn't think it mattered that he saw Bradley and Tonya together? A simple, hey, you know who I ran into?

But why would he? He never told me what my mom or Tonya said. Then, he was a kid, I get it, he apologized, I accepted. *But now?* He's supposed to be a grown-up, but he did it *again.*

Maybe it's time I had *my* say.

Starting with . . . *Tonya.*

CHAPTER NINETEEN

This Means What

$\mathcal{E}$LLIE DROPPED ME AT home and left when I promised to get some sleep. But the minute her car pulled out, I jumped in mine and rushed straight to Tonya's. I've been sitting outside her apartment for over an hour.

Watching.

Waiting.

Eating.

Tonya's apartment is dark. She's not home, but that's okay, because I can be patient. My car has heated seats. I also have hot coffee and a baker's dozen of Krispy Kremes. I've seen *This Means War*. I know how stakeouts work. And I'm officially on one.

I'm Lauren, Reese Witherspoon's character, but with the covert skills of Chris Pine and Tom Hardy. Aside from my phone, however, I lack their cool spy gadgetry.

On Facebook I notice she's unfriended me. *What a bitch.* She could have at least let me have the satisfaction of unfriending her. She's the lying cheater.

I check Ellie's friend list to see if Tonya's still listed on hers. Yup. I should post on Ellie's wall, that way she'll still see it.

Something like, *I've got a sandwich. You like leftovers, right?*

It's too nice. Maybe I'm channeling Lauren's character too much. I don't want to be nice. I don't know what I want. *Maybe a sandwich.* The doughnuts are making me nauseated.

Lauren's friend in the movie says, *Don't choose the better man, choose the man who makes you a better woman.* Well, neither do. With Bradley I was settling. And Shane is still unsettled. So I choose FDR, Chris Pine's character in *This Means War.* He likes movies and tries to know art, so yeah, works for me. *I should watch that tonight.*

Lights flash through my car's interior as an SUV turns into the parking lot. I duck, then slide up so my eyes are right above the window opening. My heart races from the hybrid surge of sugar and adrenaline.

It's *her.* And she's not alone. I can't see who she's with, though. I press my forehead to the glass and squint. *Who the hell is that?* Bradley? *Is it?* I gasp and fog the window. *It can't be.* Using my sleeve, I wipe the glass and refocus. No, not Bradley, it's . . . I don't know. They're going into her apartment. *Now what?*

I sit up and grab a doughnut. It's carb fuel for my think tank. I planned for an interrogation, not an interruption. There's no way I can go in now. I can't put everything on the line if someone's in there with her. Her apartment light flips on.

I need to know who's with her.

I'm not thinking. I'm doing. I toss the doughnut in the box, but then reconsider. The doughnut. Not the doing. I may as well finish the last few bites.

Okay . . . now I'm off. Now I'm doing.

I skulk along the walkway's edge, my collar up, my chin down. A wide step here. A low dip there. Stealthily, I creep toward Tonya's building and look around.

Thank God she's on the ground floor. I slink along the wall outside her window, inch by inch. *Shit*, the shrubbery's dense. *Ow.* The spindly branches scratch at my skin. My hair catches in its pickers and tugs as I turn my head. *What the hell kind of bush is this?* This isn't working. I try to turn . . . voices. *I hear voices!* Someone's walking up the path.

I duck as low as I can, but I'm not wearing camo, I won't blend, and they might see me.

Closing my eyes, I hold as still as possible in the shrubbery, trying to stay quiet until her neighbors pass by. Is this what a CIA spy-guy feels like? I don't know how they do it. I have an itch on my ankle.

I'm holding a weird squat position. My ankle is on fire, and after all the coffee, I need to pee.

Are they gone? I think they're gone. Okay, I scratch my leg and straighten. I *can* do this.

I turn and wedge myself flat along the wall. I sidestep between the bush and brick, backside out, hands hugging the mortar. My fingertips reach for her window, almost, I can almost . . . there. *Yes.* I'm right under it.

Slowly . . . I bring my head up. Little by little I rise, careful not to draw attention from inside. I freeze. Only the crown of my head is over. There's no weird scream, no exclamation of *Oh my God, whose hair is that?*

I stifle a giggle. That would be weird. Looking out your window and seeing only a forehead. *What would they say to the police?* You couldn't be arrested as a Peeping Tom. A forehead has no peepers.

I move up . . . up . . . and there. My eyes are now just above the frame. I see her, Tonya, and the back of the mystery man. It's not Bradley. His build is different, he has no ass. But . . . it's strangely familiar. They're arguing. Tonya's saying something but all I hear is muffled snark.

Oh! Oh, oh! He's kissing her. She's pushing him away but . . . now she's kissing him back! They've stopped and . . . why is his hand palming her belly like . . . *wait*, I thought she wasn't pregnant? Now he's *talking* to her belly.

She is pregnant!

Tonya breaks away and walks into the family room, ranting on about something. She's a pissed-off Charlie Brown adult. All I hear is *wuh, wuh, wuh wuh, wuh.* These windows really have great insulation.

Come on, *turn.*

Do it.

He's turning . . . it's . . . it's . . .

"HOLY SHIT!"

Oh! I said that out loud. The insulation isn't as good as I thought. Eyes dart my way.

I drop.

Shit. Shit. Shit. Go! I need to go! I force my way through the shrubs in record time, snapping twigs and ripping fabric as I do. I'm out. *Shit*, which way? I'm positioned like a quarterback waiting for the snap, looking to my right, then my left, then right. It's ready, set, *run!*

Trampling through a flower bed, I scramble around the corner and flatten against the wall. *Oh!* One hand's on my heart, the other covers my mouth, forcing jagged breaths through my nose.

When my heart settles, I peek around the wall. No one's come out. No one's there. One more cautionary look-see, and I make a mad dash to my car.

IT WAS RANT-AND-DRIVE THE ENTIRE way. I pull into my parking lot without remembering the ride home. I don't understand what's happening. I'm completely confused by yet another turn of fate's wheel. I'm not just upside down, I'm spinning in a complete willy-nilly cluster fuck.

I separate my keys and . . .

"Kenzi? Shit, are you okay?"

He's moving toward me, I'm frozen on the walkway, still trying to wrap my head around what I saw. What I'm seeing. *Why is he here?*

"Bradley? What do you *want*?" I can't take any more.

His hand is under my chin, turning my head, eyeing my face.

I push him away. "What are you doing?" His left eye is swollen to a mere slit, with the purple promise of yellow bruising to come.

"There's . . . um. Here." He reaches up and pulls sprigs of shrubbery from my hair. "And . . . may I?" He wets his thumb, wipes near my mouth, then examines it. "Glaze?" He looks me over, concern in his one eye.

I don't think the other one is seeing much.

Instead of a blond Gaston, he now resembles a Cyclops Quasimodo. Wiping at my face, I sigh. *Yup, glaze from the doughnuts.* When I look down I see the scratches across my legs, the rip in my skirt, and my arm is bleeding.

"Come on, let's get you cleaned up."

I don't argue. I follow him to my door and wait for him to unlock it. I need to ask for my key back.

"*Jesus.* What happened here, Kenz?" Bradley's standing in the entryway scanning my apartment.

Oh, yeah. I never cleaned up from my Bridget Jones drinkfest resulting from Saturday's symphony kiss or Monday's wedding debacle. Wow, busy week.

"I'm gonna grab a shower," I say, walking past him. I have no expression or explanation. I'm wiped. I don't even care that he's here. I don't. I'm way past the point of anger, because truthfully, why does it even matter?

Starting the water, I catch sight of myself in the mirror. *Oh, good God.* Bradley was actually being polite. I'm a Chia Pet that's been mauled by a cracked-out kitty. I sigh from somewhere deep, and rake the foliage from my hair, bit by bit.

A glass of wine is waiting for me by the couch when I emerge. Bradley's beside it with a box of bandages.

"Come here. I want to take a better look at that arm."

I hold it out for his inspection. It's a decent slice, although all surface. I don't remember feeling it happen. When he's finished, I curl up on the couch, one leg under the other, and pound back the wine in two determined swallows. Bradley takes a seat across from me, leans forearms to knees, and waits.

I make him wait a while longer.

"Okay," I say at last. "No more lies. Just truth. One chance to tell the truth. So spill."

The truth is the same as before. They had a thing before I worked there and it happened again. *Yeah, the truth sucks. He* sucks. My jaw's clenched. There's nothing he can really say to change anything.

Bradley moves to the floor in front of me and kneels. His hands reach for mine.

"She told me a couple weeks ago that she was pregnant, and . . . I panicked, okay? Then she followed me out to my car before I left for Lansing, demanding I do the right thing and marry her. *Marry her.* It was my worst nightmare, hon, you have to believe me . . ."

One blue eye earnestly looks into mine. I should probably get some ice for the bloodshot and swollen one, but I don't.

"What about what Shane said? Seeing you together at the hotel? *Not* business?" My eyes narrow.

"Hon," Bradley says carefully and slides closer. His arms are now both leaning on my lap, his hands engulfing mine. "I can be an ass—"

Thank you, Captain Obvious. I puff a breath.

He ignores it. "But if she was pregnant with my child, I'd do right by her, you know that."

I yank my hands back and straighten. *He'd do right by her?* What about me?

Bradley's brows furrow. He shakes his head. "No, what I mean is by supporting her. I'd support the baby. I want to *marry* you. And I'm pretty sure she lied about being pregnant anyway. So, it's not a concern now. Okay?"

Shit. He doesn't know about what I just saw. And it's not okay. Either way, it's not okay.

"I've been talking with Grayson about all of this—"

"Wait, *what*? My brother knows about Tonya and . . . ?" My head's not keeping up with anything. The sugar rush has crashed into a sludgy molasses drip.

"I needed a sounding board, needed to know how to handle everything. I'm sorry. I'm sorry about her. For pushing for a quicker wedding. Guess I thought if we moved things up, then somehow . . . I don't know. It'd be harder for you to walk away when I told you everything. And we could handle the situation together. *Shit,* this is a mess and I'm *sorry.*"

I'm dazed, listening to him talk, hearing the words fade in and out. Picking apart what it all means. What it doesn't. Why my heart aches.

"We can still plan the biggest wedding that anyone has ever seen, anything you want. Just give us another chance . . ."

". . . You want babies? You know I do, too. We can start right away . . ."

". . . I'll even look the other way about Bennett, okay?"

Bennett. His name brings me back. I blink and stare wide-eyed into nothing.

Bradley still wants me. *He's delusional.* After all of this, he thinks I'd reconsider? Has he forgotten I broke it off before I knew? It wasn't right then and it still isn't now.

Getting up, I search for my purse and unzip the inside pocket. *His ring.*

My voice sounds tiny, a mere wisp of words strung together in truth as I place it in his hand. "Bradley . . . I can't." This time the words don't carry a shred of indecision. "I *won't.*"

I don't know what anything means or what I want.

I just know it's *not him.*

CHAPTER TWENTY

You've Got Nerve

BRADLEY WAS GONE WHEN I woke on the couch. He left a note saying he loved me, that he was sorry, and please reconsider. That was yesterday. And that's where I stayed. On the couch. Today, I've ordered pizza, went through two boxes of tissues, watched various rom-coms, and channel surfed.

I'm thinking I may end up alone. An image of my future little girl waving a *you're fired* sign plagues me. She doesn't have to fire me . . . *I never even got the job.*

Ellie made me promise I'd do a girls' night when she dropped me off the other night and she won't let me out of it. In fact, she's here getting ready even though we don't have to leave till seven, and it's only three. All I really want to do is go back to the couch.

I've managed to get half dressed. My hair's set in hot rollers and my makeup's done, but I'm still in sweats and slippers. I don't know where we're going or what to wear. At least I know what *not to* after two hours of back-to-back episodes on TLC.

"I like it, it's pretty," I say to Ellie as she spins, modeling her dress across my living room before disappearing back into the bathroom.

Slumping at my desk, I scroll Facebook to wait. I was half hoping Ellie would've called with a location, saying she'd meet me there. Only instead of her, it would be . . . but, whatever. Not going to happen. He isn't here, he hasn't called, he hasn't done anything except disappear again.

Yeah, the movie moments are over. The credits have rolled, the ending sucked, and Roger Ebert gave it a staggering thumbs-down.

Noticing a new friend request at the top, I click. *NY152*? Who the hell is NY152? My mouse hovers to see the icon photo, but it's only the generic avatar. Clicking on it to decline, I notice the attached message.

Dear ShopGirl,
I like to begin my notes as if we're already in the middle of a conversation. I hope you consider continuing this exchange. What will you say, I wonder? I'll be online, impatiently waiting for those three little words, *you've got mail*. Or, in this instance, you have a message.

Oh my gosh. It's Shane. It's *You've Got Mail*.

I read it again, my lips forming each word. Curiosity digs inside like a spur. Clicking ACCEPT, I can see it's a brand-new account. I'm NY152's only friend.

In the movie, Meg Ryan and Tom Hanks don't know each other's real identity. They chat about basic everyday stuff. Nothing heavy. No big questions.

I have questions. But I'm not ready to ask.

I select the message icon and message link. I bite my nail and concentrate, trying to remember the movie scenes. He talks about his dog and New York in the fall . . . *what does she say?* I Google the movie script to get the perfect line.

Dear NY152,
You wonder what I will say? Sometimes I wonder about my life. Do I do it because I like it, or because I haven't been brave? I really don't want an answer. I'm just sending it out into the void.

I stare at the screen for a few minutes without sending it through. I can be brave, I can do this. *Click.*

Maybe I could be brave with everything. Maybe it's about time. Like dealing with my mom, my family . . . I tried with Tonya. I should try again. *Force* a confrontation. Then I could let it go. Maybe.

I suck a deep breath in through my nose and lean back in the chair. "Ellie? I need to use your Facebook account . . . as you. Is that okay?"

Ellie pops out from the bathroom. "Why?"

"If I go over to Tonya's she'll just lock me out or not answer the door, but if I draw her out as you, then I can ambush her."

Ellie folds her arms.

"Just to talk. I need to have it out with her once and for all." I tilt my head. "Please."

With a nod, she leans over and logs in. I select messages, click new, and begin typing a message to Tonya, as Ellie, under her watchful eye. The computer chimes.

TONYA: Hey, Ellie-bellie.

I narrow my eyes. "Oh, she'll talk to you, of course."

"What are you doing exactly?"

"You'll see." I resettle on the chair, leaving her a corner to sit beside me, and start pounding on the keys.

> **ELLIE-BELL:** I know what you did.
>
> **TONYA:** Shocker, Einstein. Everyone knows. Bradley yelled it out.

I type faster, harder, and hit ENTER.

> **ELLIE-BELL:** I saw you with him. It's NOT Bradley's baby, is it?

Return. Pound, pound, pound, enter.

> **ELLIE-BELL:** Meet me at Safia at five. We need to talk.

Ellie scootches herself closer. "What the hell did you see? I thought you were home all night?"

I ignore her. My eyes are fixed on the screen in anticipation of Tonya's response. My fingers are ready for an all-out type-off. At the bottom of the chat box it says in gray letters, *Tonya is typing* . . . it's flashing, taunting me. My heart's keeping time.

Oh my God, *what is she typing?*

Wait, now it's gone. I lean into the screen to check if what I'm seeing is right. The green light is off. I click in the chat box and the Facebook message says *Tonya isn't on chat, but you can still send a message* across the top.

What? Oh, I'm sending a message. She *will* get the message. I pound the keys.

Tonya, I know you're still pregnant and it's not Bradley's. And I know whose it is. I also know what you're up to. Be at the office at five or everyone else will know, too.

I'm actually not 100 percent sure of anything. But I have my suspicions. I grab Ellie's arm and my bag. "You're driving, let's go."

"NO, LEAVE THE LIGHTS OFF," I say to Ellie as we enter the agency.

Ellie deactivates the alarm and we scurry inside like mice.

"If I'm right . . ." I look at the wall clock. "She'll be here in less than ten minutes. I need you to get her to admit what's really going on." I don't tell Ellie about my full conspiracy theory. I'm just not sure.

It might be *too* crazy.

Ellie shakes her head. "We already know what's going on. Two guys, one was Bradley, she's pregnant."

"Just get her talking. *Please.* Then I'll confront her . . . and I can just put it behind me, okay?" Or put it on Facebook if she doesn't admit to Bradley and everyone else involved in what's really going on. I plan on recording her full confession.

"Fine, I'm all for closure, but if we go to jail, your mug shot's gonna suck. That's all I'm sayin'."

I'm still in slippers, sweats, and have a head full of rollers. *Whatever.* I drumroll the desk and glance at the clock. *Shit,* she lives like five minutes away. "We need to hide!"

We both swivel around frantically as if someone just called, *Ready or not, here I come.*

"Wait." Ellie stops, confused. "Why do I hide if I'm meeting her?"

"Because I don't want her to know you're here yet. She needs to be inside, away from the door. No escape." Okay, where? Potted plants, coat rack, desks. *Maggie's desk.* I could hide under it, since the panels reach the floor.

"*Bathroom!* Go to the bathroom," I say, pointing her toward it. "Yeah . . . that'll work. This will work. Go, go. Go."

Ellie runs down the hall frazzled, heels clacking. I slide Maggie's chair out, it rolls back with a mad spin. I lunge-step, snatch the chair, and duck under the desk, knocking my head. A roller pops and hangs half-free.

I crouch low and line my eye up with the crack to peer out. I try each eye. Left, right, left, right. Yeah, I can see. This is good. Now I wait.

I wake up my phone so I'm ready to record. I have a message. *It's from NY152.*

My heart's thumping wildly. I scan it quickly.

> Dear ShopGirl,
> Do you ever feel the worst version of yourself? Someone
> provokes you and instead of handling it with any semblance of
> class, you react. And react badly?

A nervous laugh escapes. They're lines from *You've Got Mail*, but the timing's ironic. I'm under a desk in curlers about to . . . wait, *what am I doing?*

I need to confront her, not jump up from the desk like a jack-in-the-box.

Swinging out, I hit my head, the loose roller pops and rolls. A hair coil springs wild. There's a jingle. I freeze. *Are those keys?* Keys in the door! I sprint to the bathroom at record speed, slamming the door into Ellie with a *thud*.

"Ow, *shit!* What the hell?"

"*Shhhhhhhhh!*" I whisper-shout, waving my hands in her face and spraying spittle. "She's here!"

"Then why are you here?"

"To tell you she's here! *Now, go!*"

Ellie's at the door, peering through the inch-wide opening.

"I hear a voice in the main room," Ellie whispers and swings the door wider as I creep over. "Who's she calling for?"

"You. I was you, remember? Now, *goooooo.*" More spittle.

"Wait." Ellie says too loud, spinning and hitting me on the forehead. Another curler springs loose and lands on the floor with a *clink, clink*, roll.

"*Shhhhhhhh*," we both say, smacking each other with wild hands.

I practically push her out the door.

"Tonya? Sorry, was in the restroom. I didn't think you were here yet." Ellie's voice fades in and out as the door swings shut.

I reopen it so I can hear. But I need to *see*. I flatten myself against the doorframe, slowly push it wider, and squeeze through.

"Well, you wanted to talk, so talk." Tonya already sounds aggravated.

"Um, well . . . I wanted to talk to you because . . . I know about Bradley and the *other* guy."

Yes. Good, Ellie, good. Flush with the wall, I pad toward the main room, two springy locks of hair bouncing along with each step. *Easy* . . . I need to go slow.

Tonya huff-snorts like a dragon. "I don't think you know *anything*, Ellie."

"Whatever, Tonya, I know you screwed Kenzi over."

"And?"

Bitch! I click RECORD on my phone and, using my arm like a periscope, wind it around the corner. I can't see anything. Let's hope they don't see my arm.

"And I know there are *two* guys, and I don't think Bradley knows about the other one."

Yes! *Perfect!*

The front door chimes. Wait, no, *she's leaving?*

"She contacted you, too?" Tonya asks, surprised.

Contacted who? Who's here? I lean out a little, straining to hear, needing to see . . .

I position the side of my head past the corner's edge. A little more and . . . a curler pops loose with a *snap* and lands on the floor with a *clink, clink*, roll.

Three pairs of eyes turn in my direction. My hair antennas wave hello.

It *is* him. The baby daddy.

Clive.

"Kenz?" Tonya's eyes bulge. "What the *hell* is going on?"

Let's get ready to rumble. Game on. Party time. Shake your groove thing. *Whatever.* Here we go. I straighten and strut into the room. "You. Are. *Busted.*" I use the phone to punctuate each word. "Why don't you admit it, Tonya. The baby, more than likely, is *his*—"

"Well, I wouldn't say it like that," Clive says, hands in his pockets, looking chastened.

"What? Whoa, whoa, *whoooa* . . ." Ellie's dumbfounded, her jaw is slack, palms up in the air, looking from me to Tonya and then . . . Ellie gasps. "*You're* the baby daddy?"

"You're just now getting this? Seriously?" I flip the corkscrew curl from my eye, so Ellie can fully appreciate my mock sarcasm. Then, lifting the phone in the air, I add, "Here's the whole ball of wax, ya ready?" Ball of wax? *Who the hell am I? Who says that?*

Ellie nods, eyes Cheerios round.

I take a step toward Tonya and jab the phone in her direction. "She's a lying, shitty excuse for a friend. I mean, really, Tonya? First with Shane back in—"

"OH MY GOD!" She throws back her head with crazy eyes. "Are you *kidding* me? That was forever ago. *Who cares?*"

"I care! And what about *now?* I was engaged . . . and *you* . . . and now you're *pregnant?*" I tip my head toward Clive. "And this one? He's *married*. He's your boss. Could you be any more pathetic?"

Tonya takes a step back toward Maggie's desk. I push forward, the phone aimed like a deadly weapon.

"Did you threaten to tell his wife or something? Is that why Safia's struggling? He's putting money in your pocket to keep you quiet, or is it out of guilt?" And out comes my theory.

"Oh my God, Tonya, really?" Ellie's mouth is completely unhinged. "You would really do that?" She looks like we just told her Santa was a farce.

With a dramatic flip of my hair coils, I step forward. "I'm pretty sure Mr. Can't-keep-it-in-his-pants bought her silence. Am I right? Am. I. Right?"

"Really, Clive?" Now the Easter Bunny has been debunked.

Tonya's butt bumps the desk. Nowhere to run. Cornered like a rat, and I'm only getting started. They're not denying anything. Oh. My. God. *I was right?*

"Get that thing out of my face." Tonya swipes at the phone, prompting a game of keep-away.

I hold it high, then far right, now behind my back. Her long arms wind around me and knock it loose. It's flying. It chimes in midair.

Tonya jabs a finger at my chest. "Listen, Medusa, I've had enough of this shit."

Oh no she didn't. "You've had enough? *You?*"

Ellie's got the phone. She repositions it between both hands, walking sidesaddle, hunched over. She aims it at Clive, then us. I'm not sure it's recording anymore.

"You know what?" I force Tonya back against the desk again. "Clive was going to *fire me*, did you know that? Yeah, he said we're having *financial trouble*."

Tonya's eyes are red and glossy, like she's holding back tears.

I keep going. "I don't really care what agreement you guys have. I don't. But why didn't you ever tell me you and Bradley had a thing in the first place? You said you dated someone that used to work here. *Not* the same thing, Tonya!" My voice cracks with emotion. All the pent-up hurt is hanging on each word. "And why sleep with him *now*? How could you do that to me, Tonya? Or even to him? *Why?*"

Clive takes a step toward me.

"Stay back!" Ellie's in between us. "I mean it."

What's she gonna do, chuck the phone at him?

Clive's hands are up in surrender. He arches his brows to Ellie, then looks back to me. "What are you talking about? What's going on with Bradley?"

My mouth drops. "*He doesn't know?* Oh my God, Tonya. *Really?*" Now I'm shouting. This is too much. I turn to Clive. "What, you thought Bradley just *knew* about you two? About her being pregnant?" I swing back to Tonya. "Oh shit! You don't know who the father is, do you?" I almost feel sorry for her. Almost. "Clive, Tonya's also sleeping with Bradley. So yeah, the baby might be his."

Cupid just got shot by his own arrow. Clive steps back from the impact. I almost expect to hear the Scooby Doo line: *She would have gotten away with it, too, if it weren't for those meddling kids.* Instead, a spray of papers flies into the air as Tonya wipes her hand across the desk behind her and grabs a . . . *metal bin of neon thumbtacks?*

"What are you gonna do with that?" I ask with a shrill of hilarity.

One flip and they spray out at me. *I've been tacked!* Clive is yelling. Ellie's recording. If this ends up on Facebook, I'll . . . I'll . . .

Tonya flips more paper at me.

"Oh!" I swipe up Maggie's bowl of scented potpourri and fling a handful at her. "You're the *worst* friend anyone could ever have." I'm circling, every step on tacks and dried-whatever-this-crap-is.

Tonya's face is lit with rage. "What's so great about you, Kenz? Why do they always want *you?*"

"What? If you had a real thing for Bradley . . ." I flick some more. "Then why'd you never say anything?" Even more. The smell of lemongrass fills the air.

"Because he didn't want me like that, okay? *Happy?*" Her finger's pointed in my face. "But you show up and it's all *serious* and fucking flowers and rings. *You* he wants to marry!"

I stop. "What? Oh. My. God! You're jealous?" *She's jealous of me?* "That's why with Shane, too, isn't it? And now Bradley?" I clench a huge handful and lob it at her. Hard.

"You don't deserve him!" Tonya screams. "Everyone thinks you're *so* special—"

"What?" Turning the bowl, I shake out a spray of sprigs at her.

"Stop it . . ." Her hands reach for the bowl. "Stop flinging that!"

I don't. I hurl the last few bits.

She lunges, catching the bowl's lip, causing it to spin from my hand. It whirls in the air and lands with a loud crash in a thousand pieces.

Just like our friendship.

Just like my heart.

"You've got some nerve." I look to Clive and say quietly, "I'll be working off-site to finish up my accounts." I shoot a look at Ellie to signal Let's Go and crunch through the mess toward the door.

This puts the end in friend.

CHAPTER TWENTY-ONE

Say Something

$\mathcal{E}$LLIE AND I ARE driving home on the main road, ten minutes from my apartment. I pull up my slipper and start plucking neon thumbtacks from the sole, grateful it's thick. I'm agitated and angry and—

"If it makes you feel any better, I've always hated Tonya a little," Ellie says, her face crinkled in distaste.

I give her an appreciative half-smile. Ellie's the best. She's the one who calls me, asks if I'm okay, and does things with me. In my heart, I always knew Tonya was just a frenemy anyway, a frenemy of the worst kind.

I plop my foot down and lean back. "I'm going to look for a new job."

Her eyes dart over and her hands squeeze around the wheel. "Well, then I am, too. Yeah, we'll look together."

I blink back tears and nod. "Do you mind if we stay in? I'm not really up to going anywhere tonight." My heart plummets. "And tomorrow's Ren's mini–baby shower slash engag—*shit*." I choke on the words. "Yeah, I just wanna stay in, okay?"

"Okay, sure. It's probably not a bad idea considering this, um . . . whole exploding Goldilocks thing ya got goin' on." She scans my hair and smiles.

Looking up, I push aside a straggly strand and snort.

She looks over reassuringly. "Kenz, it's gonna be okay. Everything will work out." A *beep-beep* from the car behind us barks that the light's turned green.

Out of habit, I check my phone. *The message.* There was another one. I almost forgot. Opening it, I scan and see the same one as before with additional text.

I read it out loud to Ellie in the same dreamy tone as in *You've Got Mail.* I pop my eyebrows to Ellie. "I got that one earlier. Fitting, right?"

She gives a closed-mouth smile and I keep reading. "I know this is probably a little late to be asking, but are you married?"

"Is that a line from *You've Got Mail*, too?" Ellie asks, turning onto my street.

"Yeah." I lean back to think. "Yeah, it is. Although it's Kathleen's line to Joe Fox."

Ellie's voice rises. "Oh, I bet he wants to know about Bradley. If you're going back to him." There's a spark of excitement in her eyes.

I'm busy typing a response, my heart thumping a beat or two faster. I say it out loud. "Dear NY152, What kind of a question is that? Oh wait, I get it. Your friends are telling you the reason we haven't met is that I'm married. Am I right?"

I hit SEND.

"That's Joe Fox's line." The response is almost immediate. "Dear ShopGirl, We should meet." *What?* "No." I shake my head. "He set me up for that. I'm not meeting with him yet. I'm . . . no." I still need time to think. He's lucky I'm playing along with the whole *You've Got Mail* thing. I pocket the phone and start rummaging in my bag for my keys, flustered.

Ellie pulls into my apartment complex and parks the car without another word. The only thing I want to do is head back to my couch and maybe open some wine. I'm still hunting for my keys as we get out of the car. I bump the door shut with my hip, mentally cursing the size of my purse.

"Kensington."

My heart stops. *Really?* I look up in disbelief. It's Mr. NY152. *Here* in my parking lot. There's no *let's meet*. Shane's already here.

Why is he in a suit? He smells of musk and temptation, proving the Devil does indeed wear Prada. At least I think that's Prada. Doesn't really matter. The point stands.

Shane's standing there, waiting for me to say something. I blink. This is where one of the remaining six curlers should pop and spring another hair coil. *Oh, God, my hair.*

"Hi, Shane." Ellie smiles sweetly, widens her eyes to me, then walks past to . . . *oh, great*. Rand Peterson. Gang's all here.

This is not something I'm prepared to deal with. I start walking, my hand spinning the contents around in my bottomless bag to redistribute everything. I still can't find my keys.

Where are they? I quicken my pace, without a single word or acknowledgment that he's here. Dressed like *that*, following me, dressed like *this*. It's more than embarrassing.

"You look pretty," says Rand with a bright smile to Ellie as I pass them. His face falls when he sees me.

Whatever. I'm starting a new trend. I wipe under my eyes and notice black on my fingertips. Great, my mascara ran, too.

Ellie's updating Rand on our misadventure. "And then we're in the bathroom, and Kenz, oh my God, she . . ."

"Kensington, wait, please," Shane calls from behind me, his tone warm, his expression possibly amused.

It doesn't matter, I'm not amused and I'm definitely not waiting. I just want to hide. My slipper cleats make a dull *click, click, click* with every step on the concrete. My assorted hair antennas bob and dance to their tempo. I feel like a doodlebug wearing tap shoes.

"Kensington, please. We need to talk." Shane's beside me, matching my click-shuffle pace.

I stop outside my door, reach in deep, swirl the contents like I'm about to draw a raffle ticket until my fingers brush metal and plastic. I yank my keys out, unlock the door, and move aside to let in Ellie and Rand, who are waiting. But as Shane steps forward, I cut in front, step inside, and slam the door behind me. I'm not ready to talk.

"Kensington." Shane's words are muffled from the other side.

The apartment's made of brick. So he can huff and puff all he wants. When I swivel around, Ellie and Rand are both looking at me.

"Is she drunk?" Rand asks Ellie, one hand pointed in my direction.

Ellie laughs. "Not yet. Are you gonna let him in?"

There's a *knock, knock, knock.* I ignore it. "No. I don't think so."

"Kensington," Shane says louder. Another *knock, knock, knock.*

"We need wine. Talk to him, Kenz," Ellie says and heads for the kitchen.

"I'll, um . . ." Rand motions to Ellie and follows her.

Good call. Another light knock. This time the wolf really is at the door. And what big lies he's told. Well, I guess he hasn't technically told any, but he's held back. He knew about Tonya and Bradley. The logical me says not to trust him.

But there's a persistent little voice, excitedly jumping up and down chanting, *But he's here, he's here.* It's even throwing sparkly glitter.

I close one eye and squint through the door peeper with the other. He even looks good distorted. Dark waves framing deep honey-brown—*oh*, he's looking back. I jump away quickly. He can't see me, can he?

"Kensington, can I please come in?" The handle turns left, then a half-centimeter right, before it catches.

I stand close to the door. "I don't think that's a good idea right now." I almost say *not by the hair of your chinny, chin, chin.* But I already look crazy; I don't need to sound it, too. I lean my back against the door and fiddle with my hands.

His weight jostles both me and the door as he leans from the other side. "Fine. I'm not leaving, so we'll talk like this."

"Whatever." All I'd have to do is walk away. Not stand here. But my feet are fixed in place. And to be fair, I should give him the same courtesy I gave Bradley, right? I turn so my shoulder is pressed to the door. "Here's the deal. You get one chance to tell the truth. I ask, you answer. Okay?"

"Ask."

My stomach jumps. I'm not ready. What exactly do I want to ask? Why didn't you tell me about Bradley and Tonya? Do you know about Clive? How am I supposed to ever trust you again? Why do you have my paintings? In a tiny, faint voice from somewhere deep inside . . . *How do you feel about me?*

"Kensington?"

My head rocks and clunks on the door. I leave it there. "You knew about them from the start. Why didn't you tell me about Bradley and—"

"Would you have believed me? *Really?* After everything from before? It would have only pushed you further away. No, you needed to make that choice on your own."

I did break it off with Bradley before I found out he cheated or the pregnancy thing. So I did choose on my own. And, no, I might not have believed Shane. In fact, just him saying Bradley wasn't right for me was grating. *Ugh*, that actually makes sense.

"Kensington?"

"Okay, I guess I can understand that." A surge of indignation washes through me. "But why didn't you stop me from leaving? You let me leave."

"I tried to stop you but . . . you also still had his ring." The timbre of his voice is low.

True enough. My hand splays on the door. "I don't have it anymore, Shane." I swear I can feel him through it. I close my eyes. *Just say it.* "I need to know what it is you see happening between us. What it is you want. Because I still want to get married and have a family . . . and all those things." There. It's out there. In the void. This time I need an answer.

There's a pause. The longest, most excruciating pause ever.

The door shifts, but he's not saying anything. God, say something, *anything. Please.*

I look back out the peephole. My breath catches. *He's gone?* He left. I don't see him. Angling my head from side to side reveals an empty front step and walkway. I open the door and lean out.

There's no Shane.

The excited, glitter-throwing voice is now chucking it at me, shouting, *You've ruined everything, you sounded needy and demanding and . . . he doesn't want those things.* He doesn't.

But I do.

And for once, that's all that matters.

I shut the door, confused and irritated. The couch is calling me, so I grab my phone, head over and plop down, my mind reeling. What's the point? I mean, why did he even come up here?

Clicking on Facebook, I scroll the feed. Photos of what people made for dinner and another invitation to play Texas Hold'em. I flip to e-mail. *A new message from Shane?* The subject line says "updated list." I click to read.

1. Sleepless in Seattle

2. ~~Pretty Woman~~

3. Bridget Jones's Diary

4. ~~27 Dresses~~

5. ~~Dirty Dancing~~

6. ~~Sixteen Candles~~

7. Love Actually

8. Say Anything

9. ~~You've Got Mail~~

10. ~~My Best Friend's Wedding~~

That's it? It's just the list. No note, no nothing. Reading through, I can't help but think of the movie moments with him. But I'm not sure what he's doing. I mean, he knew about Tonya and Bradley. And then he comes up here and leaves, why—*what is that?* Cocking my head to the side, I focus on the sound coming from outside. The volume starts to climb.

It's music. *Music?*

I click off my phone and listen. The lyrics and melody are familiar. I know this song. It's Peter Gabriel's "In Your Eyes."

"Oh my God."

It's *Say Anything*. He's doing *Say Anything*.

In the movie, Diane Court never looks out her window. She never sees Lloyd Dobler and his pained expression. No, she lies in bed and listens. Knowing it's the song that played the night they spent together, that he's just outside, and every word is meant for *her*.

In your eyes. I am complete.

I'm smiling through warm tears. I'm not Diane Court, I'm Kensington Shaw, and I'm looking. Walking to the front window, I slowly push the curtain to the side and peek out.

The laugh is instant. Shane's doing it. He has a boom box held over his head and . . . *what is he wearing?* A long, ill-fitting trench coat is on over his suit.

I push the curtains wider and he spots me. We stay locked in our gaze through the glass as the song finishes the last round of its chorus.

Knowing that every word is meant for me. Knowing exactly what it is I want. Maybe what I've always wanted.

In an instant, I'm at the door, tearing through it, and running to him in my thumbtacked slippers. My hair is bobbing along with each step. I stop right in front of him.

He regards my crazy hair, smudgy tearstained face, sweats, and slippers as if he had forgotten what was really on the other side of the door. I can feel the heat on my cheeks as he sets the boom box down.

My nose wrinkles. "Still want me?"

Shane steps forward with deliberate care, lifting a wayward curl from over my face. He leans in close, flecks of gold an inch away, and smiles. "Yes, definitely."

I glance up through moist lashes, making another decision. The ring's off my finger, so I ask. "Kiss me?" It comes out with a small breath, and it's captured at once by his lips.

They move slowly over mine. My hands wrap around his neck

as he pulls me close. Holy hell. Fireworks, lightning bugs, static cling . . . anything remotely electric is now zapping around inside my heart. It's a gentle tease, a sweet torture.

A really good kiss.

Shane pulls back only enough to whisper near my ear, "I know it's been tough, and tomorrow with the shower thing it isn't going to be any easier, so I have a surprise. It's *not* on our list. And you may want to change." Shane kisses my cheek, then leans out so my eyes meet his gaze. It's full of suggestion.

Snap. One of the last curlers springs free, rolls down my shoulder, and lands on the ground with a light bump, right on cue. Giggling softly, I smile.

"IT'S A VINTAGE 1955 ROLLS-ROYCE," Shane says, checking the rearview mirror. The car vibrates and shimmies as he backs out of the parking spot. "The company I rented it from said it sat disassembled for almost twenty years. They had it rebuilt."

This is my surprise. It's an old car like in the movie *Titanic*. Okay, that movie's not technically on our list, the car's not an exact replica, and the movie doesn't end happily, but who cares. That car scene was *hot*, and this works.

The inside has an aviation look with the oversized speedometer and fuel gauges in the mahogany-veneered dash. The bench seats are leather. It's just cool. "This is . . . well . . . a really great surprise," I say, smiling. "Where are we going?"

Shane turns with a sideways glance. "To the stars."

I laugh. "That's my line. In the movie Rose says, 'to the stars' and pulls Jack into the backseat, remember?"

"Then I guess I'll have to pull you into the back." Shane's eyes dance with mischief.

My insides churn wildly and I smile then look away, sure my cheeks are red.

"So, dinner? Dancing? I'm dressed for whatever you want."

Even though I've changed, it doesn't change what transpired with Tonya today. Or the upcoming interrogation about Bradley that waits for me in the morning. *Ugh*, Ren's mini-shower and what was supposed to be my engagement party. I look out the window, at early evening's sky feathered in pinks and reds, and sigh. "I'm not really up to dancing."

"Hungry?"

I look again at Shane and shake my head.

Our eyes meet and he reaches over and takes my hand. His fingers caress my palm, open against his. I bite my lip and smile coyly.

Shane smiles back, and I can tell by his expression what he's thinking. My heart's skipping wildly in my chest as I take everything into consideration.

"You know I need some time before I can commit to us, right?" I say, glancing at our fingers, now interlaced.

"Yes, and that's understandable." He takes a long, slow breath, then glances sideways. "What are you gonna do?"

"Um . . . reevaluate everything. Start over." I shrug. "Maybe paint."

"Well, if you can paint, I can wait, Kensington."

My heart swells in my chest. It's the final movie lines from *An Affair to Remember*. Well, almost. "You know *she* says the line and it's if you can paint, I can *walk*, right?"

Shane searches my eyes. "I don't paint and I'm *not* walking."

My stomach flips. I glance up through my lashes. "So you said dinner, dancing, anything I want?"

He looks over, but doesn't say a word.

My heart's skittering around in my chest. I move beside him as he drives and lift his hand, the one still entangled with mine, and bring it to my lips. Pressing a soft kiss to his fingertips, I whisper through them, "Put your hands on me, Shane."

Within seconds, he's pulling onto one of the small scenic photo spots along the White River where we were driving. It's secluded with no overhead lights. The ignition's turned off and his lips find mine hungry, wanting.

Shane's door opens and he pulls me out, only to guide me into the backseat.

"Not over?" I ask.

"This was faster," he says, his breath uneven. He's kissing right above my collarbone, my neck, just below my ear.

This is, *oh* . . . a small gasp escapes as he bites my lobe. There's a bittersweet pain pooling below my navel as he gently sucks it in. My heart is pounding hard in my rib cage. The new scruff on his jaw is coarse and bristles against my heated skin.

I run my hands along the inside of his jacket, up onto his shoulders, forcing the jacket off. My fingers nimbly undo his shirt buttons one after another until my hands are running over his bare skin. I *ache* to touch him.

He traces the contours of my body with his fingertips. It's agonizingly slow. And I need him. *Want* him. I want to give him all of me. Body and heart. My *whole heart*.

Shane has my dress unzipped and lifts it off slowly over my head, then gently lays me down. Hooded eyes of copper brown stare into mine. Whispered words and kisses follow to my closed eyelids, my brow.

We've been here before, Shane and I. And this somehow feels like coming home. It feels so good to feel happy. To just let it all go, even if it all comes back tomorrow. Because right now, I'm lost in this moment. *In Shane.* All at once, I'm overtaken with emotion. I can feel my eyes start to water, and then one fat tear breaks away.

Shane's kisses find their way to my neck, my cheek. He meets my gaze and holds it. Using his thumb, he pushes away the moisture. "Don't cry, ShopGirl, don't cry."

The next line is *I wanted it to be you.* But there's no need for words.

So I don't say anything.

CHAPTER TWENTY-TWO

Four-Letter Words and a Shower

I CRANE MY HEAD TO look at Shane. *God, he's cute when he sleeps.* He's leaned up against the door, his legs stretched out on the vintage car's bench backseat, and I'm wrapped in his arms. My legs are curled practically on top of him. He's in nothing but his boxer briefs, me in my thong. We're covered by his suit coat. This is a nice way to wake up.

Wait . . . *wake up?* Today is . . . no, *is it?*

Oh, crap!

It's Saturday.

Oh no! Fuck. Fuck, fuck, fuck! This is not good. *Please* be a dream. Be one of those really weird dreams where it lingers even after you've opened your eyes. Don't be Saturday. Please say we didn't fall asleep. I blink, then squeeze my eyes supertight and . . . open. Okay, try again. Close . . . open. Close, open. Close, open. Close, open.

We're still in the car.

Not a dream. Today is Ren's shower.

I smack him.

"Hey! Wha?" His eyes open in shock.

I sit up. "We're still in the car. It's morning. I don't know what time it is. I think it's early but . . ." I take a gaspy breath. *Clothes . . . where's my bra?*

"Okay." Shane rubs at his eyes and widens them, with a deep, slow yawn. He leisurely flips his wrist up to see the time.

I stare at him, hoping. Please be super early. *Please.* I clench my jaw and wait. His eyes meet mine. They're rounded.

"Shit!" Shane's up and already pulling on his shirt.

"Shit?" *Oh shit!* It's not super early. This is *so* not good. I find my bra and wrap it around me trying to figure out the convertible straps. I wore it racer back. *Who invented these things?*

Shane's reaching around me for his pants. I almost tie his arm in the strap.

"What time do you need to be there?"

"Um, it starts at eleven or noon? Was it noon? I don't know. Mom wants me there early. Like around ten." My bra's on, although I think the straps are crossed weirdly. One boob is awkwardly pulling left. I grab my dress and tunnel in from the bottom.

Shit, I'm stuck.

"I'm stuck!" My arms are above my head, and I can't bend them to pull the dress over my shoulders. It's all bunched. I'm really stuck. I'm thrashing about, trying to find a way to wiggle it down. My arms wave in the air like a dress monster.

"Shit! *Ow.*" I think his elbow just hit me.

"Hold still . . ." His hands have my dress and are tugging it down. With a swift yank, I'm through.

Okay, I can see again. My arms are free. I lift my rear and pull the dress down. I grab his shoes and thrust them to his chest. "*Here.*"

Shane opens the door and spills out, shoes tucked under an arm, hopping on one leg to step into his pants. The air is still morning crisp. I notice the car is steamed from the temperature difference, and handprints, *lots of them*, are speckled over the windows.

We may have gotten carried away with the Titanic *scene.*

Shane has the car started and is backing out. I climb over and fall into the front seat, scrambling for my shoes.

Shane smiles. "See, one of us got to climb over the seat after all."

I hit him again. "What time is it?"

"It's fine. I'll drop you off first, then the car. My car's there, so I'll swing back and drive you."

Oh my God. My family. We haven't had *that* conversation. I haven't told them anything. My mom, Grayson . . . they'll ask about Bradley. The vintage car is whining like a blender from the sudden acceleration. It's loud and *slow.*

"Shane, what time is it?"

He takes the corner and clips the curb, jostling me into the air. I scream. He glances over at me. His shirt is buttoned wrong, it's half tucked into his pants. He never put his shoes on, and his hair is . . . well, his hair is a perfect wonderful mess. He drops his head with an apologetic look. "It's ten forty-five."

TEN FORTY-FIVE?

"Faster, must drive faster! *Move!*" I hit him again, maybe more than once. I don't know. Since I don't have a gas pedal on my side, it's the best I can do. I can't breathe. "Faster!"

"I'm going as fast as this car will go." The old car is loudly protesting our need for speed. It's shaking wildly at forty miles an hour through the city streets. It's like we're in *Four Weddings and a Funeral*, but instead of a wedding, we're late for a baby shower, and the funeral will be mine.

This is definitely one movie moment I did not want on the list.

How will I have time to get ready? My whole family . . . the light is yellow. We're not going to make it. It's changing. "No, you got it. Go. Go, go. GO!" I'm hitting him again to help him go faster. We slide through, but it's red.

So are the lights behind us. We're being pulled over.

Are you serious?

"My wallet." Shane is digging in his pockets and coming up empty as he pulls over on the shoulder. "I don't have my . . . my coat. Where's my suit coat?" He's looking around frantically.

I spot it in the back. I dive over and grab it. Shane unrolls the window; the officer is out of his car. I'm searching his coat, desperately digging in the inside pockets, sending receipts and last night's valet ticket airborne.

"Here, I got it. I got it." I throw it over. It pings from the dash and lands somewhere on the floor.

We're breathing heavily. The windows are fogged again. Shane's reaching around to find where it landed. I'm now swatting the seat back to hurry him along. The officer is coming. *He's coming.*

"Got it." Shane has his license out and runs a hand through his hair.

"License and reg—"

The officer looks at Shane, his disarray, his mismatched-button shirt. I follow his gaze to the handprints plastered all over the steamy windows. His eyes regard me in the backseat, starting with my dress, which I just realized is inside out, and my oddly lop-sided boobs underneath. I can only imagine my hair. His eyes travel up. He locks them with mine. His widen in disbelief.

"Again?"

"Hi," I say, with a feeble wave from the backseat.

It's the same officer from the paintball caravan chase.

Fuckity-fuck, fuck, fuck.

SO I'M LATE. NOT THE worst thing, right? I didn't go to jail. That would be worse. We did, however, this time get a ticket. Well, Shane did. I got a lecture. The whole stupid affair cost us another twenty minutes. It's almost noon. I was supposed to be there around ten to help, but help what? It's not like Mom's going to cook, she's having it catered. Yes, I can be late. Showered, presentable, and late. I can.

So why can't I breathe?

My phone's ringing, again. She's called three times already. We're almost there, but I should answer it. Get it over with. I sneak another glance at the time, then at Shane behind the wheel, and reluctantly give in.

"Hi, Mom."

"Kensington, it's me, your mom."

"I know, Mom." I can hear Ren talking to Grayson in the background. Music's playing and dishes are clanking. She's in the kitchen. It's in full swing.

"Where are you? What ha—"

"I'm sorry. I know I'm late. I'm five minutes away. I'll help with—"

"Well, everything's done now. We're getting ready to sit down and eat. No, that doesn't go there, let's put that out front," she says with a huff. "And now there's nothing left to help with, is there? I had to do it all on my own. Ren, yes, it's Kensington, I found her."

I wasn't lost. Well, maybe I was. But I'm not anymore. I hear Grayson mumbling about how this is typical.

"Your aunt tried to help, but you know how that goes. Yes, we found her. She's apparently on her way."

"I'm around the corne—"

"Oh, all right. I can't talk. Just get here. It's time to eat."

The phone hangs up. I feel as if I'm spinning in multiple directions like a gyroscope. My orientation is all out of whack.

"You okay?"

"Yes. *No.*" My hand is over my mouth. My eyes are wide. *Oh, I can't do this.* I can't.

Shane's pulling over the SUV.

"What are you doing? I'm super late!" I practically scream it. I'm all worked up.

He places his hand on mine. "Kensington, you are a beautiful, smart, charming woman. It will be okay, no matter what. I promise." His thumb rubs affectionately over my knuckles. "I'm here. I support you. I see you. It'll be okay."

Keeping my eyes on his, I squeeze his hand and nod. I haven't really talked with anyone about the whole Bradley, Tonya, not-engaged thing. My stomach lurches.

This was supposed to be a special day for me. A day to celebrate an upcoming wedding and to dream about a future family. I'm so far away from that. Looking at Shane, my heart lightens a little. I'm . . . well, *happy.* A bit scared and confused, but happy. Yesterday my world shifted. Today it's in a different place. But maybe it's the right place.

Maybe I'm closer than I know.

"We can go. I'm okay." Maybe I am okay. At least I look okay. My final selection was a pleated color-block dress. I didn't have time to do my hair, so it's tied back in a loose bun. Surprisingly, it all came together nicely.

My grip tightens on my bag as Shane turns into the Village

community. There's no turning back now. We have entered . . . *the Stepford zone.*

Cars are lined up and down the street. What happened to just a small family mini-shower thing? *There's a valet?* Mom usually hires a valet service to shuttle the overflow at her annual Shaw family Christmas party. I don't know why she calls it the family Christmas party. It's everyone she knows. We're pulling up. We're here.

What is going on?

"You'll be fine." Shane squeezes my hand.

I wish more than anything he could come with me, but . . . this was supposed to be an engagement party for Bradley and me. And it's now *just* me. So it needs to be just me.

My Facebook status has gone from *In a relationship* to *Engaged* to *Single.* I should change it to *It's complicated.* Because this is definitely complicated. There needs to be a *Don't ask.*

"THERE YOU ARE. EVERYONE'S OUT back. We're ready to eat." It's Ren. She's wearing a short-sleeve jacquard dress and looks beautiful. "What the hell happened? Mom's been a wreck . . ."

I don't say anything. I'm too busy looking around. Mom's idea of a small family pre-shower and engagement party has turned into . . .

"Yeah, she invited *everyone* for your engagement party. It was going to be a surprise."

What? My stomach's on the floor. I'm surprised all right. The one time my mom decides to show an interest . . .

"Um, Kenz." Ren grabs me by the elbow and leads me to the front room, hastily. "Are you okay? I mean I know what Grayson told me, but—"

"Oh my God, Mom knows, right? About Bradley? We're not engaged. I told her, but we haven't, ya know, really talked about it." I'm shaking my head, eyes wide. "I gave the ring back, *oh . . .*" This is worse than I could have imagined. This is in front of everyone, not just the disapproving eyes of my family.

"She knows, but I think you should know—"

"Kenzi, good God, you're late. We thought you'd . . ." It's my cousin Ashlen. She's loud, opinionated, and single-handedly keeps my father's medi-spa in business with her Botox injections.

Mom is redirecting a waiter toward the patio and doesn't stop. She simply calls out to me as she passes. "That was more than five minutes, Kensington. We've started. Let's go."

"Hi, Mom," I say weakly, more to myself.

Ren leans to my ear. "Um, Kenz, I really—"

". . . Oh, did you hear about Cousin Jimmy? Yeah, I guess . . ." Ashlen won't let either of us get a word in. She's now between us, an elbow locked around an arm each, marching us toward the back.

Panic is swelling inside my chest. I'll need to make an announcement. *What do I say?* Um, excuse me, but I called the wedding off. My fiancé may have knocked up my so-called friend, but please stay on and enjoy the mini-gherkins?

Ashlen's still jabbering as we step out the sliding doors. ". . . Oh, it's beautiful, isn't it? I helped . . ."

The courtyard patio does look lovely. Mom had topiary brought in and a large tent set up with two supersized rectangular tables underneath. Draped white fabric billows in the crisp breeze, while patio heaters fight to keep it at bay. There's even a three-piece band playing on the second patio under the trees.

A mini–family shower for Ren, and a surprise engagement party for me. *For me.*

We step aside to allow a waiter with a tray of food to pass.

"Are you listening, Kenzi? Did you hear me? Oh, there's . . ." Ashlen makes a beeline for an empty seat next to . . . *Oh, shit.*

It's Liza Evans. Well, soon to be Liza Evans-Matison, with her fiancé, Ryan. Her mom is sitting beside them. Ashlen is scooting her chair in, and Liza's waving to me.

Um, hi. My ringless fingers wiggle in a halfhearted wave.

Ren grabs my arm hard. "Okay, what I've been trying to tell you—"

"Okay, let's quiet down." Someone is tapping a glass. Everyone turns to the woman up front with the helium-filled voice.

Really?

"Well, hey, if it isn't the soon-to-be Mrs. Bradley Connors, our *special-special* guest." It's Bethany Chesawit, wedding planner extraordinaire, and, I guess, baby-slash-engagement event co-ordinator.

Kill me. Kill me now.

Grayson's sitting with my dad at the end of the table. I spot Aunt Greta and smile. I think I'm smiling. My face is doing something. *Oh*, she has a new guy with her. He's thin and balding. Wonder what this one's called. Mom's standing by Dad's seat, overseeing everything.

Bethany Chesawit waves us in. "Well, come on and take a seat, ladies. You, by the proud father to be. And you, right over there to wait for your handsome groom."

"He's right there," Ashlen yells out and points toward the bar.

What?

I hear Ren in my ear. "That's what I was trying to say. I didn't know what was going on."

Walking to the table, an awkward expression on his face is *Bradley.*

"*Nooooooo!*" It just came out, and kept coming.

There's a universal gasp. The music stops, everything stops. You can hear the heads turn in my direction with a *whoosh*.

Oh. All eyes are on me.

Mom's smile is wide and forced. She's nodding as people look between us. I don't think she's breathing. I can't believe she did this to me.

"Um . . . I mean. No-o-o *way!*" A shrill chortle erupts out of my throat.

Bethany Chesawit is completely confused. Liza Evans is whispering to her mom, looking from Bradley to me.

I'm dying. *Dying.*

"Wow." I lift my hands up and shrug. "Um, *ha ha*, you got me." I raise a finger and wave it. "Great job. Oh, hi, Aunt Lindy. I like your sweater, yeah. And yours, Liza. Your dress, I mean. Obviously not a sweater . . . Um . . ." *Oh God, I'm rambling.*

Grayson's eyes are popped. Mom's mortified, motioning for me to *wrap it up*. She wants me to *wrap it up*?

"Really?" I shoot her a look of unbelief, then turn to Bradley. "Um . . . can I, ah, talk with you a minute?" I jab my finger toward the door. "In *there*?" My eyebrows spike.

Bradley looks around.

I manage a clenched smile. "Okay. Great. 'Bye," I say and turn.

Right into the path of a waiter.

We crash and tangle into a blur of arms and legs. He steps back. The tray tips. Dishes slide. Another wobble-step back and . . . food splatters. Guests squeal. The waiter stumbles onto someone's lap. His hand is where it shouldn't be.

Mine are over my gaping mouth. I've been here all of ten minutes and . . . and . . . Aunt Greta's on her feet. Dad's rolling his eyes. My cousin Ashlen's laughing loudly . . . Mom's eyes are narrow slits. Her face is red. Lips pinched tight. Her head shakes disapprovingly. At *me*. *Really?* She's angry at me? *I can't believe her.*

Suppressed hurt twists my gut, building tension until it springs loose and loud. "Are you *kidding me*, Mom?"

Oh, God.

Team Kenzi: Negative one hundred million zillion.

CHAPTER TWENTY-THREE

Love Finally

BRADLEY'S GONE. I SENT him away for good. In no uncertain terms will he be back. It's a *million* percent over. I'm shaking from his audacity. I mean, *what the hell was he thinking?* I don't know how he convinced Mom we were working things out. Okay, *yes I do.* She wanted to believe it. I get that.

Because for a long time, I wanted to believe it, too.

But holy hell, Mom.

This is awful. But I'm not in tears. I'm embarrassed. Okay, *humiliated* . . . but I'm not in tears. I'm making my own choices. For the first time ever, I feel like I'm holding my own, standing my ground. I made the choice about Bradley. I'm choosing Shane. But more important, I'm choosing *me.*

Ding. Ding. Ding. Ding. Plus one for Team Kenzi.

"Kensington?" It's Aunt Greta. Her hair's still red, only now it's a deeper shade. I didn't notice earlier.

When I turn all the way around, I see Ren beside her. I raise my hand and wave. I can't speak.

"Excellent speech, sweetie," Aunt Greta says with a sly smile.

I look from Ren to Aunt Greta. The *Bridget Jones* movie line just pops out. "I'm available for bar mitzvahs and christenings, too." A small laugh escapes, echoed by theirs.

"Well, think of it this way," Ren says, not getting the reference. "You definitely know how to make an entrance."

I look to Ren and wrinkle my nose. "Sorry if I messed up your shower."

She waves a hand dismissively. "Don't worry about it." She bumps my shoulder with hers.

Aunt Greta wraps me in a one-armed hug. "All I need to know right now is if you're okay. Are you?"

I give a meek smile. "You know, I think, yeah . . . I actually am."

Or at least, I'm working on it.

I SEE AUNT GRETA WATCHING me from across the table, doing her best to pretend she's not. I'm doing my best to keep up with polite conversation, but I can't seem to focus. It's as if the whole Bradley-waiter-speech fiasco didn't just happen. The crazy train is back on track and moving full speed ahead. I'm spooning sugar in my tea, dazed, but . . . *I'm okay.*

"So, Kensington." Dad leans on an elbow. "How are things at the agency? Heard you have a new client."

My eyes widen, the spoon hangs in midair. Does he mean Shane's restaurant? I know they had lunch, but he's bringing it up *now*? "Um, yeah. I'm working on a new movie-themed restaurant concept," I say hesitantly, and continue sweetening my tea. I peek at Mom.

She says something. I give a thin smile. I think I'm smiling. I'm at least thinking about a smile. Sinking back in my chair, I stir and take a sip. *Wow, really sweet.*

Greta's new guy is called Rolly. He turns to me, wiping his mouth with a blue napkin. "The bank is thinking of some new marketing projects. Maybe I should talk to you, Kenzi?"

Aunt Greta smiles and takes a drink. "That's a great idea, Rolly."

"Didn't you quit?" Mom asks loudly. She leans out so I can fully see her disappointment. "Tonya called last night to see if you were here. Said you weren't returning her messages. She's worried."

Ren is suddenly interested. "*Wait.* You're still talking to Tonya? I thought—"

"Complete misunderstanding," Mom answers quickly, then asks for Ren to pass the dressing.

I clear my throat. *I can do this.* "There wasn't a misunderstanding with Tonya, Mom. It's perfectly clear what she did. And I didn't quit." I look briefly to Dad for encouragement.

He gives a slight nod. That's all I need.

"I'm going freelance. I'll be finishing my projects off-site while I work up my new studio's business plan." I square my shoulders and look to Mom. "I already have one contract locked in."

"Maybe two," Rolly says and smiles warmly at my aunt.

I like Rolly.

Grayson looks from Mom to me. "You have a client contract? Who?"

I'm not quite sure how Shane's contract with Safia will work when I leave, but he said he'd hire me, so maybe future work? I take a breath and just go with it. "Well, Shane Bennett's farm, for starters."

Mom's face changes to distaste. I'm not sure if it's because of the mention of Shane or the word *farm*.

Mom puffs a breath. "I forgot his family had a farm."

It's probably both. "Yes, well, he's developed a restaurant theater and has plans to grow it into a chain. The beta site is located on his property. It's really great. It borders La Porte, that little touristy area, remember?" I take a bite and look her in the eye. My heart is thumping an odd beat.

"I like farms," Rolly says to me. "Love all the animals. Do they have horses? Such smart animals."

"How are you going to support yourself with one client, Kenzi?" Grayson then turns to Dad. "That's not feasible."

The waitress refills Aunt Greta's glass. "Thank you." She looks at Rolly. "Pigs are smarter, actually. But I'm not sure they have any animals, Rol."

"I'm sure having the Carriage House restaurant as a first client is enough to get her started." My dad regards Grayson. "Plus, she can take over the spa's graphic design work."

I smile at Dad. "Really?"

He pulls down his lips and nods. "And I expect a discount."

Rolly wipes his mouth again, now using the pink napkin. "Did you know pigs are clean? They've gotten a bad rap."

I notice Mom's quiet. There's no use in trying to convince her she was wrong. I'd only be spinning my wheels. I can't change her. But I *can* change my reaction to her. "The party was pulled off beautifully, Mom." *Even if its intent was misguided.* "It's, um, really something."

"I didn't say they were dirty, I said they were smart. Pigs are smart," Aunt Greta says to Rolly, shaking her head.

Mom's icy exterior thaws at my compliment. Mom is Mom. It's always going to be about appearances. It's how she sees the world.

I see it differently.

"Oh, well. Thank you." She flashes me a smile. "It's nice of you to notice. I wasn't sure if we should do chicken or fish, but the chicken seems to be a hit."

Rolly leans over. "Do they have chickens?"

Taking a sip of my water, I look around and catch Ren's eyes. She pops them at me with a small grin, which makes me smile. We seem to be thinking the same thing. They're all insane. But they're family. And in the end, that's what matters.

In *13 Going on 30*, Jennifer Garner's character, Jenna, wants to be thirty, flirty, and thriving. Through wishing dust, it's granted, but it's not quite as she hoped. Eventually, she gets a second chance. A do-over.

I'm not quite thirty and my life isn't thriving. But just like Jenna Rink, I have another chance to start in a new direction. Turns out, I get my do-over after all.

No wishing dust needed. Only courage.

REN AND GRAYSON ARE AT the front table surrounded by pretty packages with pink and blue bows. They're opening baby gifts from the family while the guests enjoy mini-desserts and watch. A small ache throbs from my chest as I observe them.

Mom has her hands clasped, excited to see Ren's reaction as Bethany Chesawit brings out Mom's *special-special* gift. It's not wrapped. It's the Gucci diaper bag mom told me about, overflowing with smaller gifts.

"Thank you, Mother Shaw!" Ren's in tears and they're hugging. Everyone's abuzz with my mom's generosity, good taste, and thoughtfulness. The bag is passed around and gushed over. *It is nice.*

The next one's in green paper with tiny umbrellas on it.

"This one's from . . . Ashlen," Ren says, peeling back the paper. Delicately, she slides the item from its box. "Oh, it's a bank." It's a silver turtle. "So cute, Ashlen. Thank you."

My head throws back. I removed that. Maybe Ashlen just liked it.

Next up . . . another bank. This one's a ceramic teddy bear. I *know* I didn't scan that one. It's not even cute.

"Can never have too many," Ren says with an oversized smile that doesn't reach her eyes. With every gift, Ren's smile becomes more fixed and forced.

A low, uneasy groan escapes from my chest. I sneak a look at Aunt Greta. Her brows pull down, trying to read my expression. I mouth, *I added gifts on her registry, but I removed them.*

"What?" She whispers back across the table.

Ren opens another box . . . and pulls out . . . hangers. *Plastic baby hangers?* My stomach falls. For a flash Ren looks horrified. Then she smiles. *Nope*, she still looks horrified.

My mind is desperately trying to make sense of that day. I remember deleting and scanning new items. I added beautiful designer crib sheets, tiny yellow and green neutral outfits, even a bassinet in deep cherry.

"I know I fixed it," I whisper-shout across the table to Aunt Greta. I'm shaking my head in disbelief.

Aunt Greta's mouthing, *What?* Her palms are up. She repeats the question, perplexed.

We're now mouthing an entire conversation back and forth across the table. I don't understand what happened. *Oh . . . oh, no.* Shane is what happened. He showed up, and the Fossie's lady chased us out. "*Shane*," I mouth-whisper.

She hides a laugh with a cough.

I dash to Ren's side and whisper in her ear, "I didn't save. I accidentally added things, I was going to tell you, forgot to call, but then I fixed it, but I didn't save. *I'm so sorry, Ren.* I'll return everything. I swear. Don't be mad."

Ren seems even more confused, but manages a lopsided smile as Grayson hands her the last box. Timidly, she peels back the muted yellow paper, glancing at me.

"This one's from me, Ren." Aunt Greta's right up front, camera aimed and ready.

Ren pushes aside the tissue and peers in. Her face contorts between a smile and disgust.

She lifts it out . . . *oh!*

A *click-flash* from Aunt Greta's camera blinds me.

It's the stuffed pig-monster in gaudy pink and green with buggy eyes. My gaping mouth is covered by both hands. Another *click-flash* from Aunt Greta as Ren's eyes dart around and land back on the thing she's holding.

Ren looks to me then Aunt Greta . . . *and laughs.*

Everyone does.

"Don't you dare return *that*," Aunt Greta announces, stirring more laughter.

The doorbell rings. "I'll get it," I yell out, happy for the escape. Moving toward the house, the waiter from earlier spots me and takes three long steps over as I pass. My eyes narrow. *Funny.*

Inside, I make my way to the front. Clasping the door handle, I swing it open. *Shane?* Confusion soars through me. He *can't* be here. We talked about this. I need some time on my own. Quickly stepping out, I close the door. "What are you—"

His index finger is pushed to his lips. My eyes fall to the large poster boards he's holding.

"Shane, you can't—"

Again, he shushes me. He's flipped the boards over and . . . there's writing. He flashes a shy smile and nods for me to read.

Don't say it's carol singers . . .

"What?" I whisper, confused. "Why would I—" Oh . . . I know what this is.

This is *Love Actually.*

He's doing this now? *Here?* From the corner of my eye, I catch the front room curtains move. Someone's looking out.

Shane shuffles the boards and again has my full attention.

It's the scene with Juliet and Mark. Mark's desperately in love with her, but Juliet's not in love with him. So he stands at her door and proclaims his feelings in a series of signs. It was Christmas time in the movie and he told her to say carolers were at the door. My heart is skipping erratically as he holds up the next one.

With any luck, by next year . . .

In the movie, the sign after this one has photos of models on it and says *I'll be going out with one of these girls* because Mark knows he can never have Juliet. Shane places a new sign in front. No photos. He's not following the script. Good choice. I smile.

Maybe this will be our party.

Our party? *As in an engagement party?* My eyes flick to his. I'm on pins and needles. Tingles are zinging up and down my spine as Shane swaps cards. I squeeze my toes inside my shoes.

And I will be invited in.

A laugh explodes. Another card.

But for now, let me just say . . .

I'm biting my lip through a smile, anxiously waiting to see, eyes darting from his to the card.

I love you, Kensington.

I smile with my whole heart as I stare at his words.

He loves me. Shane Bennett loves me.

I'm swooning. I almost can't breathe. Shane's hand is up. He's signaling hang on, there's more. *More?* I'm on the edge. There's nothing to hang on to. He flips to the next sign.

I'd like a date.

There's a slight tilt to Shane's head. A hopeful expression.

Valentine's Day. New York. I'll be waiting at the top of the Empire State Building at dusk.

In his eyes, I catch sight of the boy I once knew. A reckless boy with big ideas. Shane lowers the cards. It's not the boy asking. It's the man. The man he's become.

The man I love.

I nod, smiling through tears.

The door pulls open behind me. "Kensington?" It's Dad.

"What are . . . ?" Dad's eyes rest on Shane, then me.

The boards are quickly tucked under Shane's arm. "Mr. Shaw, it's nice to see you again, sir." His hand is out.

"Shane." Dad slowly accepts with a firm shake. Another look from him to me. "Kensington, why don't you go on in and see if Ren or your mother needs anything?"

"Um . . ." My eyes move to Shane's then back to Dad's. "I, ah . . ."

Dad lowers his chin. *Okay.* Backing up, I step through the door, eyes on Shane. Dad quickly pulls the door closed, shutting me out.

Oh my God. What is he going to say? What should I do? I move to the front window and yes, there's Ren behind the curtains, still holding the pig-monster. I knew someone was here.

"Holy you-know-what, Kensington!" She steps to the side so I can slide in, then leans over my shoulder.

We're both completely inside the closed curtains. Only our feet can be seen from the living room. Outside, I watch my dad's back and Shane's head. Dad's hands are gesturing as he talks, but I can't hear him. All I hear is Ren in my ear.

Her hands clasp her collarbone. "And those signs? That was so sweet, my God, it made me cry. We all knew—"

"What?" Turning completely to look at her, the words just spit out. "You all knew *what*?" My pulse is in the danger zone.

"Well, between Bradley constantly calling the house to talk with Grayson and Shane talking with your dad . . . and you know how Grayson and Dad talk." She shrugs.

Words escape me. I shake my head.

The curtain flies open with a metallic *whoosh* from the friction of the rings on the curtain rod.

We both jump. I'm clutching my heart.

"What the hell are you two doing?" It's Ashlen.

Ren and I exchange quick knowing looks. Ashlen has a big mouth.

"Nothing. Girl chat," Ren says, stepping out, the pig-monster tucked under her arm. "We were just about to go sit down. Right, Kensington?"

My eyes dart back outside. Dad's hands are in his pockets, Shane's head's moving.

Ashlen grabs my arm and we start to walk. "Great. I switched seats so I'm sitting by you guys. Liza was annoying me. She thought Bradley was British. What an idiot . . ."

I've tuned her out. Shane loves me. Dad's with Shane. Ren's being cool. My whole family knew what's been going on. Maybe not specifics, but . . .

The door opens. My heart stops. Shane's still here. Ashlen looks from Shane back to me and Ren, a curious smile on her face.

"Ren, Ashlen, why don't you two go on out back," my dad says.

It's not a suggestion. "Shane, I have a feeling we'll be seeing more of you in the future? We get together once a month for Sunday brunch. We'd love to have you."

"I hope so, and that would be wonderful, thank you, sir." They shake hands again and Dad gives me a wink as he heads toward the back.

He winked? "Um, I'll be right in," I call out, walking toward Shane.

We stop halfway down the front walk, and he takes my hand.

"What did you say to my dad?"

Shane smiles. "I informed him of my intentions toward his daughter, and that, although I'd prefer their support and blessing, this time around, I only need yours."

A sappy smile forms on my face. Dad invited him over. Shane loves me. We're going to meet on Valentine's Day.

There's a sputter then a wet blast.

I scream.

Within seconds, we're drenched. Trying to absorb the shock of the cold water, Shane and I look at each other and laugh.

Dad had the Super 3000 sprinkler system installed last spring. It blasts bursts of water up and out in record time. Mom must have forgotten to shut off the front timers.

Dropping the signs, he tugs me close and wraps me in his arms. "Guess we got our *Bridget Jones* after all."

"I may have done that one all by myself," I say with a giggle.

Shane pulls me close for a kiss. I lean up on my toes, my hands claiming his cheeks as I accept his wet lips with mine. The stubble on his jaw scratches under my fingertips. Relaxing deeper into his hold, I slowly slide down to stand on solid ground, lean back, and deliver Bridget's line complete with accent.

"Wait a minute. Nice boys don't kiss like that."

He gives a throaty laugh. "Oh, yes they . . ." He doesn't get to finish his words. They're captured by my lips. I am a happiness time bomb. I may burst into a spray of happiness confetti, adding to the water jets. *Poof.* There'll be nothing left of me.

I can hear my mom yelling for Ren to shut off the system, and pulling back, I see my family watching us from the doorway. Aunt Greta and Ashlen are laughing. Dad's smiling. Mom looks tense. She's probably worried about what people must think. Grayson's hugging Ren, and she's waving the pig-monster's paw. Rolly's behind everyone, giving excited thumbs up.

Ding. Ding. Ding. Ding. I've hit the jackpot! Team Kenzi: No longer needs to count.

I smile at Shane. His hair's curled in wet rings around his face. Drops of water are beaded in the scruff along his jaw. Flecks of gold gaze down at me and warm my heart. He wraps me tightly in his arms and lifts me for another kiss.

Only one moment's left on our Love Like the Movies list. It circles 'round to where we started.

But it's not the end.

Because life isn't a movie.

It's *better*, actually.

When Shane Met Kenzi

I'M NOT GREAT ON planes. But I'm watching *Sleepless in Seattle* on my tablet to steady my nerves and pass the time. It's the scene where Meg Ryan's character, Annie, is watching *An Affair to Remember* and Becky, Annie's friend, says my favorite line: *You don't want to be in love. You want to be in love in a movie.*

She asks Annie to read the letter she's writing to Sam, and it's *Becky* who suggests they meet at the top of the Empire State Building on Valentine's Day. It's also Becky who sends the letter.

Ellie was helping Shane the whole time. And she helped me schedule my trip to meet Shane in New York. I think she's as excited as I am. Because just like Becky, she wants what we all want, *magic.*

"Ladies and gentlemen," says a voice over the loudspeaker. The seat belt sign lights, we're asked to switch off all electronics and remain seated until we land.

I check my buckle and get my things situated. My ears pop as we make our descent. Out the window the sun's already settled low in the sky, creating a dusty haze like a blanket over the New York City skyline. I lean on the glass and watch Manhattan take shape. I've never been here. So many buildings, they seem to go on forever.

Three months have passed since Shane stood on my parents' porch and said he loved me. Not one phone call, Facebook chat, or e-mail since. Nothing. Of course, that's what I asked for. Space to get myself situated, but . . .

What if he's changed his mind?

We were supposed to meet at dusk on Valentine's Day, just like in the original movie, but just like in the movie, I'm late. My plane was delayed for two hours due to weather in Indy.

I can't wait to tell him what's been going on. Besides my dad's graphic design work, I've added two small businesses to my client list. Shane's under contract with Safia for the Carriage House, and Clive asked me to finish as a contract hire, so I did. I'm hopeful I'll still get to do the murals.

Four of my paintings are on display in a local gallery and two have recently sold. One was of a little girl that inspired me in the park and the other was the view from Shane's cottage window. Rolling hills of sun-kissed tan and yellow as far as you can see.

I haven't spoken with Bradley or Tonya. Ellie's still at the agency, although she's looking for a new job, and says things are tense. Bradley's keeping a low profile and working around the clock, Tonya's working for the competition and very pregnant, and Clive's working through divorce number two. A prenatal paternity test has been ordered.

"There's the Empire State Building," the woman in the middle seat says, leaning over. "They have it lit up for Valentine's, see?"

Where? Wait, there's a tall building with pink and white sparkles near the top. "Is that it?"

She smiles. Guess I was expecting the heart like in the movie. My ears pop again as we drop altitude, then the plane banks. *Ugh*, I'm really not a good flyer. My stomach rolls.

Closing my eyes, I distract myself by picturing the map the way they did in *Sleepless in Seattle.* The camera zooms out and I see dashed lines appearing from Indianapolis, arcing high across the states and dropping to the airport below. Not as dramatic as in the movie, we're not that far.

Too bad I still have to zigzag through Midtown in a taxi. The Empire State Building is less than ten miles from the airport, but with traffic it could take between twenty and forty minutes. I Googled it.

My luggage is only an extra tote bag to save time, and I bought an express pass online for the 86th-floor observation deck, to avoid both ticket and elevator lines, but I know there's a security check, so there's also that wait to consider.

What if he thinks I've changed *my* mind?

THE TAXI DRIVER SAID TRAFFIC'S not too bad, but what does that mean? All I see is endless streams of cars and people out walking. I suddenly feel very Midwestern and out of my element. On my phone I check the time. It's 6:15. Dusk was at 5:30. I know this because I Googled that, too. I text Ellie: Still in Taxi. Flight was delayed. Freaking out!

Oh, there it is! The Empire State Building. I lean up on the front seat and try to see the very top through the windshield. Maybe too far, I'm practically breathing in the driver's ear.

"Sorry," I say and try to see from the side. *Why have we stopped?*

We're just sitting here. Should I get out like Annie, Meg Ryan's character, did in the movie? My heart's racing, I want to be racing. *I should run.*

"Um, excuse me . . ." The taxi starts again. *We're moving.* Okay, maybe riding's better. It's actually cold and a bit dreary out. *Almost there!* I'm bouncing in my seat, I'm so excited.

I dig around in my bag for my ticket and cash for the driver. When he slows, I already have my money held out.

"Thanks!" And I'm out and off in a power walk. The air is damp and cool, the kind that gets inside your bones. At least it's not snowing or raining. *Was it raining in the movie?* I can't remember. I move with the steady stream of people toward the entrance. *How are there so many people?*

Okay. I'm here. *Wow,* this place is massive. Art Deco and marble everything, floors, walls . . . I look up: even the ceiling. American flags on either side. Elevators, *where?* I hold up my ticket to a man in uniform. "It's an express, do I . . . ?"

Glancing at my ticket, he points toward the third queue. There's still a small line. Security is what's creating the holdup. I head over and glance at the time on my phone: 6:30.

What if Shane's not there? I have his picture from college back out on my nightstand in a frame. It's again the face I greet every morning and the one I'm desperate to see. I miss him. I love him. I never said it. What if I don't get the chance?

A text chimes. It's Ellie: How close are you?

I quickly answer: Inside. Stuck in security. STILL freaki—

That's all I say, because I'm next. The guard hands me back my bag and I collect my carry-on, which is really just another bag because I knew that any kind of luggage was not allowed. *Yes, Googled that, too.*

"All clear?" I bounce into the elevator. Come on, come on,

come *on* . . . We're packed in tight, the doors close, and here we go.

My stomach lurches with the sudden rise. A voice is broadcast over the speakers, welcoming us to the Empire State Building in different languages, but with so many people talking it's hard to hear. The red LED numbers jump from 2 to 10. *Whoa.*

Twenty . . . thirty . . . *fifty floors!* The guy next to me is talking about how the entire ride is only about a minute. *A minute's too long!* Sixty-six . . . seventy . . . Now it shows each floor and I can feel it slowing. Seventy-eight . . . seventy-nine . . . eighty!

The doors open. I'm out! Straight ahead is a huge metal sign welcoming us to the observation deck. My eyes are desperate for Shane. I scan faces. *Where is he?* Quickly, I work my way through and around the inside behind the glass, then I get into the line for outside and . . .

Oh, *wow.*

I'm momentarily distracted by the twinkling lights, so many lights. I wedge myself between two people and lean up on the cement wall to peer over. It's foggy but you can see across the river all the way into Jersey. The gentleman next to me points out the Chrysler Building to his wife. A helicopter in the distance is actually below us. It's strange, but other than the chatter, it's quiet, almost peaceful.

Shane.

I spin and start circling the deck. I text Ellie: I'm finally up here, but I don't see him!

Where? Man with dark hair . . . I walk fast and . . . not him. I'm halfway around, and *no Shane.* So many people . . . It's *really* crowded and a lot bigger than I expected. When I'm back to where I started, I loop around again. Dread creeps up my spine.

Again, I text Ellie: I don't see him! Gone all the way around.

She answers immediately: Stay put. Maybe by elevators?

Oh, that's a good idea. I work my way back to the main doors, where visitors first step outside. This way I can see new arrivals or anyone leaving. Tugging my collar up, I cross my arms and tuck my chin in against the cool air.

A couple holding hands walks by. Well, lots of couples holding hands. It's Valentine's Day. *Maybe he really did change his mind?* My insides twist at the thought. I don't think I could bear another Valentine's letdown. I glance at the time on my phone again. It's so late. *I'm* so late.

A crackle pops from above. I look around just as everyone else does. *What is that?* It's coming from loudspeakers. It's . . . it's music and . . . *Tom Hanks's voice?* "It's you."

"It's me." *That's Meg Ryan.*

"That's *Sleepless in Seattle*!" I say loudly. The woman next to me eyes me strangely, but then repeats it to her friend.

They're playing the movie over the PA?

"I love that movie," says another woman.

"Maybe it's a Valentine's thing they do," someone else says.

People are looking at each other, talking about what they think is going on. My eyes are wide, looking from one person to the next. But nothing's happening except the movie's playing crisp and loud through the speakers.

"We better go," Sam, Tom Hanks's character, says. "Shall we?" The familiar song "Make Someone Happy" starts with its plucky *bomp bomp . . . bomp bomp* to end the movie. It swells louder and . . . *bomp bomp . . . bomp bomp.*

Now everyone is really craning their necks and looking around.

It's so important to make someone happy . . .

"*Oh!*" The whole crowd gasps.

I lean out to see. Two couples have spontaneously started dancing. Another couple starts spinning. Another.

"It's a flash mob!" Several voices shout out.

I've never actually seen one. The entire observation deck seems to have been staged with dancers of every age. More dancers start twirling and dipping in sync to the iconic song.

Make just one someone happy . . .

I laugh and back up to make room. *This is really cool.* I wish Shane were with me to see this. People have their phones out and are recording. Maybe I should—

Did I hear my name? I turn, but I don't see anyone. *There it is again.* I step out, shifting around to see through the dancers. They swirl to the side, and walking down the middle in perfect view is a little boy: red coat, dark hair, red-and-yellow backpack.

No way.

He stops and tugs on a smiling lady's coat. "Excuse me, are you Kensington?"

My heart slams my chest. I didn't hear that right . . . *did I?* My eyes are already prickling with tears. They're at the ready. *Really no way.*

He faces the other way, and I have to duck to see between the performers. He's talking with a woman with short dark hair. I can't hear them but I see her shake her head. Everyone's watching him, smiling, commenting. The dancers weave to the music around him, almost with him.

Now he's walking . . . *oh my gosh*, he's walking toward . . . *me.* "Excuse me, are you Kensington?"

My eyes are round. I can't get the words out so I smile and nod. I hear whispers around me. *That's her. That's the girl.* My chest is tight. I glance around as everyone watches.

"Then what's in my backpack is for you." He turns.

The raspy voice of Jimmy Durante sings on about love and clinging to that special someone. I'm at the top of the Empire State Building on Valentine's Day, talking with, well, *Jonah*. This is surreal.

I look around again and the couple beside me nudges my arm. "Go ahead, see what's inside."

I wet my lips, take a long breath to steady my nerves, then slowly lift the flap. *Oh my gosh.* It's the pig-monster. I laugh and pull him up to murmurs and laughs. There's a *snap-flash* of a camera. Then another.

Then a gasp, "His *neck*!"

My gaze drops. Threaded on a candy-disk necklace is a ring. Tears completely blur my vision. My hand covers my gaping mouth and the moisture runs over my fingertips and seeps through them. *There's a ring.*

I look up. Where is he? *Where?*

The dancers part, and waving like crazy is . . . "Ellie?" *Oh my God,* "Mom? *Dad?*" I'm beyond surprised. Ren leans out from beside Grayson, points to the monster, and grins. Aunt Greta smiles with tears, camera in hand. Another *snap-flash.*

My whole family is here. *They're all here.* My heart's swollen with happiness. He did this all for *me.* But where is—my family steps to the side.

Shane.

Dressed in jeans, gray cable knit sweater, and coat, he looks like he stepped out of a magazine. The corners of his eyes crinkle with his smile, and that's it, I'm a mess. Tears fall so fast, even as I wipe them, I can't see.

"Here, honey." Someone hands me a tissue.

I stifle a laugh, and dab. It's no use. I'm wrought with emotion.

My teeth lock hard, and I suck in a fast breath, hugging the pig-monster with a hand over my mouth.

The little boy is still beside me as Shane approaches. The music fades and a hush follows. I swear it's so quiet, it's as if the whole world is holding its breath.

Shane drops to his knee, igniting a united "*Awww . . .*"

His jaws are clenched trying to keep it together. His eyes have a glossy shine. Oh, I've missed his face.

"Marry me?" That's all he says.

My God, that's all he needs to.

It's better than any movie speech or line.

I smile with my whole heart and whisper, "I love you, Shane."

Cheers erupt. Aunt Greta's hugging Mom as she dabs her eyes, smiling. Dad's beaming. Even Grayson's eyes are moist. Ellie and Ren are crying and laughing.

I gaze into copper-brown eyes, filled with a warm, hopeful glow, and see our whole story unfold.

It's how Shane met Kenzi.

The magic of boy meets girl, the angst of catch and release, the serendipity of meant-to-be. It doesn't matter if a romantic comedy follows a predictable course, we respond because it's rooted in truth. In *magic*.

Does that mean a perfect happily ever after? *No*, in fact, I don't want perfect. I *want* the bumps. At least, the unexpected one set to arrive in about six months. I smile at Shane. Bet he's not expecting *that*.

Everyone applauds as he sweeps me high into his arms followed by the sweetest kiss. A movie kiss. A kiss that ends our Love Like the Movies list and starts our new life.

A *life* like the movies.

Real-Life Shining Stars

$\mathcal{T}$HANK YOU TO MY critique partner and friend, Kaci, who has rallied behind this story from the very first draft, and heartfelt thanks to my amazing critique and beta crew: Cristin, Amy, Stacey, Sharon, Claudia, Rox, Andrea, and Nicola. I adore each and every one of you.

Special thanks to my super-agent, Jenny Bent, for believing in this story and taking me under your ever-impressive cape. To my fabulously funny editor, Abby Zidle, and to the entire cast of people behind the scenes, who not only put this title up in lights, but made sure it sparkled.

And of course, thank you to the readers! Just like Kenzi, I think we all want a life filled with big, magical moments. *Love Like the Movies* has certainly been one of those for me, and I hope through reading, you're reminded to live yours on purpose and center stage.

Last, but never least, I thank God, the big director in the sky, for proving that when life pitches unforeseen plot twists, there's always another path to *happily ever after.*

extracts reading groups
competitions books new
discounts extracts
competitions extracts events
books new extracts reading groups
events books discounts reading groups
extracts new interviews
new titles reading groups
interviews events
books extracts events
discounts new books events events
events new interviews
discounts extracts discounts new books
www.panmacmillan.com
extracts events reading groups books
competitions books extracts new